MAD LOVE

THE SINGLE DAD PLAYBOOK
BOOK 1

WILLOW ASTER

USA TODAY BESTSELLING AUTHOR
WILLOW ASTER

Willow Aster
www.willowaster.com

ISBN-13: 979-8-9880213-9-1

Cover by Emily Wittig Designs
Cover artwork by Kira Sabin
Map by Kess Fennell
Editing by Christine Estevez

Silver Hills
The Fairy Hut
Jupiter Lane
Luminary Coffeehouse
Rose & Thorn
GROCERY
BOOKS!
Aurora's
Twinkle Tales
Wiggles & Whimsy
The Enchanted Florist
Pixie Pop-Up Market
CAFE
Starlight Cafe
Serendipity
Pet Galaxy

NOTE TO READERS

A list of content warnings are on the next page, so skip that page if you'd rather not see them.

CONTENT WARNINGS

The content warnings for *Mad Love* are death of a sibling and profanity.

CHAPTER ONE

COFFEE WITH THE DADS

WESTON

The bathroom mirror is too fogged up to see anything when I get out of the shower. I wipe it down with my towel and turn to see if any bruises are fading yet. Tomorrow will be a week since my team and I won our second Super Bowl, and it does not get old, even though my body is paying the price.

I'm young enough, I can handle it.

I'm doing what I've always wanted to do—playing

professional football. After a couple years of doing this, I'm still in shock that I'm living out my dream.

My phone buzzes and I check it. Penn Hudson. We joined the Colorado Mustangs the same season. I've made a lot of great friends on the team, but Penn and I are probably the tightest. As the quarterback and running back, it's a good thing we get along so well.

PENN

Should we bust the dad group this morning?

Why not? It's always entertaining to hear them vacillate between how great their kids are and how hard they have it as single dads.

PENN

I'm in the mood to annoy them.

You just want an excuse to hang with the greats.

PENN

You're not wrong.

The biggest draws of coming to play for the Mustangs were Henley Ward, the best wide receiver in football, and Bowie Fox, my favorite linebacker. Bonus was when tight end Rhodes Archer was drafted along with Penn and me. All of them have been at it longer than we have, and they've accepted us with open arms in every way…except for this little single dad club they have.

I'll see you there in fifteen.

PENN
Word.

The mountains look close enough to touch on this beautiful, sunny February morning. I'm lucky that I was drafted from college to play for my home state. I'd miss Colorado if I had to live anywhere else. The snow is crunching beneath my feet, and Silver Hills is just starting to wake up for the day.

It's only been a week since Valentine's Day, but every heart and cupid that took over the town is gone, and now there's green and silver everywhere I look for St. Patrick's Day. Silver Hills goes all out for the holidays.

I love relaxing mornings like this, maybe because they're rare for me. I'm usually rushing off to practice or still working out at this time. I walk into Luminary Coffeehouse with Penn on my heels, both of us scouting the place for the guys.

"Did we miss them?" Penn asks.

A bubbly girl walks up and puts her hand on my arm. "Weston Shaw and Penn Hudson at the same time? Pinch me," she says to the girl next to her.

I look at the two girls and smile, holding back my laugh when they both sigh. It's hard to tell who they're into more, Penn or me—I think they could flip a coin and be happy.

As much as I enjoy a good time, I'm still exhausted from playing so hard last weekend, the parade in downtown Denver, and all the partying that ensued afterwards.

I really just want to chill with my boys.

Or give them shit. Same difference.

You'd think I wouldn't miss the team since we've been together nonstop for months, and I don't miss all of them, but this week, with all the interviews and parties and hangovers, I've actually missed chatting with my favorite bastards.

"Is it me or is it more crowded than usual?" Penn asks under his breath.

"It's not you," I answer.

"Oh, it's you," one of the girls says, winking. "Word got out that this is where you guys meet for coffee and everyone wanted to get in on the action. We drove all the way from Boulder."

I smile politely and motion for her to step forward in line.

She turns and I exchange a look with Penn. When he looks forward again, his face lights up and I look to see what changed. He waves at Clara, the sassy owner who's my mom's best friend. She's the reason this is our place. She motions us over to the pickup line and lifts up our usual: flat white for me, caramel macchiato for Penn. Just one of the things we love to razz him about.

"Clara is too good to us," Penn says.

Clara is my parents' neighbor and decided to open this coffeehouse after her husband Jimmy died. This place has given her a reason to smile again, which is a relief. Clara is good people and seeing her brokenhearted was awful.

"Morning, Clara. You're looking lovely today," I say, taking the cup from her.

"You don't have to sweet-talk me to get your coffee," she says, but she's smiling and her cheeks are pink. She leans in and tilts her head. "I put your boys in the back room so they could have some peace."

"Ahh. We wondered if they saw this crowd and got out of here," Penn says.

"They haven't been here long." Clara motions for us to follow her.

"Thanks, Clara," Penn and I say in tandem.

I lift my foot to knock the back of his knee like my sister Felicity always does to me, laughing when it buckles.

For some reason I can never pull it off with my sister, but it works on Penn every time. He didn't have siblings growing up, so he's still caught by surprise when any of us try to torture him.

He curses under his breath and shoots me a glare as we make our way through the crowded coffee shop. It's too small for all these people, but I guess it's good for business. Clara knocks once and enters a code into the door, before cracking it open.

"I have two rug rats here who think they should be invited to the party," she says.

Penn and I step into the cozy room with the large round table and a reading chair on the side with a small bookshelf of books. Clara says it's a room for meetings, but I think this is where she comes to hide and read when it's slow out there.

"Yeah, why you gotta be so exclusive?" I ask, mostly kidding.

Bowie smirks. "Have a kid and we'll let you in," he says.

Henley and Rhodes high-five, and Penn snorts.

"I hate to tell you, but you *need* us in this little club you've got going," Penn says.

Henley raises his eyebrows. "Oh yeah? Why's that?"

"You call yourselves The Single Dad Players…and you guys just high-fived. Enough said."

Henley and Bowie look embarrassed for exactly zero seconds.

"Come on, what do you talk about in these weekly meetings anyway?" Penn says. "We've heard you when we're on the road. It's not entirely parent talk, from what I can tell."

"We go easy on ourselves when we're on the road. Then it's mostly about how much we miss the kids, and we're talking about how great they are…or how difficult," Rhodes says.

"And when you're not on the road?" I ask, playing along.

"Well, I was just telling the guys that Cassidy started her period last night when she was with me, and I had nothing in the house," Henley says, with the same gleam he gets when he goes up for an acrobatic fingertip catch in the end zone.

Penn and I shift on our feet, obviously uncomfortable.

All three of them fold their arms and look pleased.

"I had to go to the drugstore and get pads and walk her through how to use them through the door." He scrunches his brows and it's the universal sign for when Henley is about to dig deeper, be it on the field or when he's talking shit with us. "She wanted to know how to use tampons, so I talked her through that too, and then I set her up with a heating pad and—"

"Okay, okay," I say, lifting my hand.

Henley's an old dog, who has some good tricks. He knows how to dish it out like a pro.

Okay, he's not that old. He's thirty-five, and the guy gets just as much attention from the ladies as we do when we go out. Not that he's interested in any of them. His ex-wife did a number on him.

But he's a damn good wide receiver. The very best.

Henley grins. "Have a seat."

He waves his hand to the seats around the table and we sit down, not so sure we want to be here anymore but also pleased that we passed.

"Was her flow heavy?" Bowie asks, giving me the side-eye.

"Come on!" I groan.

They laugh like crazy.

"I'm mature enough to talk about periods," Penn says proudly. "I just don't want to know when Cassidy has started hers…" He sticks his lip out and does sad eyes. "She's just a baby."

"Exactly that," I say, pointing at Penn.

For some reason, that resonates, and there's a sad air that comes over the room.

"I can't believe my little girl is so grown up," Henley says sadly. "I was testing you. She hasn't started her period yet. I'd never tell you guys about that. She'd murder me in my sleep if I did. I'd be breaking dad code all over the place if I broke that news. But it *could* happen…any day now."

Oh God, maybe I'm not cut out for this. I glare at Henley, but he has my mind rolling now. I love Henley's girls. I can't stand the thought of Cassidy being that grown up either.

My phone buzzes and I look at it, frowning when I see Presbyterian Hospital across the screen. My family would go to Silver Hills Hospital if anything went wrong…

I waited too long to answer, but it rings again right away.

"I'm sorry, guys. It's from Presbyterian Hospital." I stand up and start to leave the room, but then remember the crowd out there.

"Take it in here," Penn says. "I don't think you'll be able to hear out there."

I nod and answer. "Hello?"

"Mr. Shaw?" A woman with a no-nonsense voice waits for my response.

"Yes?"

"Weston Alexander Shaw?"

"This is Weston Alexander Shaw. Who is this?"

"Your son was admitted into the ER at Presbyterian Hospital this morning," she says.

My stomach takes a dive, and I shake my head even though she can't see me.

"I don't…have a son," I say.

I'm facing the wall, but the low chatter in the room goes silent, and I can feel four sets of eyes on my back.

"Your name is on the birth certificate. The baby was born in this hospital a couple months ago, and we hoped that you were the next of kin."

I swallow hard, my vision blurring and thoughts flying at rapid speed. I've never had sex without a condom. Women I've never even met have claimed they're having my baby before, but my lawyers proved the allegations were false.

"Mr. Shaw?"

"This is a joke, right? Who put you up to this? Who the fuck is this?"

"Mr. Shaw, I assure you this is not a joke. There was a car accident this morning, and if you really are Weston Alexander Shaw, your son was involved."

"Okay, I'll play along. Where do I find him?"

"Presbyterian Hospital. Come to the ER and ask for Wanda Dixon," she says and hangs up.

I stare at the phone and turn in slow motion toward the guys. They're all staring at me in concern. Bowie is closest to where I am and he stands and puts his hand on my back.

"What was that about?" he asks.

"That was the hospital. They said my son is there. This isn't funny." I point around the table. "If I find out you guys were behind this, I'm kicking your asses."

Henley frowns. "Weston. Slow down. We wouldn't mess with you about something like this. I'd call the team's lawyers if I were you though."

"I need to get to the hospital. She said my name is on the birth certificate. That can't be right."

Bowie squeezes my shoulder and lowers to meet my eyes.

"It'll be okay," he says. "You've got this, whatever comes. Okay? I'm sure it's just a mix-up."

I nod and they all stand.

"We'll come with you," Henley says.

"No, it's okay. I wouldn't want to give the nurses a heart attack when they see all of you coming." I try for light, but my heart is racing.

"Let us know what's going on, if we can do anything," Rhodes says.

"I will. Thanks."

Penn opens the door and leads the way. "Coming through. We've got an emergency," he says.

We weave through the people still hoping to see Mustangs players, pretending we don't hear when we're asked for autographs. When we're outside, I take off in a jog.

"Call me," Penn yells, as I get in my SUV.

The drive to Denver feels longer than ever, but it's really only forty minutes or so. It may as well be another world from the idyllic streets of Silver Hills.

My thoughts are at war, divided into two camps: I can't possibly have a child, and what if I do?

CHAPTER TWO

FACING THE ENEMY

SADIE

I back out of my sister's hospital room in shock and disbelief. My eyes are too blurred with tears to see clearly as I race out of her room and down the hall, frantically searching for Caleb. I only got the call from the hospital half an hour ago, but since I live close to the hospital, I was here within ten minutes.

I was still too late.

I check my phone to see if my parents have called me

back and there's nothing. They're visiting my mom's sister in Missouri and weren't planning to start driving home until tomorrow. I've left messages, but they're not great about checking their phones when they're away, and I don't want to tell them anything in a message.

I rush into Caleb's room and see a guy standing near the crib. Dark hair, tall, broad muscled shoulders. *No. Tell me this isn't happening.* I'd recognize him anywhere. *Weston Shaw.* My sister and I have watched him play on TV every week for the past two years. I rush toward the bed and when he turns and meets my eyes, my blood goes cold.

"What are *you* doing here?" I spit out.

He reels back, studying my face. He looks confused and upset.

I move to the other side of Caleb's crib, and the tears fall all over again as I look him over and say a silent prayer of thanks that he's okay.

"Are you—" Weston starts. "Who are you?"

He holds out his hand, eventually dropping it when I ignore him.

"I'm Weston Shaw. I got a call that my s—"

A nurse hurries into the room, interrupting Weston, and her smile is luminous when she sees him. I'm not sure she realizes anyone else is in the room, including Caleb.

"Hi, Mr. Shaw. We've been expecting you," she says.

My mouth drops open. They've been *expecting* him? How is this happening? I turn, looking back at Weston with renewed fury. I'm heartbroken, terrified, and every protective bone in my body is on alert.

"You have exactly two seconds to get out of here," I say coldly.

Surprise crosses his features, and it's an expression I'm sad to admit I've already seen on his son's face.

"Look, this is a hard situation—God, I don't even *know* the situation," he stumbles around his words, "but can you please just tell me the truth? Is this my son?" he asks, looking down at Caleb asleep in the crib.

His face softens as he looks him over.

"Is he sick?" he asks the nurse.

"Would that make a difference?" I ask coldly.

I've already checked Caleb's face and fingers for any scrapes, any signs that he was hurt. He looks perfect, and Sasha's doctor assured me that he is.

"Of course, it makes a difference. What kind of person is okay with a child being sick?" he says. "Why is he here?" He glances at the nurse. "I'm sorry, maybe you can catch me up on the details. I got a phone call saying my son was here, and I wasn't aware until that moment that I had a son."

I let out a sound of derision and both Weston and the nurse turn to glare at me.

"Ma'am, I'm not sure who you are, but visiting hours are for family only," the nurse says.

"I *am* his family. More than this guy is." I stare at her defiantly and she backs down.

"Well, I'll ask that you keep your differences outside this room," she says haughtily.

I feel Weston's eyes on me like a weight dragging me to the bottom of the ocean. The need to pick Caleb up and bolt with him is so strong right now.

Dr. Williams walks through the door, and I sag in relief. The nurse leaves, happy to leave Dr. Williams to deal with this. His expression is full of sympathy when he looks at me.

"You can see for yourself that Caleb's fine, Sadie," he says softly.

Tears drip down my face and I nod. "Yes, thank you."

Dr. Williams turns to Weston and his eyes widen in recognition.

"I'm Dr. Williams," he says.

"Weston Shaw," Weston answers, shaking Dr. Williams' hand. "Is the baby okay?"

"I recognize you," Dr. Williams says, smiling kindly. "And yes, he's just fine. Not even a scratch on him. It's remarkable really. I'm just so sorry for your loss." He glances at me, his expression grave. "We did everything we could for Sasha."

"Sasha," Weston repeats. "Who is Sasha?"

His eyes fly to mine, and I can see when it all lines up for him. I'm a year and a half older than Sasha and my hair is darker than hers. She is a few inches shorter than me and has always hated that.

Was a few inches shorter.

Was.

There's no way I can think of my sister in the past tense.

No one has ever confused me for Sasha, but we look like sisters, like family.

I wonder if Weston's thinking about their night together or the way he avoided her calls afterward. If he has any idea what she went through to have this baby.

"So you're not the mother?" he asks. "Are you related to Sasha?"

Unbelievable. He doesn't even remember Sasha?

"Do I *look* like someone you slept with?" My hands are shaking, just from being in the same room with him. I hate that I'm having to talk to him at all, especially right now.

Dr. Williams turns to Weston in confusion.

I scroll through my phone until I find the picture Sasha sent of her and Weston at the bar the night of their one-night stand. When I hold it up, Weston's face pales.

"Now, do you remember her?" I spit out.

Weston swallows hard and he nods slowly.

"Can one of you please tell me what's going on?" Weston asks.

"Sasha and Caleb were in a car accident early this morning," Dr. Williams says. "Sasha's injuries were extensive and unfortunately, she passed an hour ago. We went through the usual protocol of trying to notify family and saw that Sasha and Caleb had been in this hospital before. We found the birth certificate first and got your name from that," he tells Weston before looking at me, "and then found your name, Sadie, from when Sasha was admitted for delivering Caleb."

"I was in the room with my sister when she had him," I whisper. The tears just won't stop falling. I look at Dr. Williams pleadingly.

Dr. Williams is paged over the sound system and he gives us an apologetic look. "Excuse me," he says, bolting from the room.

It's quiet for a few seconds as we both look at Caleb.

"I'm so sorry for your loss," Weston says. "Your sister. I…I can't imagine."

I'm caught off guard by how genuine he seems. But in the next second, my anger flares hotter.

"This is an opportunity for you." I grip the crib until my knuckles are white. "You didn't want to deal with Sasha when she was pregnant, but now you're all over this? No, you don't get to do this now."

He takes a step back. "I had no idea she was pregnant. And if I'd been told, I wouldn't have abandoned her. I'm not that kind of guy."

A caustic laugh erupts out of me and my face crumbles. I put my head in my hands. I've just lost my sister, and as complicated as she was, I loved her with all my heart.

I feel a hand on my shoulder and I go still. It's huge and warm and it's been a long time since a man has touched me. I'm running on fumes and no sleep, and if I could, I'd pretend I didn't despise the man for this moment of comfort, but I can't.

I've been working nonstop for the past two months because my sister couldn't and because this man wasn't in the picture, and I'm tired.

My eyes lift to his and my expression makes his hand drop from my shoulder.

"Don't trouble yourself with us," I say. "We've been just fine without you, trust me."

"Sadie, if Caleb is my son, I'm not walking away."

He stands taller and I just thought his height was intimidating before. When his eyes drill into me this way, the soft edges disappear and I see the man I'm usually watching on the TV screen when he's facing an opponent out on the field.

He walks closer to Caleb and stares at him for a few long moments.

"He's so tiny," Weston whispers.

Caleb is a two-month-old baby. I'm not sure what the guy expected.

He reaches out and touches Caleb's fingers, and his eyes are glassy when he looks at me again.

"My legal team will be here shortly. We'll do a paternity test to be certain. They're equipped to handle it and the results will be faster through them."

I roll my eyes. "It doesn't matter what the test says. You haven't been here. I have. And I'll be the one taking care of him."

"You don't know me yet, Sadie, but you will. I'm a decent person. I'm kind. Compassionate. I'm a good brother and son. A good friend. I'm not perfect. I give my friends shit, but it's all in fun. I know how to take it from them too. I don't have a great track record with women, but it's not that I'm dishonest or that I treat them poorly—it's that I haven't had the time or the desire for a committed relationship and I'm clear about that from the start. What I'm *not* is someone who doesn't take his responsibilities seriously. I'm not the enemy here, and there is no way in hell that I'm walking away from this little boy now that I know about him." His eyebrow lifts as he finishes. "Got it?"

I curse under my breath.

A thread of uncertainty weaves through me. What if he's telling the truth? What if he didn't know all this time? I grip the edge of Caleb's crib even tighter to keep standing. The one person who could set all of this straight is gone.

Would Sasha have lied to me about something as serious as this?

It wouldn't be the first time.

But no, I watched her call him. Right? She said she called him at least ten times.

She also claimed she didn't put his name on the birth certificate, and that wasn't true.

Fear settles in my chest. I've given up a lot to take care of this little boy, and I'd do it again in a heartbeat.

But I don't have a legal team. My parents are crazy about Caleb, but Sasha never told them the father's identity, and they're not in a position to help me fight this with a millionaire quarterback. Our landlord Jess has been kind to Sasha and me, but it's not like she could say or do anything that would back me up in court. *They always pay their rent on time.* How much weight does that hold?

Am I really going to lose my nephew to this playboy asshole?

I don't know how to stop it, but I know I can't ever let that happen.

CHAPTER THREE

IT'S ALL NEW

WESTON

The next twenty-four hours go by in a blur.

I'm a father.

I can't believe it.

Caleb Sebastian Shaw arrived on December fifth at 10:50 p.m., a night when I thought the most important thing in my life was the game we'd just won at Clarity Field. I was completely clueless that my son was being born across town.

He is two months, two weeks, and three days old.

He's perfect.

When he's hungry, his face curls up and he howls like he's facing the worst injustice. But Sadie picks him up and soothes him, and his tears stop.

He has a full head of dark hair and blue eyes that stare back at me, full lips that lift in a smile when I talk to him, and when he stretches and his mouth opens impossibly wide to yawn, I've never seen anything cuter.

I've stared at him for hours, captivated, and when Sadie falls asleep in the chair next to his bed, I cry.

I can't believe I've missed this much time with him.

My parents are lawyers, but I didn't want to bring them into this until I knew without a doubt that he's mine. That's not exactly right—I knew he was mine the moment I saw him, but I needed proof. So I asked the team's legal team for help and they delivered. Once they arrived, Sadie retreated to her corner like she was already defeated.

I don't know what to say to her. I feel awful for her even though I don't understand what all her anger toward me is about. I should be the one angry for being kept in the dark, but I think none of this has sunk in yet. I'm more *confused* than anything and still in shock that I'm a dad.

Sadie's lost her sister. No one should have to endure that.

And it's obvious she loves this little guy with all her heart.

I'm not trying to take him away from her, but she's going to have a fight on her hands if she tries to take him away from me.

So, I have a plan to present to her when she wakes up.

I still haven't called my family. Maybe after I've talked with Sadie, that can be the next step.

The hospital has been generous. I'd like to think they are with everyone, but I'm not that foolish. They're shaken up and doing everything they can to avoid a loud lawsuit from me. And I think everyone involved is grateful the paparazzi hasn't gotten wind of this yet—my security team is here, keeping them out. After losing the mother of my child on the ER table and knowing there was a question of paternity, the hospital has bent over backwards to be helpful. They moved us into a nice room when my lawyers arrived, somewhere we could have more privacy.

Sadie seems disgusted by the whole thing, and honestly, I can't blame her. I'm disgusted with myself for not remembering. After last year's Super Bowl win, I got a little out of control. Too much alcohol, too many women. Both were just so easily accessible all the time. But this is my son we're talking about. All of this could have been prevented if Sasha had been honest with me.

I've checked back through my phone log and texts, asked every lawyer, while looking them in the eye, whether Sasha Chapman ever contacted them. They swear she didn't, and I believe them. I don't know why she'd lie to her sister, but I didn't know her beyond a hookup. Now I wish I did.

I will be Caleb's father and protector, but holy fuck—how? I don't have a clue about what it takes to be a dad.

It kills me that he won't know his mother. And that, if not for a crazy set of circumstances, I might have never known him either.

My phone vibrates in my pocket and I pull it out, silencing it. The guys have gone nuts in the group chat since I ran out on them yesterday. I haven't told them about the test results, so they're full of questions in the thread.

RHODES

You don't have to tell us what's going on, but we're here if you need us.

BOWIE

I knew you wanted to be in the club, but this is going a little far, even for you.

PENN

Does he look like you?

HENLEY

Shit. This is crazy.

RHODES

My God, Weston. Talk to us. Do you need us there? Should we come over?

BOWIE

He's got his hands full, man. We probably shouldn't be blowing his phone up.

RHODES

You're right. My bad. But if you need us, say the word.

And then this morning…

HENLEY

How's it going over there?

BOWIE

Any news?

RHODES

I was trying to be quiet and not blow up his phone anymore.

PENN

Need some coffee?

HENLEY

You'll tell us if you're a dad, right? We're not breathing a word of this to anyone. I know that goes without saying, but…in case it needed to be said.

RHODES

I love that new baby smell.

BOWIE

And again, we're blowing up his phone.

I swipe my hand down my face and try not to laugh out loud. Figures it would be these guys who could pull me out of the dark cloud I'm in, even if for just a second.

Morning. Thanks for not saying a word to anyone. I still haven't told my parents. The team's legal team has been with me all night. He's mine. He's incredible. He's perfect. I wouldn't say no to two coffees, but we're not having visitors just yet. I'll explain more later.

Within thirty seconds, the texts start rolling in.

RHODES

What the fuck?! Who's the mom? Do you remember her? Why the hell is she just showing up now with this news?

BOWIE

That's incredible, West. You're making it weird, Rhodes.

RHODES

I'm saying what we're all thinking.

PENN

I'm shook.

HENLEY

Shut up, motherfuckers. Are you okay, Weston?

I honestly don't know. I'll explain everything later.

I stand up when Caleb starts fretting. I'm still hesitant to just pick him up anytime, so I leave him in the crib, but I know he likes his pacifier, so I put it in his mouth. He sucks it so hard it bobs up and down, but he quiets down. I stare at him and grin. My friends' excitement was contagious. Maybe I *will* be able to handle this.

Caleb will be released later this morning and Sadie and I have a lot to work out before then.

It's as if she can hear me thinking about her because she stretches and then jolts, sitting straight up, her face panicked.

I can see it the second she remembers everything. She flinches, and a cloud covers her face, her eyes filling before she straightens and rushes to Caleb's crib. By the time she's composed herself and looks at me, I've seen a thousand expressions cross her face, all of them devastating.

"Sadie," I say softly. "Can we talk?"

She nods.

"One of my friends is bringing coffee over. I asked him to bring one for you too. Are you a coffee drinker?"

She glances at the clock on the wall. Nine o'clock.

"I've usually had at least two cups by now," she says.

I smile tentatively and her eyes narrow.

Clearing my throat, I look at Caleb for courage and get distracted by how cute he looks when he sleeps.

"Is he always this fucking adorable?" I ask.

"Every second of every day," she whispers.

"You've spent a lot of time with him."

It's not even a question at this point. It's obvious, the way she anticipates his needs. She's known when he's hungry, when he's gassy, when he needs his diaper changed, the way he likes to be held. I've watched her handle him throughout the night, feeling helpless and completely overwhelmed.

I glance at Sadie and she's avoiding eye contact now. I guess that moment of sharing is over.

"Can I have coffee before we talk?" she asks.

"Sure."

She gives one brisk nod and runs her fingers through her long, dark brown hair. The light from the window casts reds and golds through it and it's thick and shiny. Her head dips, but her eyes tilt up, watchful and somewhat accusing, as she catches me staring.

I turn away quickly.

There are two knocks on the door and I move toward it, opening cautiously. So far the hospital has been good about keeping this quiet, but I don't trust it to stay that way. The sooner we get out of here, the better.

Penn's eyes meet mine under the dark bill of his baseball cap. He's got sunglasses resting on top of his cap and clothes he would usually not be caught wearing.

I snort. "You think people can't tell it's you?"

He lifts a shoulder and hands me the drink holder with four coffees instead of the two I asked for. I instantly feel bad for giving him a hard time.

"You're saving me right now," I groan. "Thank you."

"Not a problem. I stayed at a friend's near here last night, so I was close. Let me know if you need anything later."

I nod. "I will. Really, man. Thank you."

He grins and lowers his sunglasses, walking away. His massive frame makes the hospital hallway look cramped. I turn around and take the coffee to Sadie.

"He brought extra," I tell her.

She takes a cup and a few creamers and pauses when she opens the lid and sees how creamy it already is. I make a face.

"Sorry, he might've just ordered flat whites—that's what I usually get. Let me see what these are."

I check the rest and they're all the same.

"If it's coffee, I'll like it," she says.

She takes a long sip and lets out a ragged sigh afterward.

We're both quiet as we drink our coffee, and she's on her second one when she meets my eyes.

"Okay," she says.

That's it.

I sit for another few seconds waiting, but when I realize she's not going to say anything else, I finish my coffee and set the cup down. I'm leaning against the wall facing Caleb's bed and she sits on the small couch next to him. I move to the chair she was in earlier, so I don't tower over her.

But then she opens her mouth and the words gush out, knocking me sideways.

"I've been with him every step of the way," she says softly. She takes a deep breath and her voice comes back stronger. "I felt his kicks, I read him books while my sister was pregnant, I was there when he took his first breath. I was the first face he saw." Her face crumbles as she cries. "I've worked nonstop to make sure he had a roof over his head. I just lost my sister and now you want to take Caleb from me too?"

"I understand, Sadie, but he's my son and I've already missed out on so much. I never felt those kicks. I missed reading books to him, missed hearing his first breath…my face should've been one of the first he saw…"

Her face has already turned thunderous and I lift my hand, hoping to stop whatever she thinks I'm about to say.

"I don't want to keep you from seeing him." The words rush out.

Her mouth opens and closes, and her vivid blue eyes suddenly look violet in the bright light of the morning. Or maybe that's the tears in them that make them so startling.

"I don't know anything about him…or you…or Sasha. But I want to. I think we could work together to give him the best life possible—"

She wipes her face when a tear drips down her cheek. "How do you see that working?"

It sounds more like an accusation than a question, and I pause, trying not to go into defense mode.

"Well, where do you live?" I ask.

"I don't see how that's relevant."

An edge of frustration creeps into my tone. "I live in Silver Hills. I'm trying to figure out how far you are from me, if your job is by your house…what it would look like to do this."

"Do what?" she snaps.

"Raise Caleb!" I curse under my breath when Caleb wakes up and starts crying.

I try to put his pacifier in, but this time, he spits it out and wails.

Sadie stands up and starts mixing a bottle. When it's ready, she moves to pick him up.

"Can I give him the bottle?" I ask.

She takes a deep breath like I'm trying her very last nerve and I take a deep breath of my own because she's starting to try mine too.

CHAPTER FOUR

MEET IN THE MIDDLE

SADIE

I back up, holding my hand out for him to take the baby, and he steps closer and carefully picks him up. He holds him awkwardly, still tentative with him, and Caleb looks tiny in Weston's large hands. Caleb's face is red now and I don't want him to be miserable.

"Hurry." I point to the bottle and Weston is still trying to get him situated in his arms. "Here, put this arm underneath so he feels secure. And make sure to watch his head."

Weston shoots me a grateful look and then grabs the bottle, shaking it a little like he's seen me do. He sits down and gives Caleb the bottle and Caleb stops crying for a second and then turns his head, crying harder than before.

"What am I doing wrong?" he asks.

"I don't know. Sasha only nurses him…nursed." I swallow the lump in my throat. "Maybe just try putting the nipple near his lips and see if he'll latch onto it."

Weston's cheeks turn pink and the more he tries, the harder Caleb cries. He stands and holds him out for me to take. I motion for him to put him on my left side and when I have him in my arms, he hands me the bottle. Caleb fusses for me too, but I just keep teasing his lips with the nipple and he's hungry, so he eventually drinks a little.

He's cried so hard though, he gets the hiccups and I put him on my shoulder, trying to burp him. He cries and cries and a nurse comes in with a sympathetic smile.

"I'm Dana. My shift just started and I'll be checking on Caleb until he's discharged. Anything I can do to help?"

"He took the bottles from me before, but he's used to nursing by now," I tell her.

"Would you like me to try?" Dana asks.

I nod, reluctantly handing him to her. She sits down on the couch and gets him bundled up before trying the bottle again. He settles in her arms as soon as he's bundled and starts drinking the bottle when she lifts it to his lips.

"Some babies love to be swaddled," Dana says.

I curse under my breath. I knew Caleb liked that—Sasha always swaddled him—but I was so nervous around Weston, I didn't even think about it.

"You made that look easy," Weston says.

Dana laughs, her pretty eyes locked on Weston.

"I'll show you how to do it when he's done eating. It's easy," she says.

She stares at Weston for a long time and then sees me noticing and looks down at Caleb. Weston watches Caleb eat, his expression wistful.

When Weston feels my eyes on him, he clears his throat and besides the sound of Caleb drinking his bottle, the room gets quiet. After Caleb's fed, Dana changes his diaper and wraps him back up. Weston studies her technique so intently, Dana flushes with the attention and her hands are shaking by the time she finishes.

I roll my eyes, and Weston happens to catch that and his eyes narrow on me, his jaw clenching.

"Let me know if you need anything else. The doctor will be in shortly, I think, to discuss Caleb's discharge, but just press that button if you need me." She smiles at Weston and I'm not sure she even still remembers I'm in the room.

Pretty boy over here just breathes and women fall all over themselves. It's quite sickening really.

When she leaves the room, we look at Caleb for a few minutes and his eyes are already closing to take another nap.

"He sleeps a lot," Weston whispers. "Well, not as much at two this morning."

"Right. Sasha was trying to get him on more of a schedule, but it hasn't worked very well yet."

The truth is, *I've* been trying to get Sasha to work on his schedule. She's always been a night owl and since she isn't working, she stays up all night with him and then they want to sleep all day.

She's gone hits me all over again.

My phone buzzes and I'm both relieved and devastated to see that it's my parents. I hold up my phone. "My parents. I need to take this."

He nods and I leave the room, bracing myself for this conversation.

"Hello?" I answer.

"Sorry, honey, we've been camping and haven't had cell service. Is everything all right?" my mom asks.

I hear my aunt and uncle laughing in the background and hate that I'm about to turn my mom's life upside down.

"No, Mom. There was an accident."

She gasps and I talk over her.

"Caleb is okay, but Sasha…" My voice breaks and I start sobbing. "Mom, Mom, Sasha…she didn't make it."

It's quiet for a second and then I hear her cries. My dad takes the phone.

I go to some kind of numb place as I tell him the details I know. Sasha slid on ice and hit another car. Caleb's not hurt and neither was the other driver. Sasha's gone.

My dad's voice is hollow when he finally says they'll start driving back right away. It'll be a little over twelve hours, but they'll drive straight through.

I'm not sure how long I stand there after we hang up, and when I go back into the room, Weston looks at me pensively but doesn't say anything. I realize then that I didn't tell my parents about Weston.

It's probably another hour before he tries to talk to me again and I'm grateful for the reprieve. I need the time to process…I think I'll need a lot of time.

"Did Sasha and Caleb live with you?" he finally asks.

I nod.

"Do you rent or own a place?" he asks.

"What does that have to do with anything?" I frown.

He takes a deep breath and runs his hand through his hair. It falls perfectly into place again. When he looks up and his eyes lock with mine, I freeze, my heart taking a dive into the ground.

I just know I'm not going to like what he's about to say.

"I'd like the two of you to come stay with me for a few weeks."

My mouth drops and then I'm shaking my head. "Absolutely not."

"Hear me out," he says, holding up his hand. "I don't know how to take care of a baby yet. You do, and Caleb is used to you. I have a big place. Six bedrooms. You could pick out which one you want—I'm not picky. It's on a few acres. A swimming pool, pool house, a lake beyond that with a bridge crossing over the water. The place is big enough that you wouldn't have to see me all the time. We'd be sharing a kitchen, but I'd respect your space and we could figure out times to have it to ourselves if you don't want to see me. And we'd both be able to see Caleb whenever we want."

"I want to see him all the time," I seethe.

"So do I." He scowls at me, and it's the first time he's really shown his temper to this extent.

"I want to see him *without you around*," I reiterate.

"Look, I'm not thrilled about seeing you either, but it's either that or I take him home with me when he's discharged, and at the most, you get periodic supervised visits." He puts his hands on his hips and sighs, his hands dropping in exhaustion. "That's not what I want, Sadie. But I will if you force me. I don't know why Caleb was kept a fucking secret from me, but you're not getting rid of me, so either learn to deal with it," he says between his teeth, "or get yourself a good lawyer."

I step back like I've been hit, feeling like all the air has just been let out of me. The backs of my knees hit the couch and I fall onto it, suddenly cold and shaky.

He might not have wanted Caleb before, but he wants him now, and if he decided to take me to court over this, I wouldn't stand a chance in hell against the great Weston Shaw. He's Caleb's biological dad, he has more money than God, and all he has to do is smile that supermodel smile and flash those arm muscles and he'll get whatever he wants.

I've seen him practically charm the pants off of everyone who's talked to him so far.

"I want it in writing that I'll always be a part of his life." My voice is so soft I clear my throat and say louder, "Before I'll agree to anything."

"You don't get to make the rules here, Sadie."

His tone is so much sweeter than his words that it lulls me into a false sense of security at first…until I digest what he's said.

"I can't stay with you. It's too far to go back and forth from here to Silver Hills. I'm a waitress and take double shifts all the time—"

"I'm giving you my word that I want you to be part of Caleb's life," he says. "I'm giving you my word that I'll take care of both of you. We can talk about specifics once we get to the house."

He holds up his hand and taps his fingers one by one with his next words.

First finger: "But your sister kept my child from me."

Second finger: "You are not his mother."

Third finger: "And I'm not playing any more fucking games here."

He licks his lips and I watch the movement, suddenly so tired I can't think straight.

"These are your choices." Again, his tone is so deceptively kind. "We can take this to court, or you can stay with me and we'll come up with a peaceful way to get along, for Caleb's sake."

The room is silent for a few long moments.

"I love him so much," I say, my voice breaking. I lean my head back, staring at the ceiling and trying not to cry. "I'd do anything for him. *Anything*." My lips tremble and I press them together. "The night I found out my sister was pregnant, I told her to tell you right then. I never thought it was right to not tell you. And I don't know if you're lying to me and you really didn't know." I turn to look at him now. "Or if she lied to me when she said she tried again and again to reach you." I angrily swipe away the tears that keep falling. "But I know I can't win against you." My voice breaks and I lower my head, my shoulders shaking as I cry.

God, this is so humiliating, but I can't seem to get it together. When I look up at him, he's studying me with an unreadable expression.

"And I can't lose him." I wipe my nose and shake my head. "Losing my sister is…it's the worst thing I've ever known, but losing him…it would kill me."

Something flashes across his face. Compassion? Annoyance? Guilt? I don't know him, so I don't know what it is, but I take a deep breath and this time my chest fills with air…like it finally worked.

"I'll stay with you," I finally say.

He looks up at the ceiling, his shoulders lifting with his deep breath, and when he looks at me again, he's sober and intense.

"Thank you," he says.

CHAPTER FIVE

WHAT A DIFFERENCE A DAY MAKES

WESTON

Getting her to agree to stay a few weeks with me was easier than I'd expected. Once that's behind me, I step out of the room and walk down the hall until I find the stairs. When I'm certain the stairwell is empty, I call Felicity. She answers after two rings.

"Hey, I was just thinking about you," she says.

"What were you thinking?"

"That I'm going to start charging you for every cute

reporter who flirts with you during interviews. Seriously, it's gross to see your brother shamelessly flirted with on TV."

When I'm quiet, she says, "What's wrong?"

I take a deep breath. "I found out I have a child. A baby… his name is Caleb."

"*What*?"

"The hospital called yesterday and said my son had been admitted. He was in a car accident with his mom and when I got here, she had already passed. I was on the birth certificate."

"Oh my God, Weston. Who is it? She died? Why didn't you call me? I would've been there with you."

"I know you would've. His mom's name was Sasha Chapman. I didn't know her well. I've been trying to piece it together. I think we met at a party Cal Morris had not long after the Super Bowl last year." I bend over, feeling a wave of panic. "I haven't told Mom and Dad yet. I needed proof before I dragged you guys into this. The Mustangs legal team did all the tests and he's mine. But I knew when I saw him."

"You did?" Her voice cracks. "Weston. A baby boy," she says softly. "This is amazing and…heartbreaking. How old is he?"

"Two and a half months old."

"You must be in shock. I can't believe this."

"I am in shock. I don't—Felicity…what if I'm not good at this?"

"Good at being a dad? Weston, listen to me. You're going to be *great*." Her voice cracks again and she's crying when she says, "I can't wait to see you be a dad. You've got this. I know you do."

"I hope you're right."

"I'm right about this, West. I don't doubt you for a

second. Look how good I turned out having you as a big brother."

I exhale, feeling slightly calmer already. I should've called her immediately. My older sister Olivia, on the other hand…I can already hear the crap she'll give me over this. "Love you."

"I love *you*. When can I see him?"

"Soon. There's a lot to work out. Sasha's sister Sadie is… involved. There's a lot to tell you, but I just didn't want more time to go by without you knowing. I'll call you later and fill you in on the rest. I'm excited for you to meet him. He's perfect. I'll send you a few pictures as soon as we hang up."

The call to my parents is a lot harder to get through, with a lot more questions, but ultimately, they're kind and loving, as always. I let them know I don't have many answers yet, but that there's no fight for me to see my son, and that seems to ease their minds. They're excited to meet their grandson. I ask them to let Olivia know and promise to have them over as soon as we're settled.

I didn't tell my parents or Felicity about Sadie coming to the house or really many details other than the fact that Caleb's here, he's mine, and he's healthy. I already know they will think Sadie staying with me is a terrible idea. They're probably right, but she just lost her sister. I felt awful even talking about a lawsuit when she's already lost so much.

I don't know what I'd do if I lost my sisters. Olivia and I aren't even very close, but it'd still be devastating. And Felicity—she's been my best friend since the day she was born.

When I go back into the room, I can tell Sadie's been crying again. She's holding Caleb and she looks up when I walk in.

"They're discharging him soon," she says.

As she's saying that, the nurse comes in and walks us through the discharge papers. When she leaves, we gather the few things from the room and then look at each other like *now what?*

"I'll follow you to your place," I say. "We'll get a few things and I can arrange for movers to get more tomorrow."

"That's not necessary. We don't need to involve movers. I can get what I need and meet you at your house."

"Okay, I'll take Caleb with me."

Her eyes flash, a frown deepening as she shakes her head. "No. He stays with me. You don't even know what to do with him yet."

"I'll manage. You'll have to forgive me for not trusting you to take him by yourself." I lift my shoulder and she sighs.

"I'm not going to disappear with him," she says softly.

"I don't want to test out that theory."

"Fine. You can follow me, but don't judge us when you see our place." She points at me.

"I won't."

She rolls her eyes and mutters something but carefully places Caleb in his car seat. An officer came in earlier to let Sadie know they'll call when she can pick up any belongings from the wreck. When the hospital said we'd have to have a car seat before Caleb could go home, I thought I'd need to go buy one. I was surprised when Sadie said she had one in her car.

I'd like to think I'd be an awesome uncle and do whatever Felicity or Olivia needed, but I'm not sure I would ever think of keeping a backup car seat in my vehicle at all times.

I'll be needing one for my SUV anyway.

And a ton of other baby things that I have no clue about....

How the hell am I going to do this?

I pick up the car seat and we walk out of the hospital room.

"Do you mind if we take the stairs?" I ask. "Less chance of photos being taken that way."

"Okay."

We're quiet as we walk to the parking garage. Sadie gave me her address when we were still upstairs, and I can see my SUV just a few cars down from hers, so I'm not worried she'll make a quick escape.

I set Caleb in my SUV and get the base out of Sadie's car. It takes a ridiculous amount of time to figure out how to put it in my back seat, but I finally do. Sadie shows me how to click the car seat into the base and waits until I'm behind her to pull out. That small gesture gives me hope that we'll be able to work together peaceably.

I second-guess everything the whole way to her apartment.

Do I really want Sadie staying with me? Not at all.

Do I want my son? Yes.

Should I be working so hard to keep Caleb's aunt in his life full-time after she helped keep him a secret from me? I don't know the answer to that.

My parents and sister Olivia own their own practice and the Law Offices of Shaw & Shaw have an impeccable record. My brother-in-law Sutton is a judge.

But the truth is, even if I didn't have the best resources on my side, Sadie wouldn't stand a chance in court if she ever tried to file for custody. Not only that, it wouldn't take much for me to keep her from seeing my son.

It just feels wrong. Not as wrong as Sasha not telling me about Caleb, but enough that I'd hate myself for it.

We drive into a neighborhood that's older but well-kept. Sadie pulls into the parking lot of an apartment building and parks near the entrance. I park near her. Caleb is awake and I smile down at him. He stares at me intensely before smiling back and I laugh in surprise. Every single time I look at him, I get this weird ache in my chest.

"Hey there, little guy," I say like a goofy fool.

Sadie bumps into me and we both turn to look at each other, too distracted by looking at the baby to care about anything else. Her smile is bright and pretty and for a tiny second, that shadow isn't in her eyes. It quickly clouds over when she looks at me and motions for me to follow her.

Once we're inside, we take the elevator to the third floor and she unlocks the door. She's gotten increasingly anxious on the way up.

"It's not much," she says.

We walk into the apartment, and it's simple but clean. The only clutter seems to be a few small baby things.

"It's nice," I say.

"Most of his stuff is back here." She points behind her shoulder.

She walks down the hall and from what I can tell, there's only one bedroom with a twin bed and a crib. There's a changing table by the closet. Sadie opens the closet and it's full of baby clothes and I'm assuming, Sasha's wardrobe.

She flinches when she sees Sasha's clothes but grabs a bag and puts Caleb's outfits in there.

"What can I do to help?" I ask.

"Take one of these bags and get all the diapers it'll hold. They're right there." She points to the little shelf by the changing table. "And lots of wipes. I can get his clothes and toys…and pictures."

She pauses by the bed and picks up a picture. It's of Sasha and Caleb. Her eyes fill with tears and she tucks the frame into the bag and keeps moving.

When she has everything she wants from the room, she hands me another bag.

"For his books and toys that are in the living room. I'll get my things and then we can go."

We walk back into the living room and she bends down at the small chest of drawers, pulling her clothes out and packing them. I notice the pillow and blanket folded up beside the couch.

"Is this where you sleep?" I ask.

She nods. Her eyes narrow on me and I try to school my sympathetic expression. Some couches aren't the worst to sleep on, but this one looks lumpy and narrow.

"I have a few things to get from the bathroom." She tilts her head toward the hall. "There's a portable crib folded up in that closet." She points to the door.

"Okay, I'll grab it."

She nods and rushes down the hall, and when she comes back a few minutes later, her eyes are red and swollen, and her cheeks are splotchy.

Fuck.

She grabs a few more frames and tucks them in her bag and sets all her bags by the door.

"I'm ready," she says.

"I can take this stuff out and come back for the rest…if you want to make sure you have everything you want…" I watch as she swallows hard and nods.

"Thanks."

I take as much as I can carry and load it into my SUV, and when I come back to the apartment, there are a few more bags in front of the door.

"I forgot about the food." She's in the kitchen and putting food in paper bags. "I don't want it to go to waste."

I stand in the doorway of the kitchen and see her wipe the tears from her face as she hurries to empty out the fridge.

"Sadie," I say softly, "we can come back and do this another time...if it's too much."

She takes a deep breath and it's shaky. "Okay."

I take the bags from the counter and she follows me out of the kitchen. I take the groceries to the car and when I come back, we're able to get the rest of the bags and Caleb to the car in one more trip.

"Are you okay to drive?" I ask when everything but Caleb is loaded in my SUV. She's still crying. It's almost like she doesn't even realize it, the tears are just falling. "I'd feel better if we sent someone to pick up your car. My friend Penn might still be in the area and he could drive it to my place."

She's holding Caleb's carrier and looks down at him.

Her eyes are in such pain when they meet mine again.

"That might be for the best," she says.

I nod and open the passenger side for her, taking Caleb as she climbs in. Sadie's holding her keys and when I hold out my hand, she places them in my palm and I put them under her driver's seat, texting Penn when I've shut the door.

Are you still in the area?

He texts right back.

PENN

Yes, sir.

Would you be able to pick up a car and drive it out to my house sometime tonight? There's no rush.

PENN

I'm on it.

I send him the address, tell him where the keys are, and he says he's five minutes away.

You're a lifesaver. Thank you.

PENN

I've got you, man.

The drive to my house is quiet besides the sounds of Sadie sniffling and Caleb's little baby squeaks.

I don't know what the hell I'm doing, but I think we're in this together.

CHAPTER SIX

THIS ISN'T ME

SADIE

I didn't even have time to be embarrassed about Weston seeing what a dump our apartment is. I was hit so hard by the fact that Sasha is gone. Being in our place made it so much worse. It didn't feel real until then.

I would never admit this to Weston, but I don't know how I would survive if I had to stay there right now.

When we drive into Silver Hills, my spirits buoy slightly. I've always loved this beautiful little town. There are no two houses alike, and I love all the intricate detailing on the colorful homes. The small downtown area is boutique heaven, the perfect place to window shop for someone like me. But I've never even seen this side of Silver Hills…the beyond wealthy side. We pull up to a large gate and Weston puts a code in. The heavy metal gate silently glides open and we drive down the long driveway with trees lining each side. When I see his—*estate* seems like the most fitting term for it—I'm filled with a new level of dread.

How am I supposed to function in a place like this?

He pulls around to the side and I see the lake and pool in the back before we park in the garage. He's been quiet the whole drive, but I think maybe he's nervous when we get out of the SUV. He starts talking fast.

"Just leave it. I can get everything inside," he says. "Let me show you around first."

He's already getting Caleb's car seat out and moving through the massive garage.

"You're welcome to drive any of these. I'm not stingy with my things," he says, pointing to the other vehicles. "Just let me know when you're leaving…"

Is this going to feel like a prison or what?

There's an Audi and a Jeep that is so divine I'd be terrified to drive it, and next to that is a four-wheeler and a boat. And that's just what I can see as I rush past all of it to follow him. He's still talking when he realizes I'm not right behind him and he turns, waiting for me to catch up.

"I haven't been in this house long. I lived a few miles from here and it was a great house, but I was visiting a friend down the street and this was for sale for a long time. I liked the thought of more land, so…" He opens the door, and we walk through a wide hallway into the kitchen and I can't help it, I gasp.

Back before the baby came and I wasn't so sleep-deprived, I'd watch any home renovation show when I couldn't sleep, but my favorites are about the luxury homes. Get me started on those and I'll stay up all night. I've never actually seen a Viking stove in real life before, but I know what it is from those shows. The colors are black and cream and all the doors and windows are arched. It's stunning. There's a huge island and a long table nearby. When we walk into the living room, the arches are carried out in here too, only with columns on either side. There are columns on the second level as well, with beautiful iron railings between them. We keep going and there's a uniquely shaped library, again with an arched door made out of distressed wood and a glass center, and a fireplace near the built-in shelves. It's the second fireplace I've seen. We go into the foyer last, and there are double staircases leading up to the second level.

I'm speechless.

It's beautiful. There's no way I'll ever feel comfortable in a place like this.

"Front door." He points to the gorgeous arched double doors and then turns toward the double staircases. "There are bedrooms up there, and bedrooms downstairs too. Those stairs were where we came in…I don't know if you noticed the door leading to the basement."

I shake my head.

We go up the stairs and he shows me each breathtaking bedroom, and then we go downstairs and there's a movie room with two rows of luxurious chairs.

"For movie night," he says. "I haven't been in this house during the offseason yet—I mean, except for the past couple of weeks—so I haven't gotten to enjoy all the perks fully yet. Do you like wine?" He points out the huge wine cellar—I've never seen anything like it.

I nod and he stops at the large bar and island for entertaining. He bends and opens the beverage fridge—I've sort of been obsessed with those in the house shows I've seen—and holds up a bottle of water, handing it to me.

I take it, thanking him, and we go see more beautiful bedrooms and bathrooms. I think I've counted eight bathrooms.

Caleb wakes up when we're walking back into the main section of the basement, where the movie screen is set up and the bar is next to it. Weston puts the car seat on the bar and looks at me.

"Is it okay if I take him out of the car seat?" he asks.

It's funny that he asks me like I'm the expert.

"Yes. He'll probably want to eat soon and will need his diaper changed."

He takes him out of the car seat and is so cautious. Caleb gets fussy in the time it takes to get him out and Weston looks panicked.

"He's stronger than he looks," I tell him.

He relaxes a little and Caleb settles into his arms.

"What do you think?" Weston asks.

"He looks good."

"I mean the house. Do you think you can be comfortable here?"

I open my mouth, about to say *absolutely not* or something else snotty, but I pause. He's being nice and he doesn't have to be. I could be in my ratty apartment right now crying because my sister *and* my nephew have been taken from me, but for whatever reason, Weston Shaw is being decent about the whole thing.

I haven't figured him out yet, but I don't have to tonight.

It's already been a hard enough couple of days.

"Your house is beautiful," I say instead.

It's the truth, and it seems to help. His shoulders relax.

"Any favorite places you'd like to be?" he asks.

"I sort of got lost. It's big."

He gives me the first honest-to-goodness grin and it's unsettling. Makes me feel a little too off-kilter.

"You can always try out the rooms. If you don't like one, try another," he says.

"Is that what you do? Your place is so clean, I couldn't really tell which room was yours." It's not true. There's a room upstairs that looked lived in, a huge, beautiful room with a great view of the mountains.

"To tell you the truth, I haven't really settled in here yet myself. I bought it and had a decorator do most of this while I was on the road, in and out of here. My family's only come over once, and my parents live ten minutes away."

I break out into a sweat thinking about having to deal with his family. It's hard to imagine them treating me as anything other than the enemy.

"Do they know about Caleb yet?" I ask.

"I called them before we were discharged," he says. "They're excited to meet him. My sister Felicity is too. She's married and lives in Landmark Mountain. It's about an hour and a half away," he adds when I look at him blankly. "I haven't talked to my sister Olivia yet, and she'll have plenty to say about it." He laughs under his breath and the sound disappears when Caleb starts fussing.

"I have a little bit of my sister's pumped milk and formula, but I'll need to buy more formula soon," I say.

"If you give me a list, I can order it or go get it or…we could go together."

I reach for Caleb when he starts crying harder and head toward the stairs. "He gets mad when he's not fed as fast as he wants."

"Where's his milk?"

"The frozen milk is in a container in the paper bags and there's formula in there too, I think. His bottles are in the big blue bag."

He nods and when we're at the top of the stairs, he goes to the garage and jogs back in with the bags. Caleb's cry has escalated to that quiver that is the most pitiful. I hurriedly get a bottle ready and it's not fast enough.

"He is *pissed*," Weston says, sounding somewhat terrified.

That almost makes me laugh, and we both sigh in relief when I get the bottle in Caleb's mouth. He doesn't want it at first, but he must be hungry enough to try. He finally stops crying and takes the bottle.

"You're a pro," Weston says.

I snort. "Hardly. I've done my share of holding him when I get home from work or when he's fussy at night, but Sasha was with him 24/7."

"What kind of mom was she?" He winces. "You don't have to answer that. We don't have to talk about her right now…unless you want to."

I swallow hard. "She didn't think she was doing a good job, but she was doing the best she could."

It's all I can say, and it seems to be enough. He watches me for a moment and then he goes out to get the rest of our things.

After Caleb is fed and changed, we go to Weston's computer in the office next to the library and order formula and diapers and wipes, baby monitors galore and a few outfits simply because they're cute, a bouncy seat and swing…and a beautiful crib and dresser that can serve as a changing table on top.

It's been unreal to shop without looking at the price. I

tried to be conscientious about it at first, but then he'd ask if that was the one I really liked or not. Once I said what I liked most, we liked the same things, which also ended up being the most expensive.

I feel guilty that I'm here.

That I'm not treating Weston like the enemy he is.

And mostly…that I'm here and Sasha's not.

But I keep thinking of this little boy I'm holding.

All I've ever wanted is what's best for him.

"Oh, we'll need a special trash can that hides the smelly diapers," I say as we're finishing up.

He points at me. "I would've never *ever* thought of that."

By the time I put Caleb in the portable crib and crawl into the bed next to him, I'm exhausted, mentally and physically. I decided to go with a bedroom in the basement. There are still tons of windows down here despite it being a basement. It's gorgeous. And it's as far from Weston as we can get, so it feels like I'm holding on to a bit of myself in this strange new reality.

I text a few people to see if they can cover my shifts for the next week and a half at the steakhouse where I work, and once I have most of them covered, I let my boss Kim know what's going on. She's sorry to hear about Sasha and tells me to not worry about the shifts I didn't get filled, she'll take care of it. I have no idea what life is going to look like now.

It takes about an hour and a half for me to fall asleep. I toss and turn and cry. And when I finally drift off, Caleb wakes up and it's like last night—nothing seems to make him happy.

CHAPTER SEVEN

A NIGHT IN THE LIFE

WESTON

I stay up until the few shipments that were being delivered tonight arrive at the front gate and Joey calls to let me know. I walk out there instead of having him or Seth bring the packages to the house. Not that they'd mind—my security team is exceptional. But after being in the hospital yesterday and today, I have a lot of pent-up energy. Once I get these things put away, I'll go work out a while and then sleep like the dead. I'm exhausted.

All is quiet when I go downstairs and set the formula, diapers, wipes, and bottle warmer on the island so Sadie can see them. It takes a minute to figure out the bottle warmer, but it should be ready to go when she needs it. I didn't argue when Sadie said she'd sleep down here with the baby. I'm choosing my battles. But I'd like to move the baby's room upstairs once his furniture arrives. Hopefully, by then I'll know him better and he'll be used to me too.

Earlier, Caleb started crying before I'd finished showing Sadie the house. I think all that's left is the gym…and the grounds, the pool, and the pool house. The gym is in the basement, but it's far enough from the bedrooms that I don't think she'll hear anything. Just in case, I keep my music off. We'll have to test it out later and see what she can hear from her room.

I've worked out an hour when I hear something. Oh shit. Caleb's crying…more like wailing. It gets louder as I put the weights in place and rush out of the room.

I hear Sadie trying to soothe him, but it doesn't change, and I tap on the door.

"Sadie? Do you need a bottle?" I ask.

She opens the door and we both freeze, staring at each other for a few long seconds. She's hardly wearing anything and I glance down to see if my dick is out or something and realize I'm not wearing much either.

"The formula came. It's on the counter. I could mix that up or use what's in the freezer," I say.

Her eyes finally meet mine, and she nods.

I hurry to the bar and grab the packets of breast milk we put in the freezer last night. There's not much left, but enough for a few more bottles. She follows me, trying to put her arms through her zip-up hoodie while holding Caleb.

"Should I use two of these?" I ask, holding up the packets.

"Yeah." She changes positions with Caleb and he cries harder, and she cries right along with him.

It's heartbreaking.

Once the bottle is ready, I hand it to her and wipe my face and chest with a towel and throw on the shirt that I'd tossed on the bar when I came running. Caleb doesn't calm down. If anything, it makes him madder when Sadie tries to give him the bottle.

"He's missing Sasha," she whispers. "I don't know what to do."

"Would it help if I try?"

She doesn't look like she wants to hand him over, but she does anyway.

"I stink, sorry. I was working out when I heard him." I awkwardly turn Caleb until it's a little more comfortable and then try to give him the bottle.

No go.

I start walking with him, finally turning him so he's facing out, his head in the crook of my arm. His cries quieten, but they don't stop. I bounce, I rock, and when nothing else works, I start singing "Counting Stars" by OneRepublic and the second time I get to the line about losing sleep, I give it a little extra something and Caleb takes a deep, shaky breath and looks up at me, listening.

The next time through his little fist waves against my chest before it goes in his mouth, and I didn't know my heart could quadruple in size just like that. I also didn't know how a whole slew of worries would instantly take over as soon as I became a father.

How will I fuck this up?

What if I can't make him happy?

I can barely take care of me, how am I supposed to be responsible for another human?

Of course, since the song made him stop crying, I'm hesitant to stop singing, so I go through the whole thing again and when I pause, he looks up like *yes, you, strange singing man, continue*.

"I'm your dad," I sing and his little fists jump out. "And you are wide awake, aren't you?"

I turn and see Sadie on the couch. I can't read her expression, but she's stopped crying, so that seems positive. The bottle is next to her.

"Should I keep going?" I ask, tilting my head toward the bottle.

"It's worth a try." She holds the bottle out for me and when I put it near Caleb's lips, he takes it.

Sadie and I both exhale in relief.

He drinks and drinks and when he gets fidgety, Sadie reminds me to burp him. He lets out a winner. I don't think he's burped once that I haven't laughed. This baby shit is *funny*. He finishes his bottle and within minutes, there's an explosion in his pants.

I laugh again, but this one is tinged with more horror than humor. The *literal* baby shit is not so funny.

"You're doing such a good job, you may as well take it," Sadie says, smirking.

"Oh, *now* you want me to be involved," I joke.

She flinches.

"Too soon?"

She stares at me like she can't figure me out, but the stink that's coming out of this precious baby is not something that either one of us can ignore, so we both jump into action. She goes to grab the wipes and diapers, and I grab one of his little blankets that we brought from their place and look around for a softer place to lay it.

"No hardwood floor for you, no sir," I tell him, laying the blanket out on the area rug.

I get him unsnapped which is tricky with his kicking legs and my long sausage fingers. I swear, he's so tiny.

"How much did he weigh when he was born?" I ask when she tosses the diaper next to me. She sits on the floor next to him, and he grips her finger.

"He was ten pounds, four ounces, and twenty-one inches long," she says, smiling down at him.

"Wow. He's so little. What did they say he weighed last night? Fourteen pounds, two ounces?"

She snorts. "Ten pounds is *big* for a newborn. Sasha was huge and miserable." Her cheeks flush and she shakes her head like she wishes she could take it back.

I don't want to say anything that will make her stop talking, so I'm quiet. But then I look down and see something brown running down Caleb's leg.

"No," I whisper.

Sadie looks down and sucks in a breath between her teeth.

"I'm going in," I say out loud. Mostly to encourage myself.

I carefully undo the diaper and let's just say, it is not pretty. There are crevices that I've never thought about and I try to thoroughly clean each one. It's not easy, but I do it and I'm feeling pretty fucking proud of myself when warm liquid assaults my chin and nose and cheeks out of nowhere.

"The *fuck*?" I sputter, frantically reaching for the wipes.

Sadie starts laughing and Caleb looks pleased with himself.

"Did he just pee on me?"

"They do that when you don't cover them up," she says, hiding her laugh behind her fist.

"How the hell do I cover him up when I'm dealing with the poo from the bowels of hell?"

She chokes as she laughs and Caleb coos, laughing too.

"Oh, you think that's funny, huh," I say, unable to resist smiling at him. "You're all happy now…now that you've exorcised all that is foul and stinky."

He lets out a hiccupy laugh, and I'm laughing now too.

"Yeah, you have a powerful stank, but you sure are cute," I tell him.

I manage to get his diaper and jammies back on him without having any other bodily fluids touch me, so I call it a win.

"Is he always this bright-eyed at midnight?"

She nods. "Pretty much. I usually get home from work between eleven thirty and midnight, and if he's not awake then, he usually is by one. His days and nights are still mixed up."

"How do we switch it around?"

She lifts her eyebrows. "I wish I knew."

I pick Caleb up and move to the couch. Sadie stays on the floor nearby, pulling the throw I keep on the couch over her long legs.

"Where do you work?"

"Hanson's Steakhouse."

"Oh, I like that place. My family used to go there for special occasions sometimes."

She nods. "I always *wanted* to go there for special occasions, so when I got a job there, I was stoked."

I glance at her, wanting to ask questions, wanting to know

more about her and her family, but it still feels like too much, too soon. It's already weird that she's here, that I have a baby I didn't know about. It's not going to be comfortable between us overnight.

"I can sit up with him if you want to get some sleep," I tell her.

"Aren't you tired? We didn't sleep much last night."

"Yeah, but this is nice. He's being super chill at the moment." I smile down at him. "Oh, I was supposed to swaddle him. Maybe he'd like that."

I try to do it a couple times and get it close but not as tight and perfect as those nurses in the hospital. Once he's swaddled though, his eyes drift closed and Sadie looks surprised.

"We could try laying him back in the bed," she whispers.

I nod. I like holding him, but maybe he'll sleep better in his bed. We go into her room and I carefully lower him into the bed, easing away so slowly. He squeaks and then he lets out a wail. Sadie and I look at each other in defeat and I pick him back up.

He quietens instantly which I'm not gonna lie, it does something to me.

"Sorry, I guess that wasn't my best idea," she whispers.

"Sleep. I'll take him," I say.

She looks worried. "Let me know if you need help…"

I nod. "I will."

She watches us walk back into the open space and when I stretch out on the couch with Caleb on my chest, she finally shuts the door.

"Come on, kiddo. Let's try out this sleeping thing. What do you think?"

He yawns and makes little noises, and it's not long before he closes his eyes and we sleep.

For maybe an hour.

By the time seven rolls around and we've been up and down more times than I can remember, I'm more exhausted than a brutal day of training and playing an intense game *combined.*

How do people do this?

CHAPTER EIGHT

WILD THINGS

SADIE

I heard Weston and Caleb a time or two throughout the night, but it seemed like Caleb would quieten down so soon each time that I'd drift back off. It must have been a decent night. I'm a little torn about that—I don't want my nephew to be upset, but I'm not in a hurry for Weston to win him over or for my sister to be forgotten.

And the more Weston bonds with him, the more likely he'll find ways to boot me out.

I can understand why. It's already so unusual that he'd invite me to stay here. If I were him, *I* wouldn't have invited me into his home.

It will be impossible to avoid him taking my sister's place. Caleb is too young. As much as I hate this, it just gives me more determination to make sure I'm needed. I shouldn't have let Weston take Caleb last night, but I feel so much better this morning. I'll be able to function with some sleep. I actually can't remember the last time I slept that long, and it was only about five and a half hours. Sasha has always been a night owl, and with me sleeping in the living room, it wasn't like there was a place I could go to avoid hearing her and Caleb during the night.

I stretch and go into the bathroom, turning on the shower. The tears start again by the time I step into the warm water, and I try to get it out of my system before I have to face Weston for the day. I'm anxious before I've even seen him this morning.

Maybe because the sight of him shirtless when he came rushing to help with a bottle is something I can never unsee.

Or hearing him sing to Caleb. That was the sweetest thing I've ever heard.

The way he talks to him.

How hilarious he was about the diaper and then getting his face covered in urine.

Throughout everything, he's mostly been laid-back and funny, and I'm not even someone he likes.

What is that saying about keeping your friends close and your enemies closer? I'm the enemy.

That's the only reason I'm here.

If he keeps handling everything in stride, he'll soon see that I'm expendable.

When I step out of the shower, I have a new resolve to

prove that I'm needed around here. I'm not sure how I'll do that since I feel as lost about most things with Caleb as Weston is…but he doesn't have to ever know that. I think maybe I have him fooled so far.

I don't have many clothes, but I put on my nicest jeans and sweater, put a little mascara and lip gloss on, and look at myself in the mirror before I go out there to face the day.

I'm doing this for you, Sasha.

When I walk out of my bedroom, I expect to see Weston and Caleb on the couch, but they're not there. I look around, walking past the bedrooms that are open and find the gym down at the other end. It's an amazing gym, which shouldn't surprise me, but everything is just so far beyond what I could expect. It really is like one of those luxury home shows.

Do all of Weston's friends live like this? Did he grow up like this?

After I've explored the entire basement, I go upstairs to the kitchen and hear Weston laughing somewhere else in the house. I try to place the sound and decide maybe it's the library. I've been wanting to go back in there anyway, so this is a good excuse to go look without it seeming like I'm snooping.

I turn the corner and walk through the glass arched door, and there they are. They're on the plush rug in front of the fireplace. Weston is stretched out on his stomach, still in his workout clothes, and Caleb is on his back, looking up at Weston and kicking his feet. Weston is talking to him and then he leans down and blows a raspberry in Caleb's neck. Caleb laughs a new laugh, harder and louder than I've ever heard him laugh, and I just stare at the two of them in wonder for a few minutes, undetected.

Weston is telling him about his favorite book as a kid,

Where the Wild Things Are, and he talks about the monsters not being as scary as they might sound.

"I'll have to get the book for you," he says. "You'll have to see it to believe it. The monsters end up being intimidated by Max. That's the little boy's name, Max. Cool name. But so is Caleb. Also Caleb…I promise that I won't ever make you go to bed without supper. My parents never did that with me, and I solemnly swear that I won't do it with you either."

Caleb coos like he understands and I'm going to have to add this whole exchange to the list of things about Weston that are too…

He feels eyes on him and glances over, his expression cautious when he sees me.

"Good morning. How did you sleep?" he asks.

"Better than I have since Caleb was born," I admit.

He nods. "Good. I hoped you were catching up."

"How did you guys sleep?"

"We didn't." He chuckles. "At least not much. And when *he* was sleeping, I was googling about how to get a baby to sleep through the night. Controversial subject."

"I think everything is when it comes to parenting techniques."

He nods like I'm saying something wise. I'm clueless, but it sounded good.

He sits up, running his hands through his hair, and I'm glad I tried to look decent because even after sweating through a workout and staying up all night with a baby, he looks like someone the paparazzi would chase down the street. Oh right, he *is*.

I can't count the times I'd catch Sasha stalking him online. Before and after they hooked up.

Even after she claimed that she'd called him so many times and he didn't return her calls about the baby, she never seemed anything but in awe of him. It wasn't only him. She was obsessed with anyone that had star power. She lived on a steady diet of reality TV, dreaming of living that flashy life, whatever it took to get there.

It wasn't like her to let a chance like this pass her by.

I was angry at Weston. Furious, really. But she never was.

I couldn't understand it. I even asked her multiple times why she wasn't livid with him. Why she still looked at his pictures all the time…

"He's Caleb's father," she said. "And he's a good person."

She'd get this dreamy look on her face then that made me so mad.

"How can you possibly think he's a good person? The guy abandoned you when you needed him most. Who cares if he was nice to you or good in bed? He's an asshole."

"Sadie?"

I blink and Weston's looking at me expectantly. "Oh, sorry. Were you saying something?"

"I was saying my family is coming over today to meet him. We talked about noon."

"Oh. Okay," I say, dread filling my body to the extent that I need to sit down. I back into the cozy chair by the fireplace and take a deep breath. "I can make myself scarce during that time."

He frowns. "That's not necessary. Unless you're just not ready to meet them. I know you have a lot to think about right now. But if we're going to do this, I'd like all of you to get to know each other."

"I'll need to see my parents when they get into town. Actually, I should check my phone to see if they're back yet. I can't remember what time they left."

I pull my phone out of my pocket and a text came earlier

from my mom saying they should be pulling in around three this afternoon.

"I'd like to meet them too, whenever they're ready," he says. "I can go to them so they don't have to drive all this way after they've just made a long road trip."

I nod. Is he really this thoughtful all the time?

"We'll have to make funeral arrangements tomorrow, I think. There will be plenty of time to meet them in the future. We don't have to rush it." My cheeks heat and I close my mouth wishing I could take the words back. In fact, I'd like a restart on this morning. I feel like I'm drowning.

"I know the timing isn't the best, but I'd like to put their minds at ease about me," he says. "If I were them, I'd want to know who's taking care of Caleb."

"Why are you being so nice?" I ask.

I study my feet because I'm mortified.

"Uh, I don't know? Because you're my son's family. You've lost someone so important to you and important to him, and the circumstances of why I've been kept in the dark about Caleb don't matter as much right now. I'm still hurt and upset, and if Sasha were here, I'd demand to know why she did this to me, but…she's not. And I suspect you guys were just following her wishes. It wasn't your place to tell me the truth, although I'll always wish you had."

My jaw clenches. He's still turning this around on Sasha, and I just don't get it…except that it makes him look better.

"We all thought you wanted nothing to do with him," I say evenly. "My parents never knew you were his father, but Sasha didn't tell them because you never returned her calls."

His eyes narrow. "So why didn't she come find me? She found me at a party. It's been coming back to me in bits and pieces since I've seen her pictures. I'd had a few drinks that night, but I remember. She was at the party to see me. We have a mutual friend, Cal, who could've made sure she had the right number. Hell, she could've had him get in touch with me if she thought I was avoiding her calls."

I stare at him until my eyes are blurry and a tear drips down. I'm so tired of crying. It feels like the tears will never stop.

"I don't know. I don't know, all right? That's what she told me. I tried to push her to go see you or to send you a letter…to reach out to your parents' law offices."

His eyes flare in surprise.

"I know that she was terrified you'd take him from her. Even when she was singing your praises…especially when she was singing your praises, she'd say you'd win custody in a heartbeat. You saw our apartment. We got by on my tips and government assistance. But Sasha also—" I leave it hanging and he stares at me, his eyes conflicted.

"Sasha also what?" he asks.

"She struggled. She…had diabetes and she didn't manage it well. She shouldn't have…" My damn eyes won't stop overflowing. "She shouldn't have had Caleb, according to her doctors," I finally get out.

"She was sick?"

"She was doing okay. She was finally taking her insulin and avoiding all the things she should avoid…she surprised us. After she had Caleb, she got why we'd been after her to take care of herself for so long."

He looks down at Caleb for a long time and when his eyes meet mine, he seems distant again. Last night and for a few minutes this morning, it felt like we were past that, but a wall has gone back up.

"So you were planning on raising him if something ever happened to her?" he asks, his jaw tight.

"I-yes. I promised I'd take care of him no matter what.

She'd ask often, even before she had him, if I'd raise him like he's mine. To the point that I told her to stop talking that way. She was doing well, she didn't need to think like that. I'd say, '*Just take care of yourself, that's all you need to do.*'" I shake my head and clasp my hands together to keep them from shaking. "She wasn't satisfied with that, so yes, I promised her I would."

"So I'm a huge inconvenience to your plans," he says.

I glare at him. "I didn't *have* a plan. I never wanted my sister to die. She tried to talk about it and I'd shut her down. And since I didn't think you wanted him, I vowed to be Caleb's everything if the day ever came when she couldn't take care of him. Mostly to get her to stop talking about it."

I duck my head and grab a tissue from the side table.

"You're not doing it alone," he says, his voice softer. "It's important to me that Caleb has a relationship with you. Just don't ever try to cut me out again. I am a nice guy, but I'm a father now, and I have limits."

I shiver and don't say anything back. I'm not sure if we'll ever come to an agreement about this. If we think the other is lying or didn't do enough to make the truth be known, is there any way past it?

CHAPTER NINE

INTRODUCTIONS

WESTON

Very little sleep happened last night, but I'm running on adrenaline.

I have a son.

God. I still can't believe it.

I've never been so fucking tired in my life.

I held him most of the night, staring at him and talking to

him and dozing off, only to dream that I was crushing him. I woke up sweating and in a panic. He went in his crib after that.

I've never thought much about having kids, being so far from settling down in a committed relationship. The whole thing has always felt really far off. A huge what-if that I wasn't sure I'd ever experience.

And I've been thinking about Sasha a lot.

I'm so curious about her. I wish I could remember more about her. She was cute, nice, and seemed down to earth, but there wasn't much of a spark between us. She made the first move, was outgoing and fun, and I was all too willing to give her what she wanted. I've been too willing to give a lot of girls what they want. I'm not proud of that. And it's not like I've turned over a whole new leaf.

I still like to get laid.

But I'm getting tired of the meaningless fucks.

I don't even love how easy it is anymore—at first it was appealing to have constant access to beautiful women who were eager to please. Now, it might feel good in the moment, but the hollow feeling I get afterward isn't worth it.

If I were to meet Sasha now, I doubt I'd even consider sleeping with her…so maybe I've changed more than I thought.

The guys have been texting this morning, wondering when they can come meet Caleb. In my last text to them, I suggested we talk later this afternoon. Maybe they can come after my family spends time with him. I can't wait for the guys to see him, but my family deserves to have first dibs.

My housekeeper Amy comes twice a week to clean and to leave a few meals that she prepares in my kitchen. But since family will be trickling in throughout the day, I order a bunch of takeout—pasta that will still be good reheated, large salads, fruit, and a few desserts.

When Ed, one of the daytime security guards, calls to say the food has arrived, I ask him to bring it to the house and leave it on the island because I'm watching Sadie give Caleb a bath. We're in the largest bathroom upstairs and his little tub is sitting inside the bathtub. Sadie handles him almost as carefully as I do, like she's still tentative around him too, but she still knows what she's doing more than me.

He loves the bath. He'd started fussing a little, but when he got in the water, he instantly stilled.

"It's like he's in a Zen state," I say, chuckling.

"Sometimes I'd hear Sasha giving him a bath in the middle of the night when he was having a hard one," she says.

As always, she's quiet after she talks about Sasha, and I want to tell her to say whatever she wants about her sister.

When she doesn't say more, I clear my throat and pat Caleb's hand. His fist clasps around my finger while Sadie washes him.

"One of the articles I read suggested waking them to eat every few hours during the day. And limiting interaction during the night…which I totally screwed up last night, by the way. But he's awake now," I say, smiling when he smiles up at me.

She tilts her head. "We can try it. I already know I'll feel bad waking him up though." She smiles at him too.

She finishes washing him and then we just watch him kicking his feet in the water for a few minutes. He sort of shivers and I reach out to feel if his stomach's cold and get peed on again.

Sadie surprises me by cracking up at this. I think she

surprises herself because it ends almost as quickly as it started.

"We clearly don't have his bathroom habits down yet," I say, washing my hands.

When I turn back around, I catch her trying to hold back a smile.

"Looks like you're a target," she says.

I scrunch up my face. "You mean he's never gotten you before?"

"No." She laughs.

She carefully lifts him out of the tub and I hold the towel up. She holds onto him, exhaling when I wrap the towel around him.

"Baths make me a nervous wreck because he's so slippery," she says.

I motion toward the bed and she lays him on it, making sure he's thoroughly dry before she puts on his diaper. I picked out his outfit. He doesn't have many clothes, but what he has is cute and soft.

"Did you grab a onesie?" she asks.

"What?"

"A onesie."

"No idea what that is, but tell me and I'll go grab it downstairs."

"It's a one-piece short-sleeve thing that snaps and goes under his outfit."

"Is this outfit also called a onesie?" I hold it up.

Her lips pucker out. "Mmm, more like a one-piece or a playsuit? I don't know actually."

"I'll never get it straight. I like that outfit though." I point toward the door. "Okay, I'll go look for a onesie and be back."

"I can just bring him downstairs too, he'll be warm enough."

I hesitate and then follow when she bundles Caleb back up. I go back for the outfit still on the bed and catch up with them.

"Is work okay with you missing shifts?" I ask.

"They're being great about it, fortunately."

"That's good."

We get downstairs and I say, "Ahh," when she holds up a onesie.

"Now's probably not the right time to talk about it, but…I have more time off right now than I will once the season starts. I can watch him when you go back to work, and then we should talk about what to do when I go back. We have a few months to decide."

She looks conflicted and I regret bringing it up so soon, but the subject is unavoidable.

We finish getting Caleb ready. She works on all the snaps while I put on his socks, and when I pick him up, inhaling his sweet baby scent, she fluffs his hair.

My phone buzzes and I answer it.

"Your parents and Olivia are here," Ed says.

I curse under my breath. "Thanks. Send them up."

The doorbell rings a minute later and I curse again.

"How do people get anywhere on time? We didn't even leave the house and I thought we still had at least another half hour." I nuzzle Caleb's cheek and smile when his mouth turns to suck on my cheek. "Sorry, little guy, I need to shave for you."

I walk toward the stairs and go up slowly, muttering about how I haven't even showered yet. Then I turn and see Sadie still standing back, looking uncertain.

"You don't have to worry. My family will be fine. Well,

unless Olivia is in a mood, but I'll keep her in line. I talked to everyone more this morning, told them you'd be here…"

She still looks hesitant but nods and moves toward me. We walk up the stairs and to the front door. I open it wide and all three sets of eyes zero in on Caleb.

My parents' eyes soften, my mom gasps, putting her hand on her heart, and Olivia studies him like he's an alien from outer space. Her eyes flicker from him to me to Sadie and then narrow. It's about what I expected from her.

"He is absolutely beautiful," my mom says.

When she can finally tear her eyes away from Caleb, she looks at Sadie and gives her a reserved smile.

"Hello, I'm Lane and this is my husband David and my daughter Olivia."

"Nice to meet you. I'm Sadie, Caleb's aunt." She lifts her hand awkwardly and drops it. "I guess you already knew that."

"We're really sorry for your loss, Sadie," Mom says.

"Thank you," Sadie says, focusing on Caleb.

My dad tags onto that, adding his condolences while nodding pensively, and Olivia just stares at Sadie. I shoot her a look and motion for them to come in. Once they're inside, my mom touches Caleb's hair and her eyes fill with tears.

"He looks so much like you did, Weston," she whispers.

"Come on back. I ordered lunch, but it arrived a while ago, so it might need to go in the oven for a while."

We file into the kitchen, Sadie trickling in last.

"So tell us everything," my mom says.

Sadie and I look at each other, something like panic on her face, and I don't know why I feel a sudden need to protect her. I did not see that coming.

"Let's ease into this, okay?" I say. "Sadie's been through a lot the past few days. Caleb was born on the fifth of

December and I'm probably partial, but he's the best baby that ever lived, aren't you?"

Caleb makes a sound like he's agreeing with me, and my parents laugh.

"Would you like to hold him?" I ask my mom.

She nods eagerly and I carefully pass him to her. She looks down at him in awe as she holds him, and her eyes are overflowing when she bends down to kiss the top of his head.

"I'm your grandma," she whispers against his hair. Her eyes lift to mine and she gives me a shaky smile. "Weston, he's a dream."

I swallow the lump in my throat and nod, too overwhelmed to speak.

"I just don't get why your sister didn't tell him about the baby…but now you're living here?" Olivia says.

"Olivia, let's not do this right now," I warn.

"But is that wise? You don't even know each other," she pushes.

"It was an abrupt decision, yes, but the priority is Caleb, so we're doing our best to put aside our differences and work together for his sake."

"That's all very progressive of you, but they kept your son from you, West," she says.

"Enough, Olivia," Dad says.

I glance at Sadie to see how she's handling this, and her eyes are glassy, but she's standing tall.

"My parents and I were led to believe Weston didn't want to have anything to do with the baby. They don't know yet that Caleb's his." Sadie looks at me. "My dad is a big fan." She looks at my family again and presses her lips together. "And honestly, I'm still trying to make sense of what really happened."

Everyone's quiet for a second and my mom speaks first.

"I hope we can all continue to be a united front for Caleb." Mom looks down at him and blinks back tears. "You don't know our son well enough yet, but I can promise you that he will love this child with his whole heart and do his best to take care of him. The fact that he had you move in here should prove that."

She glances up at Sadie and Sadie nods.

"I'm starting to believe that," she says softly.

CHAPTER TEN

THE GRILLING

SADIE

God, this is torture.

Weston's family is nicer than I expected, but there's still a lot of resentment under the surface.

I can't blame them for that.

If I were in their shoes, I'd hate me.

We eat and Caleb snoozes as his grandparents hold him. Olivia shakes her head when Lane tries to hand him to her. I'm not sure what to make of Olivia, but I'd be protective of my sibling too—I guess I already have been. And seeing Caleb being so loved, it seems like my protectiveness of Sasha may have been to Caleb's detriment.

When Weston's sister Felicity and her husband and son arrive, the mood lightens considerably. Owen is nine and so cute and funny, and Felicity and Sutton are warm and friendly. It's hard not to stare at them because they're beautiful people and so obviously in love. Weston and Felicity's closeness reminds me of Sasha and me, where they're hugging one minute and she's tripping him the next. But most of all, they are ecstatic about Caleb.

My parents call to say they'll be later than three. I'm restless and don't know what to do with myself. As the day goes on, I wonder even more what I'm doing here. Weston clearly has backup. He wouldn't need me to make this work. And when his parents and Olivia talk about work, I'm reminded that they're all lawyers, and Sutton is a freaking *judge*.

"What do you do for fun, Sadie?" Felicity asks.

"The past couple of months, it's been all about this guy," I say.

Her smile is pure, without any of the blame that they must all think I deserve.

"She works at Hanson's Steakhouse," Weston says.

I nod while they go on about how much they love the place.

"We don't get to go as often—well, I live in Landmark Mountain now, so that's part of it. But we hadn't been there for a long time before that even. We'll have go back," she says.

Olivia rolls her eyes, but Felicity misses it because she's smiling at me.

"You should bring Caleb out to meet everyone sometime soon," Felicity says, looking at Weston and me. "Sutton has a huge family and they're all crazy about Weston now." She laughs.

"They're great," Weston adds.

"Is that all you do?" Olivia asks, looking at me.

"All I do?" I repeat.

"For work?" Her eyebrows lift.

"Oh. Yes. I work a ton of hours and then try to help with Caleb when I'm off." I shake my head.

She's gone echoes in my mind.

"So this must feel pretty great, staying in this nice house indefinitely," Olivia says.

"Olivia, you need to leave if you're going to keep being like this," Weston says.

She lifts a shoulder. "I'm just stating the obvious. No one else seems to be telling the truth."

"It's okay," I tell Weston, standing up. "I'll be downstairs if you need me." I look at everyone. "It was nice to meet you. I'll give you some time together. I know all of this is a lot to take in."

"You don't need to go," Weston says softly.

"It's okay." I move past him and rush out of the room.

When I'm almost to the stairs, I hear Weston say, "She just lost her sister. While you're here judging her about staying here, she's about to have to face her parents, who just lost their *daughter*, and help them plan a funeral. Have some fucking mercy, Olivia. Sorry, Owen. Grab a dollar from the kitchen for your swear jar. You know where the stash is."

I jog down the basement stairs before Owen gets to the kitchen and don't stop until I'm in the room I slept in last night. I fall back on the bed and can't fight back the tears any longer. My phone rings before I can delve too deep into all my feelings.

"We're back," my mom says. "Where are you?"

"There's something I need to tell you."

About an hour and a half later, my parents arrive at Weston's. I feel awful for one more minute that they had to drive to get here after their road trip, but their need to see Caleb after everything that's happened outweighed their exhaustion. When I mentioned to Weston that they were back and wanted to see Caleb, he invited them to come here, but he also offered to go to them. I told him I'd let them make the decision and once they heard that his family was here, they said they'd come.

When they walk through the door, we fall into each other's arms and I just thought I had cried before—it's like a whole new dam of emotions floods out of me when I see my parents. After a few minutes, my mom pulls back and starts tending to me the way she always does, pushing my hair back and reaching in her purse for tissues. She passes one to me and my dad, and we all blow our noses and try to get our bearings.

I feel my dad's attention shift when he realizes Weston is in the room, and he clears his throat, nodding at him.

"Hello. I'm Chris." My dad holds out his hand and shakes Weston's. "And this is my wife, Pam."

Weston nods and shakes Mom's hand next.

My parents are unfailingly polite, so even though their shoulders are stooped with the weight of the loss of their baby girl, I know they'll make an effort to be kind to Weston.

Out of all of us, Sasha has been the free spirit, never confined to a box. If she didn't feel like being polite, she wouldn't be. I've always admired that about her.

When my parents get a good look at the entryway with

the grand double staircases, their eyes are as wide as mine were yesterday.

My dad is a combination of awestruck and distrustful, meeting the quarterback of his favorite team after he's taken them to the Super Bowl two years in a row, who also happens to be the father of his grandson and hasn't been around at all.

Weston gets it out of the way right off the bat, before we even leave the foyer to join his family. He hands Caleb to them, which makes both of them cry, the grief about Sasha so raw it's brutal.

He's gracious when I introduce him to them. He tells them he's sorry for everything that's happened. He's so sorry for their loss. And that he didn't know he had a son until the hospital called him on Saturday. My parents are as shocked as I was, even more so finding out it was *him*, and I think they're so genuine that I can see on Weston's face that he truly believes it.

What shocks *me* is that they believe Weston didn't know.

I think maybe I was wrong to ever jump to that conclusion, especially knowing how Sasha could sometimes twist the truth. I just always wanted so badly to believe whatever she told me.

"We're sorry," my dad says. "I wish I knew what Sasha was thinking. There were times she didn't…make the best choices." His cheeks flush and he looks down at Caleb as his eyes fill with tears. "But she was a good person, Weston, and she loved this boy more than anything."

"When you're ready, I'd like to hear more about her," Weston says.

That makes my mom cry harder, and I hug her and then my dad, while Weston stands there quietly, being there but giving us space at the same time.

When we get our bearings, my mom looks at Weston and

says, "I'm not sure if you can trust us after all of this, but we're here, and we'll do whatever we can to help. We want to be part of Caleb's life and if this gets to be too much, we could also take care of him. We'd never keep you from seeing him."

"I appreciate you saying that," Weston says.

I wasn't sure if it would make him angry to hear that or not, but he's calm.

"I won't keep you from seeing him either. I want to raise him, but that's part of why I asked Sadie to stay here and help me. I don't want to take him from the only family he's known. He needs normalcy and I don't know how long Sadie is willing to do this with me, but as you'll see, it's a big place, so she could stay here forever and it'd be okay with me."

My mom's eyes meet mine and I can see her mind whirling as much as mine is.

"What happens when you meet someone?" she asks, still looking at me and then at Weston. "Eventually you'll both fall in love with someone and they might not be okay with this arrangement."

"I'd like to have it in a legal document," I say. "That way, you'll trust that I'm not going to take him from you when I go to the store, and I'll feel better knowing I won't get the boot when you get a girlfriend."

For a second, there's a flash of indignation in his eyes, but when he nods, it's gone. "We can talk to my parents about it tonight. I can have my family draw up paperwork—they're lawyers. And you can look it all over and see if you agree to it or if we need to keep tweaking it. Sadie mentioned before that she needed it in writing and I should've made sure it was done then. But if the day comes when we are in relationships, and I'm nowhere close to that, by the way, I'd still want Sadie to raise Caleb with me. It sounds like that's what Sasha really wanted—for Sadie to raise him—and I'd like to think that since she put me on the birth certificate, she'd be okay with me raising him too."

My mom opens her mouth, but nothing comes out.

"Thank you," I whisper.

"Are you guys hungry?" he asks. "There's a lot of food in the kitchen."

"I don't think we'll stay," Dad says. "We're exhausted and not good company right now, but I'd like to meet your family before we go."

They go into the living room and meet everyone, and it's strange how well everyone gets along. When my parents start to leave, Lane and Felicity both hug my mom.

I walk my parents to the door and they study me intently.

"Are you really going to be okay here?" Dad asks.

"I think so. The whole thing is crazy, but I'd rather be here than living without Caleb."

They nod solemnly and we all hug each other.

My mom pats my cheek when I pull away.

"I think you're in good hands," she says.

And the craziest part is I'm starting to believe she's right.

CHAPTER ELEVEN

COOLER THAN THAT

WESTON

By eleven o'clock the next morning, my parents have drafted a custody agreement, probably one of the more bizarre ones they've ever done. It basically states that Sadie and I are raising Caleb together. Technically, I have full custody, but I won't keep Sadie from seeing him whenever she wants. If we ever need to renegotiate the terms, we will, but for now, she has full access to him and so do I.

Something eases between Sadie and me. Almost instantly. At first I was offended that she needed it in writing, since I'm doing a lot here to be conciliatory when I wouldn't have to be, but I think I needed it too. Building trust will take time.

"Should we grab some lunch?" I ask.

"Actually, I—" She looks nervous again and I turn to face her.

We've just left my parents' office and it took a huge effort to get out the door on time…after another night of little sleep. We both have dark circles under our eyes and I feel like I could go for a power nap right about now, but my stomach's protesting.

"What is it?" I ask.

"I need to meet my parents at the apartment and then go to the funeral home. They've decided the funeral will be the day after tomorrow and there are a lot of arrangements to be made."

"Can I do anything to help?"

Her features soften, her full lips puckering as she bites the inside of her cheek. "Thanks, Weston. If you could—I mean, if you wouldn't mind, I—" She takes a deep breath and makes a face. "I'm not good at asking for help."

"It's okay. I'm offering."

She nods. "Can you watch Caleb while I'm gone?"

A hesitant smile breaks out across my face and she looks startled by it. Her cheeks flush and she looks so damn pretty, I end up being the one to look away first.

"I can do that," I say. "You sure you trust me to handle him?"

She exhales again and nods, her smile shy. It does something to me. It makes me want to see her smile more often.

"You're getting there. You'll be okay," she says.

She gets in the SUV as I walk around to my side. When I turn the ignition, she keeps going.

"He'll probably want to eat again by the time you get home." Her cheeks turn pink again. "And need a diaper change before you lay him down for a nap."

"Got it. Do you need me to drop you off at your place? Caleb and I can pick you up whenever you need."

She turns to look at me. "No, that's okay. I don't want to tie up your day. This is already a lot." She spreads her hands out, waving them around.

"I don't mind. Whatever is easiest for you." I don't want to admit that I'm a little nervous about having him on my own. It's different than when I'm with Caleb during the night and I know Sadie is close by.

She's quiet for a moment. "For someone who's such a—" She clears her throat. "You sure are a lot nicer than I expected."

I'm stunned for a second and then laugh, keeping my eyes on the road as I drive toward home. "Thank you, I think? What were you going to say? Such a what?"

She looks out the window, but I can still see her smirk.

"Such a player." She wrinkles her nose and looks at me.

I finally nod. "I deserve that." I make a face back at her. "But I've been trying to amend my player ways for a while now."

"Hmm," she says skeptically. "You don't need to say that on my account. We already signed the papers this morning." She lifts her shoulder and her lips quirk to the side like she's trying not to smile. "I'm stuck with whoever you are and whoever you're with."

I snort, more surprised that she's going there than anything.

"I'm *not* saying it for your account. I'll prove it. Besides my family, you are the only woman who's been in my house."

She scoffs. "Oh, *okay*, you've lived there, what, about a minute?"

"I moved in around the end of September...mid-September actually. A solid five months."

"Oh." Surprise flashes across her face and then she's smirking again. "But there's still plenty of opportunity for you to sleep around on the road. I've seen you with at least five different women since September."

My eyebrows go sky-high. "You've been keeping track of who I'm photographed with?"

Her mouth hangs open, color tingeing those cheeks. Her smile and making her flush is kind of addicting.

"It's hard to miss when you're the darling of Colorado…"

"Darling of Colorado..." I crack up. "That's a new one for me. You think I'm the darling?" I look over at her and grin and she rolls her eyes. "I'm touched, Chapman."

"Don't be, Shaw," she says, but she's for sure grinning when she looks out the window.

We get home and she holds the baby while I get his bottle ready. I'm sitting in the comfy chair in the library feeding him when she taps on the door.

"I'm heading out," she says. "Text or call if you need anything. I should be back by five or five thirty."

"Okay. I'll see you then."

I have a moment of anxiety when she leaves that I'll mess something up or that Caleb won't be happy with me for all that time. But for at least the first hour, he's content.

The guys have messaged every day. There's a constant stream of texts going between us, but today is the first day that has been more open for them to come see Caleb, so I let them know. Rhodes is the first one to respond.

RHODES

It's about damn time.

BOWIE

What he means to say is that we'll be right over.

RHODES

I said what I said. And we'll be right over.

HENLEY

I've got a little time before I need to pick up the girls. Pretty boy, you in?

PENN

I'm in. I'm dragging this morning, but I'm in.

HENLEY

It's eleven, PB. You all right?

PENN

It was a NIGHT.

RHODES

Was it that girl who wouldn't stop texting you yesterday?

PENN

<smug emoji>

RHODES

Damn. I miss getting laid.

BOWIE

What's it been, a week?

RHODES

I wish, man. I wish.

I've got a good idea. Why don't we continue this conversation in person?

RHODES

Okay, Snarky. I'm gonna let that one slide because you're a new daddy and I know you're tired.

He's awake right now and he's pretty fucking cute awake. Or asleep. Get over here.

BOWIE

He's a dad for two minutes and already showing off.

RHODES

He's always been that way. It's the quarterback in him.

I'm still chuckling at the messages when my phone buzzes to say Penn is here. I have to laugh that he's the first to get here after saying he's dragging.

I let Blake know to let Penn through and that Henley, Rhodes, and Bowie will be following soon.

"That was fast," I say when I open the door to Penn.

He grins when he sees me with the baby. "Holy shit, West. It's gonna take time to get used to seeing you with a kid, Shaw."

"I know. Trust me. It's hard for me to get used to it too."

"What did your family think?"

"They freaked out." I laugh. "Already obsessed with him. Everyone but Olivia, but that's par for the course." I lean down and kiss Caleb's head. "And he was a champ, getting passed around and handling it like a pro. The only time he gets out of sorts is in the middle of the night."

Penn winces, and the rest of the guys trickle into the house.

They all start talking at once. And a bunch of huge football players sliding into baby talk is fucking hysterical.

"You are so cute," Henley coos.

"What a guy," Bowie says, in the highest voice I've ever heard come out of him. "Yes, you are." He grins when Caleb's fist flies in the air. "Gonna have your dad's arm."

"He's a good-looking boy. Must look like his mama," Rhodes says and then shakes his head when Bowie reaches out and twists his nipple. "*Ow*. My bad. I didn't mean it. It came out before I'd thought it through."

I shoot him a look and he relaxes when Bowie lets go.

"He's great, man," Bowie says. "How did he do last night?"

"Another sleepless night," I say. "I think he misses his mom. He wants to sleep during the day, but at night, he's alert and looking for her."

"That's the saddest thing I've ever heard," Rhodes says.

"I know." I look down at Caleb, who's fighting to stay awake.

He got jarred awake when the guys came in, but now that he's used to the noise, he's conking back out. I bounce him a little to see if he'll stay awake.

"Guys, I don't know if I'll ever get used to this." I look around the room. "Why don't they have a playbook for single dads?"

Henley's eyes narrow as he tilts his head. "I would've given anything for one. You got a spare notebook lying around?"

I shrug and nod. "Sure. One sec."

I go into the library and grab a large blue spiral notebook and a couple of pens.

When I get back, they're still talking about sleep. I toss the notebook to Henley and he opens it and stares into space before he starts writing.

"Levi didn't sleep through the night until he was seven months old. I thought I was gonna die," Rhodes says.

Rhodes' son is two and looks just like him, which is a good thing for the kid because Rhodes has been on *People* magazine's *50 Most Beautiful People* list for five years and running. The guy has superstar in his genes. His dad is British, multi-Oscar winner Troy Archer, and his mom is Amara, African supermodel and founder of several successful businesses in the beauty industry.

All of us but Penn have been on the list, which we love to razz him about, but he's not quite twenty-four, so it'll happen. Henley's been on it eight times. I've been on it twice, which is something I never imagined happening, especially since I'm not an actor and I'm only twenty-six. We're not a bad looking bunch, and it's only a matter of time before Penn makes the cut. Dude looks like a model himself—hell, if we believed the press, we all do, but we make more fun of it than anything. The ridiculous title has coincided with our ages and how long we've been playing, which makes sense since we were relatively unknown before football changed our lives. Regardless, we give each other crap about it all the time, and it's become a mock competition. Rhodes is thirty, so he has fewer under his belt than Henley, Bowie is twenty-eight and has been on the list three times. He's also practically as famous as Mozart in Austria, where he was raised until he was twelve.

"Gracie was like that too," Henley adds. "The first two made it seem like we were sleep whisperers. They slept through the night right away and once they were done breast-feeding, it was like eleven hours. And then Gracie comes along and bucks the whole system."

We all laugh. Gracie is five and a little spitfire. It's no surprise that she came into the world that way. Audrey is eight and quiet. I don't think she's ever caused a moment of grief. And Cassidy is twelve and from what Henley says, she's the typical oldest child. She wants everything to be in order and can't stand it when it's not.

"He'll adjust," Bowie says, his eyes warm as he looks at Caleb. "It'll just take time."

Bowie is the most patient person I know. He's massive and gruff and looks like he has a chip on his shoulder most of the time, but he's a marshmallow inside. At least he is if he likes you. If he doesn't, it's a different story.

His daughter Becca is one of the cutest kids I've ever seen. She's seven, always smiling, and she has Down syndrome. Watching Bowie and Becca together gives me hope in humanity. She can be having a bad day, but when she sees Bowie, her whole face lights up and she runs and leaps into his arms like it's been years since she's seen him, even if it's only been an hour. I know it's been difficult to get the right care for her, especially with taking her on the road, but I've never heard Bowie complain.

"I'm so glad you guys are here," I tell them. "Come on back."

"Mind if I grab a beer?" Penn says.

"Of course not. Help yourself."

"Everyone want one?" he asks.

We all chime in that we do and go sit in the living room, and Penn comes in a few minutes later and passes each of us a beer. Henley passes the notebook to Bowie and when Bowie reads what Henley wrote, he chuckles and starts writing.

I turn on a basketball game and we halfway watch it but

mostly talk. It's weird, the amount of pride I feel when they hold Caleb and talk about him.

"How's it going with the girl?" Henley asks as he holds Caleb.

"Sadie?"

He nods.

"We're keeping the peace for the most part." I lean forward, my elbows on my knees.

"What's she like?" Penn asks.

"Guarded...protective of her sister and Caleb." I lean back, thinking about how I'd be if the roles were reversed and how I'd be protective of my siblings too. "She loves Caleb. There's no question about that."

"He's the priority," Rhodes says, nodding.

"I think it's commendable that you're working together right now," Bowie says.

"Fuck yeah, it is," Henley adds.

We're all quiet for a moment, processing everything.

"Guess you got yourself into The Single Dad Players, Weston. Aren't you jealous, Penn?" Rhodes asks, his shit-stirring grin in full effect.

Penn holds up his hands. "I don't need to be part of The Single Dad Players, thank you very much. I'm just fine on the outside looking in." He lifts his beer bottle.

"You know you want to be," Henley scoffs. "Because we're so dope."

Penn puts his fist over his mouth as he cracks up. "Okay, Pops. Do you hear yourself?"

"Watch it, Pretty Boy," Henley says, his look teasing but still fierce enough that Penn's cocky grin fades. He's in awe of Henley and loves to give him shit but gets afraid when he straddles that fine line.

"It's pretty great being on the inside," I say, shrugging.

They laugh and as we hang out talking about kids and nonsense, I can't stop thinking about how glad I am to have them in my life.

It's only been a couple of days, but my whole world expanded when I realized I had a son.

Life is short and could turn upside down at any moment. I need to figure out a way to not miss out on a moment of it.

CHAPTER TWELVE

THE GUYS

SADIE

After another painful day, the last thing I want to do when I pull into Weston's driveway is see anyone. My mom took one look at me earlier and pulled out her concealer. I cried it off at the funeral home and she reapplied before I left.

So something in your life will feel normal, she said.

I don't know how concealer will help the way I feel, but when I see four honking SUVs parked in the back, I'm glad for my mom's help. I don't normally give much thought to how I look, but even I know I was looking rough earlier.

I step in the back door wondering how I can get to the basement stairs without anyone noticing me and I walk into a madhouse.

The first thing I hear is the string riff that I think everyone alive knows. That line throughout Britney Spears' "Toxic" is being sung way up high and a couple are singing it as low as they can go. I think it's Weston singing the chorus in a high falsetto.

I walk into the kitchen and see five very large men dancing their asses off and singing, while they're surrounding Caleb, who's on a blanket on the table getting his diaper changed. When I realize who they are, I'm stunned and on hot man overload, but the sight is too hilarious. Penn Hudson and Rhodes Archer are dancing like they were meant to be Britney's backup dancers, and Rhodes is the one singing the high string line, while Penn just throws in random lines while he focuses on his dance moves. Henley Ward is twisting his hips and taking the bass, and Bowie Fox is bopping his head, also singing bass. Weston's changing the diaper, but his hips are swiveling like Channing Tatum on whatever that dancing movie he was in that made me look at him with new appreciation. *Magic Mike*, yes.

I start sweating, but I also start laughing…hard.

They immediately turn, Weston lifting Caleb up to his shoulder, and the singing and dancing comes to an abrupt stop.

"Please. Don't stop on my account," I say, trying to rein in the hysterical laugh in my gut.

My insides are shaking with being face-to-face with some of the players I've loved for years. Henley Ward is an *icon*. I mean, all of them are. I still haven't gotten over the fact that I'm living in Weston Shaw's house, but we've sort of been thrown into a situation where I have to deal. But holy fucking hell.

One by one, they come over and introduce themselves, shaking my hand. Their earlier humor is gone, earnest expressions on their faces.

"I'm so sorry to hear about your sister," Rhodes says.

"Weston told us what the two of you are doing together, raising this little guy," Henley says. "It's commendable. It really is. And we're here to help whenever you guys need it."

"It's hard to say who Caleb looks like more now that I've gotten a better look at you," Penn says. "But your dark hair and blue eyes…I think it's you."

My cheeks are on fire by now. Sasha always said she thought Caleb looked more like me than her, which I loved so much, but now I wish he looked like her.

"It's really nice to meet you," Bowie says. "And like Henley said, we want to help."

"That's so kind of you, all of you. Thank you."

"It feels wrong that we're carrying on like this with what you're going through," Rhodes says.

"No, it's not wrong," I say. "I haven't laughed that hard in a long time. My sister loved that song, and she was a huge fan of all of you, so I only wish she could've seen that for herself." I smile at them, my eyes reaching Weston last.

His cheeks are flushed which makes his blue eyes stand out even more. His hair is messy, and he looks sexier than I've ever seen him, which is saying a lot because he looks hot *all the time*. But now his expression is tentative, like he's concerned that I don't really mean what I'm saying, and I feel bad that we've had such a sad, tumultuous beginning. If we'd met any other way, I bet we would've been friends. Maybe we'll get there, I don't know.

"We were just gonna order pizza," Weston says. "What's your favorite?"

"I like Hawaiian."

"Yes," Rhodes says, coming over to bump my fist. "We're keeping you. I can't ever get anyone on board with Hawaiian."

"Because it's wrong," Bowie says.

Rhodes lifts his eyebrows. "If loving it is wrong, I don't wanna be right."

When I laugh, he bumps my fist again.

"So, did Weston tell you anything about us?" Penn asks.

"A little," I hedge.

"We've been occupied with other things," Weston grumbles.

"These two kept trying to butt in on The Single Dad Players," Rhodes says, smirking. "Now there's just one left. What are you gonna do about it, Penn?"

"I need to hang out with Jeremiah, Samson, and Free more," Penn mutters. "They don't give me this shit." He winks at me.

"We hang out with them plenty," Rhodes scoffs. "Don't forget Reed. That boy knows how to have a good time, on or off the field. But when you need some nurturin', you come to The Single Dad Players."

"The Single Dad Players," I repeat, glancing at Weston and smirking. "Like football players or playboy players?"

"Whatever works for you." Rhodes gives me a sexy grin.

He is so hot and so *trouble*.

"Back off, Archer." Weston rolls his eyes. "They named it that long before I was inducted," he says to me.

I lift a shoulder. "Seems like you fit right in, whichever meaning intended."

"Damn," Bowie says, laughing. "She's got your number, Shaw."

Weston's eyes narrow on me. "I've turned over a new leaf, Chapman. Tell her, boys."

"Now that I think about it, he has been hanging around me and Bowie more when we go out, rather than those two," Henley says, nodding at Rhodes and Penn.

Weston looks at me like that's proof that he's on the straight and narrow.

I lift an eyebrow at him but don't say anything. It doesn't matter what I think anyway.

"Nah. Don't let Penn make you think this is something it's not," Rhodes says. "These guys saved my life. I didn't know the first thing about being a dad when I got drafted to the Mustangs. When we realized we were the single dads on the team, we started meeting to talk about the trials and tribulations of fatherhood, and the rest is history." He pounds Henley's fist and then Bowie's…and then lifts his eyebrows and pounds Weston's.

"Here, catch," Bowie says and tosses Rhodes a blue notebook. "Your turn."

Rhodes grins and nods. "All right. It's time to wax philosophical, folks."

Penn groans. "These papas think their little club is all that." He smirks and shakes his head. "Just because I can wrap it up well doesn't mean I should be left out."

"No, you did not just say that," Rhodes yells, laughing, and then he looks at the baby, apologizing for being so loud. "For the record, I wrapped it up very well. I just didn't know Carrie was swapping out my box of condoms for ones from the early 2000s…and not taking the pill like she said she was."

Whoa. Carrie has the balls of a bull.

"I was having kids with my wife, not realizing that she didn't want to be married to me anymore," Henley says, his voice low.

No way. Who in their right mind wouldn't want to be married to Henley Ward?

"Sorry, man." Rhodes clinks his beer bottle to Henley's.

"I didn't know my girlfriend couldn't handle a child with special needs," Bowie says.

Oh my god.

"Fuck, you guys win, okay?" Rhodes says.

My heart has dropped more with each new revelation, but Bowie and Henley laugh and clink their glasses.

"They get me with that shit every time," Rhodes grumbles.

"Hey, we're only telling the truth," Henley says. "This is how we deal with our pain. We laugh about it."

"I'm not laughing right now," Rhodes says. "That's some depressing shit, man. Makes Carrie sound like a saint."

They all laugh at that.

"Carrie is not a saint," Penn says.

Rhodes wipes his eyes, laughing harder than all of them. "I know that's right. That woman is terrifying, but she's a good mama. She wanted a football player baby daddy and that's what she got."

"A damn good one too," Bowie says.

"Aw, you goin' soft on me, Bow?" Rhodes acts like he's going to kiss Bowie on the cheek, and Bowie has him in a headlock in the next second. Rhodes screams like he's dying and Caleb starts crying. "Fuck, I'm sorry," he says, ducking out of Bowie's hold in an instant. "I swear I'm an adult when my son is with me." He looks at me solemnly.

"I believe you." I reach out for Caleb and Weston hands him to me. I close my eyes as I hold him close. He quiets down and nestles into my neck and it's the best feeling in the world.

"These guys are the best dads I know," Henley says. "And you will be too, Weston. You're already blowing my mind. It took me at least fifteen minutes to change a diaper when we had Cassidy." He looks at his watch. "Shit. I've gotta run pick the girls up." He smiles at me. "Sadie, it was a pleasure."

My cheeks flush and I mumble something back, and Weston walks him to the door.

One of the guards brings the pizzas when they arrive, and it's good that I got my three slices right away. Weston asks if I'd like more before the last few pieces are taken, and when I say no, they swoop in. They inhale six large pizzas.

Weston's groaning afterward. "I know we're in the offseason, but I still shouldn't have done that."

"You'll be all right. You guys want to meet at the gym tomorrow?" Penn asks.

"I could if it's earlier in the day." Bowie looks at his watch. "I better head out. Becca will be home soon."

"I can meet you," Rhodes says. "Carrie has Levi today and tomorrow."

"I'll pass this time," Weston says.

"I can watch Caleb if you want to go," I tell him.

He smiles. "Thanks. I'm not quite ready to leave him yet." He sees the look on my face, and adds, "Not because I'm afraid of leaving him with you. We've got papers now, remember?" He bumps my hip with his and my insides flood with heat.

When I glance away, Penn, Bowie, and Rhodes are all staring at us with interest.

Rhodes grins. “You two have got a cute little thing going on already, you know that, right?”

“Shut up, Rhodes,” Weston says.

“I’m just sayin’…”

“Well, don’t.”

Weston shoots me a nervous look and my heart skips a few beats. I act unfazed and tuck my head against Caleb’s.

I wish I could say that Weston doesn’t affect me, but I’d be lying.

CHAPTER THIRTEEN

A WAY WITH THE LADIES

WESTON

When I come downstairs wearing a suit the morning of the funeral, Sadie stares at me in confusion.

"I should have made sure it was okay that I come to the funeral," I say sheepishly, dragging my hand along the back of my neck.

"You're going to the funeral?" she asks.

"I was planning on it. If it's okay with you and your family."

She swallows hard and nods. “That would be nice. Thank you.”

“Of course. I want to be there.”

She’s wearing a blue dress that matches her eyes and her long, dark hair falls down her back like a thick curtain. She looks beautiful. And exhausted.

“Did you get any sleep last night?” I ask.

She makes a face. “Not much. But thanks for taking Caleb. How did he do?”

“He actually had a little better night. Cried for a while when I took him from you at one and again at three, but not as long. We talked about a few things, took a stroll around the house…I think maybe he’s starting to get used to me.”

Her smile is faint and sad, but it’s there.

“He is,” she says.

“Can I drive you to the service?”

She hesitates for a second, and I’m certain she’ll say no.

“I’d like that, yes. I just need to get Caleb ready. My mom gave me a cute outfit for him to wear. Where is he?”

“I put the portable crib in the library.” I point at the baby monitor. “And every monitor on this level and upstairs is at the highest volume. If he takes a deep breath, we’ll hear it.”

Again, she smiles, but her heart isn’t into it. I honestly don’t know how she’s still standing here, looking so brave and strong when it’s obvious she’s suffering. A little sound comes from the baby monitor and her eyes light up. She takes a few quick sips of her coffee and grabs the prepared bottle, diaper, and outfit I didn’t notice until just now, and makes her way to the library.

The decent thing to do would be to turn off the monitor since she’s in there with him, but when I hear her talking to him, her voice quiet and singsongy, I can’t resist listening.

"Hi, sweet boy. You ready to eat? Come here and see me. I love you," her voice breaks, and I can't do it.

I turn the monitor off and text my sisters.

Hey. I love you guys.

FELICITY

I love you too!

OLIVIA

Who is this?

Very funny.

OLIVIA

<eye roll emoji> Love you too, b-hole.

I groan and laugh under my breath. My parents wouldn't let Olivia call me an asshole when we were kids, so she tried a-hole. No go. But for some reason when she pulled out b-hole, they thought that was the funniest thing. Naturally, it stuck. She's been calling me this since I was nine and she was twelve.

I'm unsure if I should go help Sadie get Caleb ready or if she needs this time with him. I decide on the latter, and when she comes out with him half an hour later, he's all dressed up in a grey sweater outfit, looking adorable.

"Look at the two of you." I hold up my phone. "Can I take a picture?"

Her cheeks flush and she blinks. "Sure. Or you can just get some of him."

"But you both look so great."

She smiles down at him. "He does look so cute, doesn't he? It's the softest sweater, and he's the perfect size. It's like cuddling with a teddy bear."

I snap a few pictures, pausing when she kisses his head, her eyes closing for a second like she's breathing him in. And then I hurry to catch the moment, my heart thrumming in my chest.

I hear more about Sasha during the funeral than I have yet and feel like I have a better sense of who she was. Funny, compulsive, and a little bit reckless, caring, and stubborn. Her friends and family talk about her like they never knew what she was going to do next, but that she made them want to be along for the ride. I also hear about how crazy she was about Caleb, and that's the part that nearly brings me to tears. I hate that Caleb will never know his mother.

Caleb is sitting with Sadie and her family, and I spend most of my time watching them. Caleb because since I found out he existed, I haven't wanted him out of my sight, and Sadie to see how she's reacting to all of this. She looks even thinner than she did when I met her a handful of days ago. I need to make sure she starts eating more.

When the service is over and Sadie sees that my parents and Felicity came, as well as the guys, she bursts into tears and hugs everyone. She reaches me last and the look in her eyes both surprises me and breaks my heart.

"Thank you," she whispers.

Overcome with emotion myself, I just nod and reach out to hug her. As I do, I feel her take a deep breath and relax into me, and something almost as fierce as when I saw Caleb for the first time happens inside of me. I don't know her well at all, but I want to take care of her. I want to protect her from pain and to be someone she can turn to. I want to trust her and for her to trust me in return.

A little bit shaken by the intensity of these feelings, I don't know what to say when she finally pulls away. We could've been hugging for seconds or minutes, I don't really know. Time sort of stood still for me.

I don't know how to explain it, and I don't feel the need to try. Both of us are in a fragile state, for different reasons, but the common root is our love for Caleb. That's bound to put more gravity on any interaction I have with her.

I notice her hands are shaky when I let her go.

"I'll ride with my parents to the cemetery," she says, finally meeting my eyes again. "You don't have to come to that. It's just family, and they can bring me back to Silver Hills. Caleb too, if that's okay."

"Of course, it is. I don't mind staying close and taking you both home though," I say.

"Thank you. I think I'll ride with them. You're probably sick of seeing me cry by now and I have a feeling the cemetery is going to bring out the ugly cry."

"I think you're one of the strongest people I've ever met," I tell her.

She stills, her gaze fixed on mine. When she blinks, the spell is broken and someone calls her name. She turns and lifts her hand to wave. I tear my eyes from her to see a good-looking guy walking toward her.

"Thanks, Weston," she says, before walking away.

I go out to eat with Felicity and the guys, but my mind is a million miles away.

"You okay?" Felicity asks under her breath.

"Yeah, I'm sorry. I'm…distracted."

"You worried about being away from Caleb?"

"I don't like being away from him, but no. I trust that Sadie will bring him home tonight."

"I like her. She seems straightforward and honest to me,

despite the way she came into your life." Felicity takes a drink of her Coke and turns to face me. "And she's really hot."

I roll my eyes. "I can't believe you're taking it there. The guys didn't even do that after they had pizza with her the other night." I was actually shocked that they didn't. Rhodes flirted with her, but he flirts with everyone.

"Well, don't tell me you haven't noticed," she says. "Are you going to be okay with her staying at your place? She is *really* attractive."

"She's all right," I say.

Felicity snorts before I've even gotten the words all the way out.

"What, do you want to date her?" I tease.

"I'm a happily married woman, thank you very much. I just know you have a way with the ladies and unfortunately, as much as I'd love to see you settle down, you haven't been in any hurry to." She lifts an eyebrow at me.

"No argument there." I hold my hands up.

"Is she really going to be okay with all the women you parade through your house?"

Felicity stayed with me for a few weeks after she graduated from college, so she thinks she knows all about my lifestyle.

I frown. "I've changed since you stayed with me. That was over a year ago. I didn't like who I was becoming," I admit. "And finding out I had a son and didn't even know about it—that's only underscored the fact that something needed to change."

"That's not on you, West. Sasha should've told you. But back to Sadie…are you interested in her?"

Felicity is like a dog on a hunt when she's digging for information. She ended up not going to law school despite being accepted in all the top schools. She chose a different career path, and it's suiting her well, but she can get to the bottom of the truth better than anyone I know.

"No, I'm not…interested in her." That feeling I got when I hugged her comes back to me and I push it down. "I can't be mad at her for Sasha's choices. I want to get along with her. I want us to raise Caleb together and hope that we can develop some sort of friendship while we do that."

Felicity leans in. "And she's pretty."

I groan. "Yes, she's pretty, but so are a lot of women. It doesn't mean I have to get in their pants."

"Whose pants are you getting in?" Rhodes asks, perking up.

Shit. I thought they were deep in conversation over there, but when I look around, everyone is focused on me.

"No one's pants. In fact, I've not been in anyone's pants for longer than usual, and I'm okay with that. It's been on purpose. And the subject is closed. My sister is right here and even if she weren't, I don't want to talk about it."

"That's usually when we need to talk about things the most," Bowie says.

"Oh really." I give him a droll look. "How about we talk about your dry spell then?"

Bowie glares at me and looks down at his plate.

"Thought so." I chuckle and take a long swig of my water.

I glance at my watch for the hundredth time, wondering if Sadie is done at the cemetery yet. How is she holding up? What time will they be home? Should I have food waiting for her when she gets back?

I run my hands through my hair, exhausted by my thoughts.

"Why would you purposely go through a drought?"

Rhodes asks, not willing to let the subject drop. "We need women to survive."

"Maybe he was tired of the flooding," Henley says, smirking. "He had so many women, he needed a break to dry out and get his house in order."

"And it's a good thing, because now there's a beautiful woman in his house," Bowie says, grinning before he takes a drink of his beer.

"Oh, I was hoping we'd talk about that," Rhodes says, his full-wattage smile coming out.

"No, we're not talking about that," I say.

"But I really want to," Rhodes says with a mock pout.

"Me too. I'd love to talk about that," Penn chimes in.

"Too fucking bad." I stand and toss my napkin on the table. "Thanks for coming out today. I think it really meant a lot to Sadie that you all were there."

"Wait. Don't forget this." Rhodes holds up the blue notebook they've been writing in. It says The Single Dad Playbook in large block letters on the front. "I had to take it home to finish my entry. We'll add to it when we meet again."

"Thanks." I take it from him and wave it slightly. "Can't wait to see the nuggets of wisdom in this thing," I tease, but I'm actually looking forward to seeing what they've come up with so far.

"You're leaving?" Bowie asks. He gets up and squeezes my shoulder.

"Yeah, I need to get home."

"He's got a beautiful woman to get home to. I'd be rushing off too," Rhodes says, laughing under his breath.

"We're not going there," I say, lifting my hand. "I don't even see her that way."

Bowie's eyebrows lift.

"Really?" Rhodes says, looking thunderstruck. He leans

over the table and whispers loudly, "She has curves for days, man. That ass in those jeans and her tits are the perfect—"

I slam my hand down on the table.

"Enough," I say a little too loudly.

I glance around, grateful that we're in a little alcove to ourselves.

When I turn back to look at the table, I point at Rhodes. "Don't talk about her like that."

Rhodes looks satisfied.

"That's what I thought," he says, smirking.

I groan and get out of there.

CHAPTER FOURTEEN

REPERTOIRE AND DRINKS

SADIE

For at least three weeks following the funeral, I'm in a fog. I thought I was dealing with losing Sasha and what that meant for my future and Caleb's, but I don't think I had even scratched the surface yet.

It all comes crashing down. It's a struggle to get out of bed. I feel weak and sick and everything hurts. I can't eat. All I want to do is sleep, but I force myself to stay awake to see Caleb.

Weston hovers nearby, trying to get me to eat and asking if I want to go on a walk or if there's anything he can do. He's been thoughtful, but he's also given me space when I've needed it. I don't know how he knows when I've hit my limit with being around people while I'm grieving, but he's observant and perceptive. I don't know why I keep being surprised by him, but I am.

I went to work twice and both times I started crying and couldn't stop, so Kim sent me home. But now she's starting to call again, asking when I'll be back. I'm too deep in this dark pit to call her back.

Weston's covered the nights and the three of us are together most days. I know he's worn out, but he hasn't said a negative word about it. He and Caleb have bonded with all this time together. When Weston walks into the room, Caleb rocks back and forth, excited and reaching for him. I can see how ecstatic it makes Weston and it makes me happy for him, and yet, I can't help but feel like it makes me lose my sister a little more each day. Caleb won't even remember her. And at the rate I'm going with him, he's not going to remember me either if I don't step it up pretty soon.

I take a long shower and put jeans and a sweater on, a step up from the leggings and baggy sweatshirts I've been wearing every day.

When I walk upstairs, I can hear Weston singing to Caleb. I smile when I hear that it's "Houdini" by Dua Lipa. This guy's musical repertoire is bizarre, to say the least. Once I reach the kitchen, I see Weston playing peek-a-boo as he's singing. Caleb throws his head back and cackles, and Weston's laughing too. When Caleb lets out a really loud laugh, Weston loses it and can't keep singing because he's laughing so hard. A laugh bursts out of me, and Weston turns in surprise. His eyes light up when he sees me, and I almost retreat back down the stairs. I don't want to ruin the mood with my sadness.

His face falls when he sees my expression and he holds out his hand. "Hey, come join us."

I don't know if he meant for me to, but I take his hand and it feels like a lifeline. I let him tug me toward them and he throws the blanket over my head and says, "Where did she go?"

I play along, staying hidden for a second before pulling it off and saying, "Boo!"

Caleb laughs so hard he gets the hiccups, and it brings me so much joy to see him this happy, I almost forget to be sad.

I think Weston doesn't want to lose this opportunity, because he says, "Why don't we get out of the house for a while? Want to go to the park? It's nice out, feels like spring. Or we could take a drive…my sister's been wanting us to come see her in Landmark Mountain."

"I don't feel like I'm good enough company to go there yet, but maybe a drive closer to home would be nice."

"Yeah? I know a place you might like. Get your coat and some comfortable shoes and I'll work on putting some food together."

I'm already rethinking my decision, but the hopeful look in his eyes forces me to keep that to myself. I nod and go grab my comfiest boots and coat. When I come back up, Weston has Caleb's bag packed and is making sandwiches. I pitch in and help, the monotonous task a nice reprieve from my thoughts.

We're in the car within half an hour and Weston won't tell me where we're going.

He's quiet, almost as if he's afraid to break the spell.

"You're doing great with him," I finally say.

He turns to me, a pleased expression on his face. "You think so?"

"You really are. I'm sorry I've been—"

"No, don't be." He faces the road again. We're going up a mountain and the curves are getting more intense. "I've been worried about you, but I think I'd be more worried if you weren't reacting to this loss. It shows me how much you love your sister, how deeply you care about the people you love."

I think about that as I stare out the window.

"I need to do better for Caleb," I say softly. "I will do better."

"He's all right. He loves you and he'll be right here when you're feeling yourself again."

I turn to look at him. "You really are a decent guy."

He grins. "That's what I strive to be. Decent."

I'm rolling my eyes when he glances over and his smile grows.

"Hey, at least you'll never get a big head when I'm around." I lift my shoulder and he laughs.

"True. My family will be pleased about this."

"I should probably get back to my apartment soon. It's been a little more than the few weeks we talked about, and I don't want to overstay my welcome," I say.

I never wanted to stay in his house, but it's so hard to think about leaving Caleb.

"Don't worry about that right now. I'm in no hurry for you to go, and your rent is taken care of through the end of your lease, so you don't need to worry about that either."

"Weston! You didn't need—"

He holds up his hand. "I told you I'd take care of you. And I want you to stay as long as you can."

"Thank you," I say softly.

We're almost to the top of the mountain when Weston

parks. When we get out, he puts a hat and coat on Caleb and puts him in a baby carrier I didn't even know we had. Caleb's head rests against Weston's chest and they both look content. I'm surprised by the ease in which he handles Caleb. It's changed a lot in the past month.

We grab the food and a blanket and walk until we've reached the crest. It's only a short walk up, and when we get there, I gasp. The view is incredible. We're not even close to being on the tallest mountain, but we're high above the trees, the clouds feeling close enough to jump on one and float away.

We set down our things and walk closer to the edge of the mountain.

"Silver Hills," he says, pointing to the left.

From here, I can make out the pretty church and the water tower with ivy painted around it.

"So many places to see," I say.

"You haven't even been to my favorite coffee shop yet, Luminary. Or my favorite place to get a drink—don't tell anyone…" He leans down to whisper, "At The Fairy Hut."

I bite back a laugh and look up. He's closer than I thought and we stare at each other for a beat without saying anything.

"The Fairy Hut?" My voice sounds breathy and I clear my throat.

"It's exactly how you'd imagine," he says like he's annoyed.

"I can't say that I've ever imagined a fairy hut."

"Well, it's awesome. It's kind of dark inside with all these lights everywhere, some that look like lightning bugs flying around. And all the drinks have these weird names, but they're delicious. My brother-in-law can barely choke them down, but the last time we went, he chose Tink's mead and was happy."

"Tink's mead," I repeat, unable to hold back the smile.

He points at me and Caleb reaches out to grab his finger. He laughs and continues to point with Caleb's fingers latched on. "You look like a Beyond the Goat Hollow kind of girl."

"I'm…uh, I'll have to take your word for it."

"Maybe a Who Let the Frogs Out…but those are strong. I'm not sure how well you handle your liquor."

I giggle. "I'm not sure if I should be offended that you're linking me with these particular drinks. They sound terrible. I very rarely drink, but when I do, I'm a lightweight."

He gives me a huge grin. "If you're game, we'll go after our picnic. They serve great food too." He lifts a shoulder. "Maybe we'll be hungry again after all this fresh air. Their Bubbling Brook soup is my favorite."

"That sounds a lot more appetizing than the drinks."

"Well, their Cow Slobber soup is also good, but I think that one is seasonal."

I choke back a laugh. "I'm not touching that one."

"It's good, I swear."

"You're always thinking about food, aren't you?"

He looks at me incredulously. "Isn't everyone?"

I shake my head, laughing again.

"Hmm. I didn't know that." He turns and puts his hand on Caleb's stomach as he bends to pick up the blanket.

"Let me help." I take the other end of the blanket and we smooth it out.

We sit down and keep taking in the view. When I turn to say something, he's already looking at me. He startles slightly and starts taking food out. There's more than I thought. Besides the sandwiches, there are chips and fruit and brownies.

"Those look great. Where are those from?" I ask, pointing at the brownies.

"Clara makes them. She's the owner of Luminary. You'll love her. Sassy and so dang cute…and she can make a helluva coffee and pastry…and brownies." He waves his hand. "Everything she makes is good."

A curl of unease twists in my stomach and I try not to react. Does he like Clara? Maybe I need to go to Luminary and see this girl. Just to see who could possibly be in the picture at some point.

"Dig in," he says, handing me a plate.

And despite not thinking I can eat very much, I manage to eat a little bit of everything. Weston looks so pleased with himself by the time we're done, I think maybe he was telling the truth. Maybe he really was worried about me.

We stay a little longer, but the wind picks up, so we decide to go.

"The Fairy Hut?" he asks when we drive down Jupiter, the main drag in the cute and tiny downtown area.

"Sure, why not?" It's been the best day I've had in a long time. I'm not quite ready to cut it short.

We stop at a light and there's a woman with long blonde hair that looks like Stevie Nicks' younger sister, singing with her guitar on the corner. Weston lowers the windows and we listen.

"She's good," I say.

"Yeah, Tiana's a sweetheart. Went to Woodstock and said it changed her life."

I turn back to look at her as we pull away. "She's old enough to have been to Woodstock?"

"She's in her seventies," he says.

"Unbelievable."

He points out his favorite places along the way. Twinkle Tales, an adorable bookstore, where the highlight besides an incredible book selection, is Hank the orange tabby cat.

Starlight Cafe, a retro diner that is more than just burgers and shakes, they also have every pie imaginable and their soups are great too. Rose & Thorn, a fine dining experience…he kisses his lips when he says this and it makes me laugh.

"Along this whole street, every Saturday, summer through fall, vendors come from everywhere and the Pixie Pop-Up Market takes over." He shakes his head when I try not to laugh. "I know, I feel like an idiot every time I say the names of anything around here. Twinkle Tales? Come on."

I can't help but laugh then.

"But the Pixie Pop-Up Market…it's amazing. If you like to shop even a little bit, you'll love it."

"You really love this town, don't you?" I ask.

"I grew up here, and there's nowhere else I'd rather be. Landmark Mountain is incredible too, though. I didn't know another place could come close to this, but it does."

The Fairy Hut is even better than Weston described, although he did a pretty great job. He didn't tell me that the servers have pointy ears and wear fairy clothes. The girls are wearing little tutus and wings, and the one guy I see is wearing a scalloped edge shirt over tight black pants.

"Do you ever get the urge to dress like a fairy when you come here?" I ask.

"Uh…no. Those pants are too similar to the ones I have to wear playing football. I don't love my junk getting on those websites highlighting bulges as it is. Can you imagine if I wore pants like those that don't have as much compression?" He shudders.

Meanwhile, I'm picturing his bulge. I'm sorry to say I'm quite familiar with those sites and his bulge.

CHAPTER FIFTEEN

YOU COULD HATE ME

WESTON

After our day out, Sadie has been around more. She still seems so sad and tentative, but she has color in her cheeks and she's eating more often too.

I got an email that Caleb's furniture should be arriving today, so I'm going to broach the subject of moving his room upstairs. I've been sleeping on the couch downstairs more often than not…or the chair in the library. Somewhere close enough that I can reach him before he wakes her up.

I'm a little nervous about bringing it up with her, but I don't know why. She's been more open. She's not looking at me like I'm the bad guy as much anymore. I still don't think she fully trusts me, but I don't think she hates me either.

We're somewhere in the middle of a peaceful place.

Still, I make pancakes to soften the atmosphere. I've discovered that if Sadie doesn't want anything else to eat, she'll say yes to pizza or pancakes, and since it's nine in the morning and they're one of the few things I know how to make, I'm going with pancakes.

Sadie comes up with a happy Caleb. After being up with him last at six, I put him in the portable crib downstairs by the couch while I worked out in my gym and snuck upstairs just a little while ago to grab a shower and make coffee. He's still waking up during the night, but the intervals between are getting longer and the length of time awake is getting shorter.

Sadie looks better today. She looks amazing, actually. She's wearing a cute sweater and jeans, and her hair is pulled back in a ponytail. I've tried my damnedest not to give it any thought, but Rhodes is not the only one who's noticed the way her ass fits in her jeans and the way her tits are a perfect handful. Her legs go on for days, and her long neck is an expanse of graceful elegance. And that's just her body. Her face…God, her face. Her eyes, her mouth.

Get a grip, Shaw. Get a fucking grip.

I'm determined to not blow this with Sadie. I cannot fuck this up.

The circles under her eyes are almost gone. She looks more rested than she has in days, and she's smiling down at Caleb. When she looks up at me, her eyes widen when she sees what I'm doing.

"You made pancakes?" She smiles.

"Does that sound good?"

"Always."

"Well, dig in. They're still hot."

When she walks over, Caleb grins his huge, gummy smile at me and I lean down and nuzzle his neck. Sadie freezes and Caleb laughs.

"Sorry." I take a step back. "I can't resist his neck."

She relaxes and grins. "I can't either. His little chubby neck…and wrists and legs…and cheeks…" She laughs. "I guess I can't resist anything about him."

I grin at her and she seems taken aback for a second. Her cheeks are flushed, and she focuses on grabbing a plate.

"Want me to take him while you eat?" I ask.

"Have you eaten yet?"

"I had a protein shake a few minutes ago."

She stares at me, pausing the syrup midstream. "You made these just for me?"

I lift my shoulder. "Yeah. It didn't take long. And you seem to like them."

"I love pancakes," she says softly. "Thank you. You didn't have to do that, especially if you're not eating them."

She hands Caleb to me and I hug him close.

"It's no trouble. Maybe I'll have a couple with peanut butter in a little while." I laugh. "I had a good workout already."

She lifts her eyebrows. "You eat them with peanut butter? Doesn't it stick to the roof of your mouth?"

"Well, my favorite way to have them is with Karo syrup and peanut butter, but I try to avoid that kind of sugar most of the time. Today I might just drizzle honey over the top."

She nods like she's considering trying it.

"That does sound good."

We go to the table and sit down, both of us focused on Caleb for the first few minutes.

"His furniture is supposed to come today," I finally say.

"Oh good. I was wondering when that was arriving."

"How would you feel about…what if—" *God, why is this so hard? I'm never nervous around women, but I'm nervous around her.*

"Spit it out, Shaw." She laughs.

I swipe my hand down my face. "I don't know why I'm nervous."

I look at her from the corner of my eye and her face drains of color. She sets her fork down and folds her hands, waiting for me to come out with it.

"Just say it," she says.

"Would you be okay if we move his room upstairs? You could move up there too. Or if you really prefer downstairs, we can keep it as it is. I just…I want you to sleep well, and I thought it'd be fun to have a real bedroom set up for him."

She sags against the back of the chair and then throws her napkin at me. "I thought you were going to ask me to leave."

I frown. "Wasn't it just yesterday that I told you how much I want you to stay? Are you getting more comfortable? I know it's been an adjustment."

She takes a bite and finishes it before she speaks. "When I first got here I didn't think I'd ever be comfortable here, but you've made it easy to adjust. And you need to get some sleep too. Have you even slept in a bed since we got here?"

I slowly shake my head.

"If you prefer being upstairs, let's move his room up there. How would you feel about me staying up there too? I'd like to be more helpful than I've been."

"You're being plenty helpful," I tell her. "I've loved having that time with him. It hasn't been a hardship." I smile down at him and his hand slaps onto mine as he waves his arms. "I like how bright it is upstairs and the view of the mountains out the windows is a little better from up there. And of course, you can move up there too."

"I don't want to invade on your space."

"Do you hear us? If we get any more polite, halos will appear out of thin air."

A shocked laugh bursts out of her.

"Or tiny horns," she sasses.

I grin. "That's more like it."

She rolls her eyes but is still laughing, and two pink splotches appear on her cheeks. "Okay, I'll move my things upstairs, but on one condition."

"Let's hear it."

"I'll start taking half of the night shift."

I make a face. "The thing about that is when my season starts back up, I'll need to take you up on that more often. But for now, I have the time, and I like that I'm getting to know my son and that you're catching up on sleep."

She finishes another bite and pushes her plate away, studying me carefully.

"I actually believe you when you say that," she says.

My head tilts. "I'd hope so."

She shakes her head. "I can't believe you're not angrier… or more bitter. You could hate me, but I don't think you do."

"Of course I don't. Would you stop saying that? Have you ever really thought I hated you?"

"At first I did. I just thought you were good at hiding it."

"And now?"

"I think you're genuine and when you say something, you mean it."

I swallow hard and nod. "Thank you. I try to only say what I mean."

"I need to get back to work soon. My boss has been amazing, but I'd totally deserve it if she fired me."

"Unless you love the job, you wouldn't have to go back…" I cringe slightly, not knowing how she'll take this. "Please only hear this how I intend it. In several months, we'll have to find help with Caleb. I don't want you to feel pressured to do more than you want to do…or to talk you into anything, but if you wanted to take care of him full-time, I could compensate you for it. If we don't do that, we should consider looking into people now so that he's covered in a few months."

"I already feel like I'm freeloading off of you," she says, shaking her head.

"You're not. I don't feel that way at all. I wanted you here, remember?"

"I'd take care of him because I want to, not for money."

"Would you feel that you're missing out on something you love if you do that?"

"I don't love my job, but it was a necessity."

"If you're open to this, we should definitely discuss it more. Whenever you want to, I'm in." I laugh when Caleb lets out a loud burp. "You're a great icebreaker, aren't you?" I kiss his temple.

"I'm in too," she says.

So, over the next hour, we come to an agreement. I'll pay her a small stipend and all of her expenses. She'll take care of Caleb while I'm at work and they'll travel with me some too. We haven't come to a conclusion about where she'll live yet, but I assure her I'm not rushing her out of here.

"I sound like a full-time nanny," she says, smiling.

"More like a work wife without the benefits…or maybe *with* benefits, depending on how you look at it." I laugh awkwardly. "Taking care of things without having to put out." I groan. "I'll shut up now. I've made this awkward."

Thankfully, she laughs too. "Yes, you have."

Her cheeks are rosier than ever when I look at her again. Her full lips are pink and distracting and her eyes are bright and playful. A pang of desire hits me hard. I feel it all over. My head, my heart, my dick—my entire being feels like it's reaching out for her.

No, this cannot happen, I tell myself. *I cannot be attracted to her. I cannot fall for her. I absolutely cannot.*

But when her lips lift into a smile meant just for me, I know it's already happening.

CHAPTER SIXTEEN

ARE YOU SERIOUS RIGHT NOW

SADIE

We spend the rest of the day clearing out the room that we choose for Caleb. It's upstairs between the massive room I put my things into and Weston's. When Weston put out the word among his friends and family that he had new furniture that he doesn't need anymore, he had several offers to take it off of his hands within the hour.

Henley's daughter Cassidy wants the furniture and they come over to pick it up. Cassidy tries to play it cool, but it's obvious she has a crush on Weston and that she's beside herself to own something that belonged to him. When Henley tries to pay Weston for it, Weston refuses, and I think about how amazing that must feel to be able to just give things away like that.

Before they leave, Henley says, "Hey, you got that notebook?"

A smile breaks out across Weston's face. I think Cassidy and I both stop breathing.

"Yes, I do," he says. "It's gold, man."

Henley laughs. "Grab it for me and I'll bring it to our meeting tomorrow."

"Oh, I forgot I'm actually invited now." Weston laughs. "Where are you meeting?"

"Luminary…"

Weston looks at me and pauses. "I'll wait and see how it's going here. Unless you'd like to see my favorite coffee shop?" he asks me.

I nod. "I could do that. I wouldn't have to be part of the meeting…Caleb and I would get our own table." My eyebrows lift. "*Oh*, is this a Single Dad Players meeting?"

"Single Dad Players?" Cassidy says, her eyes flying to her dad.

I want to laugh because it's said in the typical *are you serious right now* teenager voice.

"It's coffee with the guys," Henley says.

He shoots me a look that makes me feel like I'm in trouble, but for some reason, I still just want to laugh. I can only imagine what Rhodes would be saying right now.

"We'll be there." Weston grins at me like we're in on the joke together.

Henley grumbles and Weston helps them load everything in a moving truck. Another huge bonus of being filthy rich:

access to whatever you need at the snap of a finger. This would've taken me rounding up at least three friends' vehicles to *maybe* get the furniture to my place safely.

While Weston's finishing up with them, I call my boss Kim. She answers on the second ring.

"How are you, girl?"

"I'm feeling a little more human these days," I say.

"How's that baby doing?"

"He's growing like crazy. He's doing better too. We're both adjusting, but it's taking a while."

"Aw, sweet boy. I miss him…I miss both of you. Sasha too," she says softly. "I think about you guys every single time I drive past your apartment…so all the time. I'm glad to hear you're both adjusting," she says. "It'll take time."

"I'm sorry it's taken so long for me to call you back. I'm really sorry. You've been amazing about all of this and I've let you down."

"No, you haven't. I can't imagine how hard this has been. And we've done okay here. Esther and Carla wanted more shifts anyway. I always gave you first dibs because you're the best and I love you, but they're getting the job done." She laughs. "The job is here when you want it, but…we'll be okay, Sadie. You've got a little boy to think about now." She clears her throat. "Well, that's nothing new—you've been thinking about him nonstop since he was born and working your ass off to take care of him. You put the rest of us to shame as a big sister."

I lower my head and wipe the tears from my face. "Thank you, Kim. I love you too. You've been the best boss I've ever had, and an even better friend. You took me under your wing when I really needed it, and I'll always be grateful for that. I…" I take a deep breath and forge ahead. "I have an opportunity to take care of Caleb full-time, and I think that would be good for us, at least for a while."

"Are you kidding? You've been the best employee I've ever had. You saved my ass when I became manager. And this sounds like an opportunity you can't pass up. You have a job with me anytime, so I think you're set for job security." She laughs. "I'll miss you though."

"I'll miss you too. I'll have to come see you sometime when things get a little more normal around here. I'm staying in Silver Hills right now, but I miss everyone."

"I'd love that. Bring the baby. It's been too long since I've seen him."

"I will."

I hang up feeling like a load has lifted off of me. Caleb goes down for a nap, and when Weston comes back in, he stretches his arms over his head. I look a little too attentively at the muscles in his shoulders and biceps, the little strip of skin showing under his shirt, and I force myself to look away.

"We got that stuff out of here just in time," he says. "Caleb's furniture is here. I'm just going to let them in the front."

He jogs to the front door when the doorbell rings and I wonder, not for the first time, where he gets all that energy. I'm not sure when he's sleeping.

The guys come in with the furniture, out of their minds with excitement when they realize this is Weston Shaw's place. There's just one problem: no crib. When they've checked the order and we've checked it on our end too, we realize we bought a changing table, a chest of drawers, and bookshelves, but we didn't actually buy the crib we'd picked out.

"Damn. Guess we'll have to go shopping," Weston says, making a goofy face at me.

After they've set up the rest of the furniture, going the extra mile to put it all together, they ask for his autograph. He's good-natured about the whole thing, making them feel relaxed and yet still keeping it professional. When he's ready for them to go, he thanks them again for all their help and leads them to the door.

"Wow, you are really smooth with that. I like how you got them out of here in a hurry without making them feel dumb."

He wrinkles his nose. "Was I that obvious?"

"No! I don't think they had a clue. You're just a lot more laid-back when it's us here or your friends and family."

"Free once had a fan show up at his house. It was right after he signed with the Mustangs, before he had a good security system, and when he got home, the girl had taken all of his family pictures off of the wall and had them surrounding her in the living room."

"No," I gasp.

"She started taking pictures with him…she wanted to fill all the frames with the two of them."

"*Wow.*" I make a face.

He nods. "Yeah. I think we all learned to keep a healthy distance from then on."

"Except for with the women…"

He flinches slightly and I regret saying it.

"Yeah," he says eventually. "I haven't always made the best decisions when it comes to women."

"Did you have any desire to see my sister again after your night together?" My heart starts pounding like crazy. I don't know why I'm bringing this up, and I'm not sure what I want him to say.

He leans against the kitchen counter. We've gotten all of Caleb's things from the basement and paused to get a drink of water before taking them up.

"Honestly?" he asks.

I nod. "Yes, please."

"No."

I look down at my water bottle. "Why not?"

"We had fun at the party…we drank, we danced and fell into bed together. The next morning we didn't share numbers, we didn't kiss goodbye. We both knew what the night was, just a good time."

To hear Sasha tell it, it was the hottest night of her life. It's kind of sad that he viewed it so differently, but I can't say it surprises me. He could have anyone he wants. There's also something about hearing this that relieves me…in a twisted way that I'm not proud of.

It doesn't matter. Who he sleeps with is none of my business.

"Have you ever felt more with someone you slept with?"

These questions keep pouring out of my mouth like it's my prerogative to know.

It's not.

But he doesn't seem bothered by it.

"No, not really. If anything, I've avoided women that I might connect with too much. I've been focused on my career. Sex has been an outlet, a good time, and anyone I've slept with has known that. I've never made promises of anything more." He lifts a shoulder. "But I'm tired of all the partying and sleeping around. I'm not a kid anymore, and I don't know…maybe I don't want to have sex just for the sake of having sex."

I'm finding it hard to breathe fully. I never thought I'd be talking openly about sex with Weston Shaw.

"What about you?" he asks.

"Me?" I squeak. "Uh, it's been a while for me and I wouldn't mind having sex just for the sake of having sex."

His eyes light up as he laughs. "Is that right?"

My face flames. "No, probably not. I mean, yes. No!" I shake my head. "Ugh. Um. I usually find it easier to connect with sex than having a conversation. That probably doesn't surprise you. I'm not the best at making conversation." I hold my hand up. "Not that you're thinking about me having sex." I put my head in my hands.

He coughs, trying not to laugh.

"How did we get on this subject?" I groan.

He pulls my fingers away from my face and my breath hitches. When I look up, he's smiling and he's stepped closer. A lock of his dark hair has fallen over his forehead and I'm tempted to brush it back.

"I'd like to be someone you can talk to easily…about anything," he says. "I like it when you open up." He lifts his shoulder. "I'd like to know everything."

My insides warm. "What do you want to know?"

"Do you have good friends in your life?"

My mouth opens and closes. I wonder if I seem pathetic to him.

"Not many. Sasha was my best friend…and other than my friends at work, I didn't really spend time with anyone else. I hung out with my boss Kim outside of work occasionally. She's a good friend. Well…my former boss now. I haven't told you yet, but I let her know I most likely won't be going back to Hanson's. I have a standing job with her whenever I need though."

"Have you ever wanted to do something besides waitressing?" he asks.

I snort. "Of course. Don't get me wrong—it's been a great job. But I would've loved to go to school for interior design. It just hasn't been feasible."

He's quiet as he studies me. And then, "Who was the last guy you had sex with?"

I laugh. "That's what you want to know?"

He shrugs. "You started the sex talk."

I groan. "Drew."

I watch his Adam's apple as he swallows. "Who is Drew? Wait..." His eyes narrow. "Is that the guy who came to the funeral?"

"He was there, yeah."

He takes a step back. "So, he's still in the picture?"

"No, not really. I mean, not at all like that. But he's a friend. We worked together."

"At the restaurant?"

I nod.

"Did you care about him? Did you want it to be more?" His expression is intense when he waits for me to answer. "Do you want it to be more now?"

"No. *No.*" I laugh awkwardly. "I'd put an end to it already. We were done and I was good with that. I cared about him, but he was too much of a flirt with everyone for me to take him seriously. It was fun while it lasted, but he was more of a friend than anything. He acted sad when I ended things, but I didn't really buy that." I smile and watch the muscle in Weston's jaw clench and unclench.

"I guarantee he was sad," he says softly. His eyes roam over my face and linger on my mouth.

What is happening right now? He almost looks like he wants to kiss me...but no, I'm sure I'm reading that wrong.

I start to sweat.

"Why do you say that?" My voice is shaky.

"Because you're a rare kind of beautiful, Sadie," he says. "I've never seen eyes like yours, violet and luminous and haunting. Your mouth is what supermodels pay their plastic surgeons to have." He looks me over and my entire body starts thrumming. "But then you're also smart, kind, unassuming…and you love with your whole heart. Any guy would be crazy not to hold onto you with everything he had."

No one has ever said anything like this to me before. I want to wrap up his words and carry them around with me, pulling them out any time I'm having a hard day.

My mouth parts, and in the distance, I can hear the clock ticking as we stare at each other. Caleb makes a sound in the baby monitor and the spell breaks.

I point over my shoulder. "I'll go check on him."

He swallows and licks his lips before nodding. "I'll bring the rest of his stuff up here so he can sleep in his room tonight."

He smiles like he didn't just turn my world upside down, and he leaves the room, taking my heart with him.

CHAPTER SEVENTEEN

TEETERING

WESTON

What the fuck was that?

You are teetering into dangerous territory, Shaw.

I drag my hand through my hair and try to focus on putting Caleb's things away, but I can't stop thinking of the way Sadie looked at me just now.

I came *this* close to kissing her.

What the fuck am I thinking?

I have a feeling we'd be explosive together, and then what?

She barely trusts me now. If things went south, we'd be stuck co-raising Caleb and we just think this has been hard already? It'd be ten times harder if our feelings got involved.

I'm glad that we're getting to know each other and that it feels like the walls between us are finally coming down, but a surefire way to ruin all of that would be to make a move on her. Whatever this is that I'm feeling needs to be placed in the far recesses of never, and we need to stay firm in the friend zone.

Without thinking it through enough, I text the guys.

Do we ever do impromptu Single Dad Players meetings?

HENLEY

I just saw you! Why didn't you say you needed a meeting today?

I wasn't thinking about it then.

PENN

The Single Dad Players are an ongoing resource of vital tips and information. That's what I've heard anyway. I wouldn't personally KNOW. But I can be over in twenty. Just finishing up at the gym.

RHODES

I'm with Penn. We'll be right there.

BOWIE

It must be dire if it can't wait until tomorrow.

Shit. I forgot we were getting together tomorrow. It can wait. Never mind. It's best that it's not at the house anyway.

HENLEY

The curiosity will kill me if I have to wait until tomorrow.

It's nothing. Forget it. I'll see you tomorrow.

RHODES

We're on our way.

HENLEY

I'll be there in more like thirty.

BOWIE

Same.

No, don't come. Sadie's here and I don't want her to hear this.

HENLEY

You're killing me.

RHODES

By tomorrow you'll have talked yourself off of the cliff and will have toned down the angst, which truly sucks because I am in need of some DRAMA. Has it really only been a month and a half since we won the Super Bowl? I'm dying here. At least give us a fucking hint, Shaw!

I chuckle, my earlier urgency already feeling a little more under control.

But now they're texting every few minutes.

PENN

Did you walk in on her taking a shower?

RHODES

No way. Shit. Did you???

BOWIE

No, he did not walk in on her taking a shower. He has like seventy billion bathrooms—why would he walk into hers while she's taking a shower?

RHODES

Uh, because she's in there! Taking a shower!

I didn't walk in on her taking a shower. I'm not a skeeze.

RHODES

Neither am I, but I am horny, dude. It's been too long. I need someone to be getting some.

PENN

I'm getting some. Why aren't you? You're usually keeping up with me. You really don't need us now, Weston?

RHODES

I don't know what's wrong with me. I need to go find a willing body. Elle is going through crap with Bernard, so I'm trying to be there for her, but I'm in a constant state of pissed off. I can't stand that dude.

BOWIE

I can't believe she's still with that guy.

RHODES

Trust me. I can't believe it either. She's been my best friend forever and is the smartest woman I know, but when it comes to Bernard, she's got blinders the size of Texas.

We all love Rhodes' best friend Elle, and Rhodes is right, Bernard is a douche. I personally think Rhodes and Elle belong together, but Rhodes doesn't even let us tease about it. He shuts that down *fast*.

HENLEY

She needs to dump that asshole for good. West, call it. You need us now, we'll be there.

I'll see you tomorrow. Crisis averted for now. Thanks, you guys.

I get everything put away in Caleb's room and then drag in the surprise I've been hiding in my room for the past few days. It's a rocking chair that's comfortable and pretty, something I didn't realize would be so hard to find.

When Sadie walks into the room with Caleb and sees the rocking chair in the corner, she gasps.

"I love it," she says. "I didn't know you'd bought this."

"It was a little surprise. Try it out," I tell her, motioning for her to have a seat.

She sits down and grins when it rocks. "So good." She looks at Caleb who's jabbering excitedly. "What do you think of your room? You love it too, don't you?"

She glances around the space, taking it all in.

She stops rocking when she sees the picture. It's one that I grabbed at the apartment while she was in another room. Sasha is holding a tiny Caleb and kissing him. I hung it by the rocking chair, low enough that when we're rocking Caleb, we can see it.

"It's perfect, Weston. Even better than I imagined."

"It will be once we get a crib." We both laugh. "The stores are closing soon. Should we go pick one out tomorrow after coffee?"

"That would be great." She smiles and nods. "Weston, Sasha would've—" She pauses. "She would've loved it, but actually, this is more my taste than Sasha's." She makes a face. "I don't know why I feel bad saying that. We would've talked about it if she were here, so it's not like I'm…talking behind her back." She sighs and shakes her head. "I still don't know how to talk about her like she's not just away on vacation or something."

"I get that. You can talk about her however you want," I say. "I like hearing about her. I want Caleb to know everything about his mom."

She takes a deep breath and her lips tilt up, and for the first time since I've known her, she doesn't cry when she talks about Sasha. "She would have characters on the walls, and it would be cute, but I like how classy everything looks without them. Instead of that one adorable bunny that is the cutest," she points to the floppy stuffed bunny propped up on the bookshelf, "there would be stuffed animals *everywhere*. She liked things to be over the top, and I like that it's still obviously a baby's room without being hit over the head with cutesy everything."

I smile. "I know what you mean. I like that about it too. We could add a few characters for Sasha if you want though."

She laughs. "That's sweet, but no, it's okay. This is much better." She looks at the picture of Sasha and Caleb. "And she's still a part of things too."

"My interior designer is Autumn Ledger—she's the one

who helped me find the rocking chair and almost everything else in this house. She'd call this understated elegance."

She blinks up at me. "Did you say Autumn Ledger? Like Zac Ledger's wife?"

I nod, grinning. "I know. I freaked when I met them. I was always a huge fan of Zac's. He's the true GOAT of the NFL, in my opinion. And he's such a nice guy. There's a weird connection with our families now—well, more like my sister's family. Zac's brother Jamison is married to my brother-in-law Sutton's sister, Scarlett."

She moves her fingers up like she's calculating and then shakes her head. "Wow. So you're saying Autumn Ledger has been in this house?"

I nod and she gives me a huge smile.

"That is amazing. I *love* her. I think I've seen every magazine and every show she's ever been featured in…"

"You said you would've gone to school for interior design?"

"Yes. I don't know that I'm any good at it, but I'm way into it."

"Your apartment was decorated nice."

She makes a face. "Thank you. That didn't feel like my best effort, but I can make something out of very little." She laughs. "My mom and Sasha both like a little more," her lips twist as she tries to come up with the right word, "clutter… more knickknacks than me. I love the way you have a place for everything and it's cozy without feeling cluttered."

"I'd say thank you, but I have Autumn to thank for that."

"I bet she asked what you liked and based everything around that, though," she says. "So I'm sure you played a part in how it turned out. And I've been here long enough that I would've seen you make messes by now if that's the way you kept your house."

"She did grill me endlessly, trying to pinpoint what I like. And I loved everything she did so much that I haven't wanted to screw it up." I smile at her and then we both laugh when terrible sounds come out of Caleb.

She holds him up, scrunching her nose.

"I think it's time to try out your new changing table, little guy," she says.

It takes both of us to work on the mess the little dude has created, and when we're done, we go downstairs and raid the fridge. There's been a different vibe between us today, really since we went on that picnic together. I think I showed my hand too much when I told her she's a rare kind of beautiful, but I stand by what I said. I get the impression that Sadie struggles with low self-esteem, or maybe it's not that, maybe she's just not been comfortable around me until now.

Since we're talking more freely with one another now, I want to know everything about her. And that scares me. Because I don't remember ever feeling this invested.

I keep telling myself it's the situation we're in.

It's living in the same house.

Raising Caleb together.

She's in a vulnerable state after losing her sister.

I'm in a vulnerable state finding out I had a son I didn't know about…

All of it pointing to *proceed with caution*!

But it just feels so good to talk to her. Each new piece of information I cull out of her feels priceless.

Caleb coos happily in the swing next to the table.

"I went out to see the pool house the other day," she says, before taking a bite out of her sandwich. "I hope that's okay. It's beautiful out there too."

"Of course, it's okay. I want you to feel like this is your

home too. You know, you don't have to ever go back to your apartment."

She looks down at her plate. "Thank you. It's helped to be here, but it would take time for this to feel like home. I'm grateful that I get to be with Caleb." Her eyes meet mine and then she glances away quickly. "I'm still having a hard time believing I'm here," she admits. "And having a lot of guilt over it."

"Guilt, why?"

She sets her sandwich down and dusts off the crumbs. She seems far away suddenly, her eyes distant as she stares outside.

"It should've been me," she says softly. "I should've been the one to go, not Sasha. She deserved a better life, and Caleb deserves to know his mom. I've never talked about this, but…I was supposed to watch Caleb that morning. Not for any particular reason except to give Sasha a break. But I got home really late from work the night before and overslept. I don't know why she didn't wake me up…or why she left in the first place. She rarely went anywhere. She wasn't comfortable driving in gross weather, so it's even more confusing why she went out that day when it was icy."

She blinks and a tear drops down her face.

"I haven't been able to go through all of her things yet. I helped my parents go through some of it at the apartment, but I'd like to keep anything of hers that's special and give it to Caleb when he's older. There's no way he will remember her, but I want him to know everything about her too, for him to still have her presence in his life. You know?" She looks down and more tears fall. "This house is a dream. Caleb has everything he could possibly want. But I can't help but feel like I'll never belong here. I'm taking the space that should've been my sister's."

I reach out and take her hand. It's small in mine, but the instant our palms touch, an awareness crackles through me. Sadie looks up at me. Does she feel it too?

"It will never make sense that Sasha is gone," I say. "But that doesn't mean you don't belong here. That's a space that only you can fill…in Caleb's life, in mine, in this house. We will talk about Sasha to Caleb, I promise you that. He'll know about her and he'll know how much she loved him."

I bend so she meets my eyes and she nods slightly.

"I'm not one of those people who says *everything happens for a reason*, because that's too conflicting for me to wonder why so many suffer. Why do horrific, inexcusable things happen to children and good people? Everything happening for a reason would make it seem like there's a higher power out there pulling strings to make certain people's lives the *worst*." I clear my throat, a lump building in my throat from seeing all the tears falling down her cheeks. "But I do think good things can come out of tragedies despite how awful they are. Sasha shouldn't have died, and equally as true…you should not feel guilty that you didn't."

She looks at me for a moment and then her face crumbles. She buries her face in her hands and I move until I'm kneeling in front of her chair. I push her hair back and then pull her toward me. Her head leans against my chest, and my arms wrap around her as she lets it out.

After some time, she gets quiet and I keep holding her. Every now and then, she'll take a deep, shuddering breath, but she doesn't pull away.

When we finally break apart, my legs are stiff from being in the same position for so long. But I wouldn't change a thing.

"Thank you for saying that, Weston," she says softly. "People kept saying that at the funeral—everything happens for a reason—and it made me so angry. I don't think I've ever heard anyone say what you just did and it"—her voice shakes and she takes another deep breath—"it really helped. Thank you."

I push her hair back from her eyes and we stare at each other for a few long seconds. Finally, I get up and move away from her because the urge to kiss her is too strong.

CHAPTER EIGHTEEN

ALWAYS ON MY MIND

SADIE

I take a shower before bed, my mind replaying my recent interactions with Weston. There have been a couple of times now when I thought he might kiss me. It could totally be my imagination…in fact, I'm sure it is. It's probably just me wanting that.

When exactly did I start to see him differently?

When did it become impossible to stay angry with him?

I have to dig deep to even have negative feelings toward him right now when he's being so good to Caleb and me.

It's still wrong for me to be having any *feelings*, or whatever this is…because *he slept with my sister.*

But they weren't an ongoing thing. They didn't have a relationship.

Downplay it all you want, but you know how hurt Sasha would be to know you're even thinking these thoughts about him.

That's the thing though—none of this would be happening if Sasha were still alive.

She obsessed over Weston Shaw, but she also equally obsessed over Timothée Chalamet, Robert Pattinson, and Ryan Reynolds, to name a few. Weston was just a little more accessible than some of her other obsessions.

I was shocked that when she got pregnant with his baby, she didn't camp out on his doorstep and demand that he take care of her and the baby. It was out of character for her not to do that. It seemed like she got what she wanted—time with Weston, his baby—and then she was afraid to make one wrong move that might take Caleb away from her.

Knowing Weston the way I do now, I know he wouldn't have taken Caleb from her, but my sister didn't know that.

Regardless of what Weston and Sasha were to each other or what they might've been eventually…they have a child together.

I have no place in Weston's life beyond being a caretaker of Caleb.

I wash my hair and body distractedly and then step it up in case Caleb wakes up once more before I get in bed. I slide under the covers, sighing when I feel how soft the sheets are. My satin tank and shorts feel like heaven against my skin after my hot shower, and the soft sheets are the cherry on top.

My eyes close and my mind once again goes to how it felt to have Weston's arms around me.

Caleb starts crying and I jump up, hoping I can get to him before Weston does. I feel bad for how much Weston has been up with him during the night this past month. Caleb is quiet before I reach his door and I carefully crack it wider, my breath catching in my chest when I see Weston barechested and—*are those boxer briefs?!*— rocking Caleb in the rocking chair.

He's singing softly—"Little Blue" by Jacob Collier—and it's so poignant and beautiful, I stare at them like I'm being lulled into a trance myself.

His eyes lift, and he pauses his singing for a second, his eyes slowly taking me in from head to toe. My nipples pebble under his gaze and his eyes get stuck there before trailing down the rest of my body. I rushed in without a robe, so I'm hardly wearing anything…but then again, neither is he.

I can't force myself to look away. When he lays Caleb in his crib….when he stalks toward me, his eyes predatory as he advances closer…I can't tear my eyes away. I know the way his broad shoulders and muscular arms felt holding me, but seeing them is on another level. His chest is spectacular, and the eight-pack leading to the V makes my mouth water. My eyes venture lower and the bulge sightings on the websites did not do this justice. All of this is seen through a nightlight, but it's bright enough for me to see him get bigger right before my eyes.

He stops within an inch of me. I swallow hard and look up. His breath skates across my skin when he leans in and my peaks brush against his chest.

"Looking good, Chapman."

He moves past me, and when I get to my room, I'm shaky as I get under the covers. It didn't mean anything, right? He can compliment me without it meaning he wants me. Although that doesn't explain him getting hard when he saw me. But that's probably just because he hasn't had sex in a while. He hasn't had time to since Caleb and I moved in.

I force myself to not think about the way he looked stalking toward me, the way his breath felt against my ear as he whispered that I looked good. I shiver and eventually fall to sleep, dreaming about all kinds of X-rated activities with Weston Shaw.

I wake up the next morning, feeling surprisingly ready to face the day. I jump out of bed with more energy than I've had in a while, and after I check on Caleb who's still sound asleep, I get ready to go to Weston's favorite coffee shop. I haven't worn eyeliner or anything more than a little mascara and lip gloss since the last time I worked a shift, and it feels good.

If it works out, I might go to the apartment after the coffee shop and get more clothes. I don't have much more than what I brought, but I'll get some of Sasha's clothes and bring anything that's left of hers to go through here. Somehow that feels easier to handle than trying to do it in the apartment where I can only see all the places she's missing.

Caleb is cooing in his crib when I walk out of my room, and the way he smiles up at me when I reach him fills my heart up.

"You are so adorable," I tell him.

His smile widens and he starts babbling, which is new. I crack up, wishing Weston could hear this.

"Are you trying to talk?" I lean down and tickle his neck softly, and he laughs. "I'm so lucky to be in your life," I whisper as I pick him up. "I love you so much."

I change his diaper and wash him with a warm washcloth. I'll give him a bath tonight before bed, but he loves the warm washcloth, so I always do that in the mornings. I've noticed that Weston does that now too, and the thought makes me smile. He's a good dad. We've both gotten better at all of this in a short amount of time. It's amazing what a trial by fire can do, but I still don't feel like a pro and doubt I ever will.

After I've checked the weather, I pick out the long-sleeve grey and white romper that looks like a baseball jersey. It has a C on it. Sasha got it at her baby shower, and it's one of Weston's favorite outfits on Caleb. But when I try to put it on, it's too little.

Just another thing that makes me tear up. I try really hard to pull it together, but I shed a few tears while I pick Caleb up and look in his closet for something in a bigger size.

"Mornin'," Weston says.

I turn and his smile drops.

"Did something happen?" he asks.

I wrinkle my nose and shake my head. "Everything makes me cry these days, I guess. Caleb's outgrown our favorite outfit." I point to the romper, and Weston frowns.

"Aw, not that one. Are you growing too fast, little guy?" He reaches out to pat Caleb's arm, and Caleb bucks, waving his arms wildly when he sees Weston.

I laugh and hand him to Weston, who immediately dives into Caleb's neck with raspberries. Caleb cackles and we both crack up. I settle on an outfit and Weston places him on the changing table, making faces at Caleb while I get him dressed.

"I can't believe this fits him already. I bought it before he was born and then when I saw him, it seemed like it'd be forever before he could wear it," I say.

"It's really cute. I think it's my new favorite. You have good taste, Chapman." He laughs when Caleb starts babbling. "What are you saying? What?" He looks at me, still laughing, and he looks so beautiful it halts my breath for a few seconds. "Are you hearing this?"

I laugh. "I was hoping you'd hear him. He was doing it before you came in too."

"Our boy is trying to talk, yes, he is," Weston sings, smiling down at Caleb, and my heart flutters inside before it catapults to the floor.

Our boy.

A whole slew of emotions takes over—joy, pain, elation, and guilt.

Always the guilt.

I know Weston doesn't mean anything bad by saying that. My nephew *is* my boy, but it's becoming increasingly harder to not feel like I'm his mama too, and I just don't know what to do with that.

I mask my feelings and keep a smile tacked on my face, knowing if I let it drop even slightly, I'll crumble for the rest of the day.

For the first time, I wonder how Sasha would've dealt with losing me if our roles were reversed.

She probably would've hidden her pain by partying every night. That was her go-to for anything. If she was down, party. If she was happy, party. If she wanted to get laid, party. If she needed free drinks and food, party.

We were always the opposite of one another. Where she was confident and the life of any room, I was shy and awkward, preferring one-on-one time with her. She had a lot of friends, but I really only needed her. She was jealous when I started working and made new friends, but she'd disappear for days with her friends and not understand why I wanted to know where she was. I was older, but she lost her virginity first. She never met a stranger and could talk people into anything. I, on the other hand, take a while to warm up to someone and if I tried to talk someone out of something, they were sure to do it. She was charismatic and charming and beautiful, and I was the smart, practical one.

For once, maybe I should take a page out of Sasha's book and see if maybe she had the right idea. I don't need to go as far as partying, but trying to have a little fun wouldn't hurt.

"Where'd you go?" Weston asks, bending slightly to meet my eyes. "You look nice, by the way." He smiles and my mouth goes dry.

"Thank you. I, uh…I was just thinking it'll be nice to get out of the house for a little while."

"Ahh. I'm so glad you're coming with me. You'll meet Clara. I already know you'll love each other."

Right. Clara. I'd almost forgotten about her.

We feed Caleb and change him again before we leave for Luminary, and even though we were up in plenty of time, we're still twenty minutes late.

CHAPTER NINETEEN

THE VAULT

WESTON

Luminary Coffeehouse is buzzing when we arrive. I wave when I see Clara and she hurries around the counter toward us. When she reaches us, she beams. She only has eyes for Caleb.

"I've been dying to meet this guy," she says. "I can't believe you haven't been in to see me before now!" She stares at him and shakes her head, clasping her hand to her heart. "He is so perfect. I can't get over him." She swats my arm. "I don't want to miss out! He needs to know his Auntie Clara, yes, he does," she coos.

"Sorry, Clara. We've been staying close to home, trying to get used to…all that comes with taking care of a baby…"

I look at Sadie and she has an odd expression on her face. I nudge her with my elbow.

"You okay?"

She nods absentmindedly, smiling at Clara. "You're Clara? Hi," she says, her smile growing. "I'm Sadie, Caleb's aunt."

God, when she smiles, the whole world looks brighter. It's blinding and makes my chest feel weird. I try to rub away the ache in my chest, frowning.

"Hello, Sadie. I've heard all about you from Lane. We're BFFs—do people still say that?" She laughs and Sadie giggles, looking fucking delighted, and I stare at her as if I'm seeing her for the first time.

I'm not.

Clearly.

I saw every inch of her in those short shorts and that skimpy tank top last night and have had two sessions in the shower to deal with the aftermath of that, but fuck me, what is going on here?

She's stunning and completely oblivious to the fact. She's smart and insightful and quietly shines in everything she does, whether it's taking care of Caleb or talking about interior design or packing her things from the apartment she shared with her sister. Even her grieving is stoically graceful.

She has a much larger personality than she realizes.

If I weren't trying to do away with my player ways, I'd go out and get laid to dull these thoughts, but it wouldn't work. It feels like a betrayal to even consider it, but that's bullshit.

It's not like we're contemplating a relationship. We can't go there, and I'm sure she wouldn't want to anyway.

But I can't stop thinking about her.

Sadie Chapman is under my skin.

I've been in denial about it for a while now, but it's not going anywhere. It's only getting more intense.

"I came out to see what you might want to order, Sadie." She leans in and talks low enough so only we can hear. "Business has been booming since the guys have been coming in. I've hired two new employees."

She points and we look at the pink-haired barista by the espresso machine and the tall, lanky guy at the cash register. She grips my arm and I realize she expects me to follow her. She proves it when she tilts her head toward the room we met in last time. We start walking fast, trying to keep up and still hear her. She hasn't stopped talking.

"I didn't want you to have to wait in line because people will start asking for autographs and then you'll never get out of here." She puts in the code and slips inside, opening the door wide enough for us to squeeze through and shutting it quickly. She leans her head against the door and exhales.

"Jeepers," she says. "I'm not sure I'll ever get used to this hustling. I've lived in Silver Hills my whole life and it's always been quiet. I like it that way." She laughs and motions to the guys who are looking up at us, amused.

"Jeepers," Penn says, grinning. "I like that. Do you mind if I use it, Clara?"

Her shoulders shake as she laughs. "If you want to sound ancient like me, have at it," she says.

Sadie smiles and waves at Levi, Rhodes' little boy.

"Hi, I'm Sadie," she says.

He grins and waves before putting a Cheerio in his mouth.

"He is so cute, Rhodes," Sadie says.

Rhodes grins and tousles Levi's curly hair. "And t-r-o-u-b-l-e."

We laugh. I reach my hand out and Levi high-fives me.

"Just like your daddy, aren't you, buddy," I tease.

"Daddy!" Levi yells, his fist holding up a bunch of Cheerios that he then crams in his mouth.

Henley gets up and holds out his hands for the baby. I hand him over and Henley starts talking to him in that high baby voice that never fails to make me laugh.

"I don't know if I haven't been a parent long enough or what, but is there going to be a certain point where I start sounding like a baby when I talk to the little guy?" I say.

Henley cuts his eyes over at me and his mouth twitches.

Sadie snorts. "You do it too every now and then." Her voice changes to falsetto, as she says, "Yes, you do!"

The booming sound of laughter reverberates throughout the small room. Rhodes laughs so hard he's wiping his eyes.

He points at Sadie and looks at me. "She has got your number, Shaw."

I roll my eyes, grinning. "Whatever. I still don't sound like the rest of you fools."

They laugh at that too.

"Yeah, right," Bowie says.

"You just wait. You'll be doing all kinds of things you never thought you'd do," Henley says.

"Baby talk, Peppa Pig, competing with yourself for how fast you can change a diaper…" Rhodes ticks off his fingers.

"I think my fastest time was thirty seconds," Bowie says.

Rhodes backs up his head like he's affronted. "But was she clean after that? We're not talking how fast you were and still leaving behind streaks."

Bowie looks offended. "Hell no. What do you take me for? A novice?"

Rhodes lifts his eyebrows and shakes his head. "Too bad Levi's potty-trained. I need to work on beating your time."

Henley bounces Caleb and makes a face. "We've got a baby here that you can practice on."

"Oh, I'll go change him," Sadie says. "I wasn't intending on staying back here anyway. I just wanted to say hi."

Everyone starts talking at once, trying to convince her to stay.

She laughs and shakes her head. "No, I'd be breaking the rules even more than Penn is." She smirks as everyone laughs.

"You want your usual, Weston?" Clara asks.

"Yes, please."

"And what about you, Sadie? What do you like?" she asks.

"I'll come out there and see your specials. I like to mix it up."

"A girl after my own heart," Clara says. "Come on, I'll show you my favorites."

Sadie takes the backpack we're using as Caleb's diaper bag and reaches out for Caleb. He goes to her, feet kicking and his gummy smile so big it makes all the guys go on about how cute he is.

She lifts her hand and waves, her eyes on me. "Have fun, guys."

"You really don't have to go," I tell her under my breath.

Her eyes are smiling when she says, "It's all good, Shaw."

My heartbeat stutters and I watch her until she's out the door.

"Holy shit, man," Rhodes says, his eyes wide. "I'm feeling some vibes…"

"No shit," Penn says. "Are you guys—"

"No," I interrupt. I hold my hand up and then hustle to the chair, dropping into it. "Don't even say it out loud."

"Don't say what out loud?" Penn frowns.

"Whatever was about to come out of your mouth?"

"Are you guys hooking up?" Penn says, tilting his head.

I growl and motion for him to cut it off right there.

"Why can't I say that?" he asks.

"Because I don't even want to put it out into the universe. It cannot happen. I can't be thinking about it. Just no." I put my elbows on the table and tug on my hair with both hands.

"Well, it's obvious you are thinking about it," Rhodes says. "And why can't it happen?"

"Because we're trying to raise Caleb together and if it went south, it'd be the worst."

"It's not great when things go south, but we're all examples of what happens when you're a parent and the relationship with your significant other goes south," Henley says. "With the exception of Adriane," he gives Bowie an apologetic look, "we've all managed to co-parent with our exes. It's not easy, but it can be done peaceably. If it didn't work out with Sadie, you'd put Caleb first just like you already are."

"Well said, Hen." Rhodes says, pointing at him. He looks at me. "Any relationship is a risk. And yes, it becomes more complicated when you're raising kids together, but that doesn't mean you don't give it a try if the feelings are there."

"It's probably just an attraction that will fade…but I'm not used to this feeling. You know me—I've slept with my share of girls that just want to be with me because I play for the Mustangs. The attraction doesn't last. Is it because I haven't slept with her yet? And then how awful would that be if I slept with her and my feelings weren't the same?" I lower my head. "I don't think she'd ever go there with me anyway because I slept with her sister," I admit.

It's quiet for a second.

"West," Bowie says, his voice low.

I look up and meet his eyes.

"Get to know her. If these feelings grow and you think she feels the same, give them a chance. You'll regret it if you don't. Adriane broke my heart, but I don't regret the time I had with her that was good. I think we'd all say that about our exes…even Rhodes."

Rhodes snorts. "Yeah. You're right, man. As much as Carrie drives me crazy, she gave me the best gift of my life. I can't regret that."

"And it's not like you were in a relationship with her sister," Penn says.

"We just made a baby," I groan.

"That you never even saw when she was alive. The sister is a non-factor," Penn argues.

"It might be a factor for her, and I'd understand if it was," I say.

"Cross that bridge when you come to it," Bowie says. "For now, don't agonize over this attraction. Get to know her and see if that's even what you're feeling…if it goes beyond attraction. You've never stuck around a girl long enough to know."

I swipe my hand over my face, groaning again, but he's right. I've imagined I'd think about a relationship sometime in my mid-thirties after I've enjoyed my career a while and I'm ready to settle down. The interactions I've had have been with women that I didn't expect to feel more for—the girls just down for a good time in high school and the jersey chasers from then on. It's kind of gross when I think about it now, but I always thought it wasn't hurting anyone since they went into it knowing it was just a one-time thing.

Getting a stranger pregnant knocks that theory out of the water.

"What Bowie said," Henley says, smiling at us. "That's sound advice." He laughs and shakes his head. "I've gotta say though, it's sure fun to see you in this state."

The rest of them laugh and chime in their agreement.

Bastards.

"I'll agree to get to know her better, but I'm going to bury this," I wave my hand over my body, "whatever this is, way down deep and not let it out again. Thanks for letting me talk it through. It helped." I let out a shaky breath.

They all look at me like I've lost my mind.

"Shit. You didn't hear a word we said." Rhodes scowls.

"I heard you. I just...I have my hands full learning how to be a dad. I don't think I can learn how to be in a relationship too."

CHAPTER TWENTY

A DAY OUT

SADIE

I adore Clara.

The exuberance I felt when I found out she was Weston's mom's age and not some hot young thing…well, it was hard to contain.

I don't even want to think about what that means.

After I've changed Caleb, Clara hands me a mug. "Here you go, honey. It's a Solar Latte. I saw you perk up when I mentioned it has lavender in it."

"Oh, I'm excited to try it. Thank you so much." I take the mug and blow before taking a sip. I close my eyes and hum. "That is *amazing*."

When I open my eyes, she's beaming at me and then lights up when someone catches her eye behind me.

"I didn't know you were coming in today," she says.

I turn and see Weston's mom, Lane. Her mouth falls open into a happy smile when she sees Caleb and me. She hugs Clara and then squeezes my shoulder, leaning down to say hello to Caleb.

"Isn't he the cutest thing you've ever seen?" she says.

"He really is," Clara says. "You told me, but I didn't believe he could be *this* cute."

Lane laughs in delight and pulls her scarf off. "I wanted to surprise Clara and I'm the one who got surprised instead."

I move the backpack and tap the chair. "Join us."

Her head tilts as she grins at me. "I'd love to."

I offer Caleb up for her to hold and she nods excitedly. As she's moving to her seat with him, I hear bickering and turn to see two ancient men at a nearby table.

"It's better than it ever was, Marv," one says.

"No, it's not. Football ain't what it used to be," the man I assume is Marv says. "It used to be simple. You know I'm right, Walter. We'd go watch a game, eat a hot dog and grab a beer…come home at a decent hour. Now, it's thousands of people with their chests painted and wearing the dumb things over their heads. The players do those herky-jerky dances when they make a touchdown like that's not the whole point of the game."

"You're right, you're right," Walter says. "They do look like idiots. And I can't stand how long it takes to get out of there. I'd rather just watch at home."

Marv harrumphs his agreement.

I snort and turn quickly when Marv glances over and narrows his eyes on me.

Lane winks at me and says, "Hey, Marv and Walter, good to see you this morning."

They both grumble a hello and look like they swallowed something bad.

"Why's it so crowded in here, Clara?" Walter frowns.

Clara lifts a shoulder and grins. "The good people of Silver Hills like my coffee, I guess."

"Then why don't I recognize half of them?" Marv says.

"Aw, come on, it's kind of nice to see some new people around town, isn't it?" Clara says. She laughs and puts her hand on Lane's shoulder. "I'll bring you a coffee in a sec."

"Thanks, love," Lane says. She leans closer to me and whispers, "Those old codgers complain about the sky being blue."

I giggle and sip my coffee.

"So, how's it going? Are you getting settled in at Weston's? Adjusting?" she asks.

I feel my face heat when she says Weston's name and I hope Lane doesn't notice.

"It's getting easier," I admit. "Although both of us are still catching up on a lot. His new furniture came and we realized we didn't actually order a crib. He's got this beautiful room now with a Pack 'N Play for his bed." I roll my eyes. "We've got more shopping to do," I add.

Lane's head falls back as she laughs and Caleb laughs too, which makes her so happy.

"Oh, you are the cutest thing," she coos at him. "Well, I'm off today if you and Weston wanted to go shopping." Her attention turns to me and she smiles. "I'd love more time with this guy."

Lane and David have stopped by the house often since

meeting Caleb, and they're both great with him. They raised three kids, so it's not really a surprise.

"I understand if you're not ready to leave him just yet," Lane says.

I swallow and look at Caleb, happily waving his little teether.

"I'd like him to have time with you," I finally say. "Weston is with his friends in the room back there." I point over my shoulder. "We can ask if today works for him too."

"Wonderful." Lane beams, first at me and then Caleb. "We'll have so much fun."

After Weston and I go over what Caleb likes and doesn't like and when he'll be ready to eat and nap, Lane laughs and waves us off.

"He'll be okay, I promise," she says.

Weston puts Caleb's car seat in her car and Lane gets in the driver's seat and looks amused when she glances at us.

"I'll call if there are any problems, but I don't anticipate there being any," she says. "Have fun, you guys. Take your time. Caleb and I will have a blast and your dad will be disappointed if you pick him up before he gets a chance to see him."

Weston nods and looks like he wants to say more but just nods again. "Thanks, Mom. Let us know how he's doing, okay?"

"I will."

We're both quiet for a few minutes as we drive through Silver Hills. It's rare that we're alone with each other.

Weston clears his throat. "I messaged Autumn earlier and she recommended a place in Denver for his crib. But she also said she'd heard about a great place here in town for cute clothes and unique toys. Want to stop there first?"

"Sure. That sounds good." I glance at him and his smile is sweet, which makes my stomach take a nose-dive.

I've got to shake off whatever this is, *now*.

"It feels weird without the kiddo, doesn't it?" Weston says.

I laugh. "Yeah, really weird."

He pulls in front of a boutique and parks. It looks like a place I could never afford to shop in and for the zillionth time, I can't believe that I'm experiencing this life.

"My mom will take good care of him," he says. "And she'll call if he seems unhappy."

I nod. "I'm not worried. I guess all parents…I mean, all *people* feel this way when they leave their baby for the first time." I shake my head. "I know I'm not his parent. I didn't mean that…and I've left him before…obviously. It just feels different now."

"You don't have to call it that if you're not comfortable with it, but I think of you as his parent. You're taking care of him, day in and day out. We're co-parenting him."

I look down at my hands, willing myself not to cry. Taking a deep breath, I let it out slowly and turn to him. "Thank you," I whisper. And then louder, I say, "Let's do this."

He grins. "Fuck yeah, let's do this."

He lifts up his hand and I clasp it, both of us squeezing for a few seconds and grinning like crazy for no apparent reason.

The boutique is one of the cutest places I've ever seen. Cute clothes and cute *everything*. At first I'm reluctant to pick anything out, but Weston keeps holding up adorable outfits and I get dreamy eyes and he laughs and drapes them over his arm. He has quite a pile going already.

"He doesn't need so many clothes." I laugh.

"I'll get a bigger size in this one. Or hell, both sizes," Weston says. "It's fucking adorable."

The salesperson giggles next to us and she waves when we look at her. "Hi, I'm Marcy. Would you like me to set those aside for you?" She stares up at Weston and gasps when she recognizes him. "Weston Shaw," she breathes. "You are…I am…you are incredible."

Weston smiles at her like he's used to being told this all the time, but when he glances at me, his cheeks are pink. "Thank you. Couldn't do it without my team," he says. He lifts the arm laden with clothes. "We're not done shopping, but we'll take these. Tell me where and I'll set them down."

In a trance, Marcy points to the counter.

He nods and walks them over. I start looking at the items on a bookshelf and laugh, picking it up.

"What did you find?" he asks.

"You've gotta have this," I say, holding up the tinkle tent.

"What is it?" He frowns, studying it. His eyes widen when he gets it and he cracks up. "I had no idea babies needed so much shit. Yeah, we're taking that." He grabs three more and laughs again when he looks at them.

He pauses in front of an orange and white device. "What the hell is a baby shusher?" he whispers.

I giggle. "I have no idea. Try it."

He turns it on and we both look at each other wide-eyed.

"No," I whisper.

"Hell no. Is it me or is that creepy?" he whispers back.

"Totally. I'd rather him listen to waves or something nice than a constant shush. That makes me think of the librarian at school, shushing everyone all the time."

"Agreed. Oh look, what does this one sound like?" He plays another sound machine and it has waves and rain. He looks at me like *can you believe this?* "Did you not just say you wanted waves? It's a sign."

I laugh and he picks up the boxed one behind the display. I stop saying what I love because he picks up everything I like and puts it on the counter. By the time we leave the store, he has dropped bank and we haven't even gotten to the crib yet.

We chat all the way to Denver, the vibe way more comfortable between us now, and according to the directions, we're almost to the store Autumn recommended when Weston pulls into a large bookstore parking lot.

"A bookstore?" I ask.

"I feel so wrong going here instead of Twinkle Tales, but…we're here and they'll be closed by the time we get back to Silver Hills. Caleb needs a few more books, doesn't he? I like the ones he has, but I'm ready for some variety."

I press my lips together to keep from laughing, and we go into the store. He has a stack of a dozen books when I hold up *Where the Wild Things Are.* He gasps and I can't stop smiling.

"I was looking for that one. It's my favorite," he says.

I almost tell him I overheard him talking to Caleb about it, but I just grin and say, "I thought you might be into this one."

He takes the book and holds it reverently, flipping through the pages.

"I can't wait to read this to him," he says.

I'm able to take him in more freely while he looks at the book. His long eyelashes, his full lips, the way his hair curls around his ears now that it's a little longer. His childlike excitement over everything we've bought for Caleb, but the way his broad shoulders fill the aisle of the bookstore is all man.

I've thought vile things about this man, and they've all been wrong. He's a good man. A good dad. And when he meets the right person for him, he'll be a good partner.

That thought sobers me up, and I turn away from him, looking at books but not really seeing them at all.

CHAPTER TWENTY-ONE

BOOKS AND MOVIES AND SOUND MACHINES

WESTON

By the time we're driving home with Caleb in the backseat, we're flying high. We found so many great things today. When I told my mom what all we'd bought, she laughed and said she guessed I could afford it.

"But geez, save some for his college fund," she teased.

His crib will arrive tomorrow morning, so after I've read a few of his new books to him, saving *Where the Wild Things Are* for last, I start to place him in his portable crib.

"Only one more night in this thing and then you'll be sleeping like a king in your new bed," I tell him.

Sadie walks by and then comes back and stands in the doorway.

"Want to give him one more kiss goodnight?" I ask.

She nods and walks toward us, smiling as she bends to kiss him.

"Love you, sweet boy," she whispers.

I put him in his bed and Sadie turns on his new sound machine. We grin at each other when we hear the waves and move quietly out of his room.

"I wonder if he'll sleep any longer with the waves going," I whisper.

"I hope so," she says.

We look at each other, still standing in the hallway. I like having her and Caleb upstairs now. I didn't realize how empty this house felt before they got here.

"Want a glass of wine or anything?" I ask. "We could watch a movie."

She looks surprised. "Oh. Sure. Yeah, that sounds great actually."

I grin. "We've had a long, hard day of shopping. We deserve this."

She laughs. "If that's a long, hard day, I'll take more of those, please."

We go downstairs and I point toward the basement staircase. "Want to help me pick out a bottle?"

She shakes her head. "I wouldn't know what to pick. I trust you...and I like everything," she adds.

"I don't have a bunch of fancy shit, despite my fancy wine cellar," I say.

I jog down the stairs and grab a bottle of red. Hopefully she'll like this one.

When I get to the kitchen, Sadie is putting a bunch of crackers and dried fruit out on the long, pretty board Felicity gave me for Christmas. She slices cheese and winds it around the crackers and then adds prosciutto and salami.

"That looks great," I say. "My sister gave me that thing and I've never used it. Now I don't know why I haven't."

"I've never used one either. But this is what they do on some of the home shows I like. They have a massive charcuterie board sitting on the table or kitchen island when the family comes to see their remodeled home for the first time. They're usually piled higher than this, but this is a good start for the two of us." She laughs. "It always looks delicious… and it's pretty."

"It is." I nod.

She glances up and catches me staring at her. I hold up the bottle of wine.

"This okay?"

She nods without looking at the bottle and I chuckle, moving to grab two stemless wine glasses. I pour wine into each of them and when she steps back from the tray, I hand her a glass.

"These are pretty too. Did Autumn pick these out?"

"No, Olivia gave me these. I've never used them either. First time for everything." I smirk and lift the charcuterie board and my glass and take it to the movie room downstairs.

Sadie turns up the baby monitor and looks at the screen. I set the board down and move to look at the screen with her.

"He is *out*," she whispers.

"I can't believe how much he's already grown," I say.

We move toward the two chairs in the middle and sit down.

"Do we need plates? I can go grab some." I motion toward the bar down here.

"I'm good without one," she says.

I turn the TV on and Sadie laughs when she sees *The Proposal* playing.

"I love this movie. Have you seen it?" she asks.

"It's been forever."

"You're probably not into rom-coms. We can watch something else."

"I don't mind a rom-com," I say. "I have sisters, you know. They had to put up with sports and I had to put up with rom-coms."

She laughs. "Well, I don't want to put you out or anything…" Her voice is playful and I reach out and poke her in the side. She yelps and my eyes widen.

"Oh, you're ticklish?" I do it again and her mouth drops in shock.

"Hey, watch it," she says, and she pokes *me* in the side.

I jerk away and grab her hand when she laughs and tries it again. We freeze, staring at each other, both of us breathing hard. I weave my fingers through hers and pull our hands to my chest. I wonder if she can feel how hard my heart is pounding.

She licks her lips and my eyes track the movement, and before I can stop myself, I'm leaning in and claiming her mouth with mine. Her lips are soft and sweet. She tastes like mint and apricots and her mouth feels so fucking good. I deepen the kiss and she whimpers. I keep her hand in mine and with the other, I slide into her silky hair. Her free hand does the same, tugging my hair as we kiss and kiss and kiss.

When I finally let go of her hand, it's to touch her jaw, her neck, and then I grasp her hips to lift her until she's straddling me. She gasps when she feels how hard I am for her and it's fucking bliss. When I start rubbing her over me, I lose my fucking mind. My hand wanders up her shirt, and I palm her tit before sliding her bra to the side to thumb over her nipple. The sound she makes goes straight to my dick and I do it again and again, tugging it between my fingers and then rubbing away the sting. She gasps into my mouth and our movements become more frantic. I tug her leggings down and she lifts up to help me, and I do the same for her until there are fewer layers between us and we're just in our underwear. It's unbelievable how good it feels. When she rocks against me like this, we both shudder. Every time I rub against her clit, I hear her sharp intake of breath and it makes me more determined than ever to make her sound like that again.

She clutches my shoulders, pulls my hair, and I feel the heat of her against me. I pulse up into her, my fingers moving beneath her panties to touch her, and it only takes a few small circles over her swollen bud before she falls apart. When her head falls back with a moan, I kiss down her neck and she swivels her hips to get more friction and that's when my orgasm barrels through me. It's blinding, and it's like time pauses and the euphoria of how incredible this feels goes on and on.

But then, I open my eyes and she opens hers, and the next thing I know, she's climbing off of me. She stands in front of me, her nipples raised proudly right at my eye level. My mouth waters. I'm desperate to get my mouth on her, but when I look up and meet her eyes again, I freeze.

"We shouldn't do this," she whispers. "This can't happen."

I run my hand through my hair and exhale. "Right. Okay. I'm sorry. I shouldn't have—"

"No, I was right here with you," she says. "It just—"

She puts her hand up to her mouth and glances down, her cheeks pink as her eyes dart away. I adjust myself, cursing under my breath.

"I'll keep my hands to myself," I tell her. "Come on. We'll eat and watch the movie." I hold up my hands and wave them. "Hands off. I promise."

She looks hesitant still, but then the scene comes on where they arrive in Alaska and Sandra Bullock meets the mom and the grandma. She puts her hands to her cheeks and takes a deep breath before she sits back down.

"Okay. I can't resist this movie…and I am hungry."

"Great," I say, turning up the sound. "I'll be right back."

She still hasn't looked me in the eyes again, but I'm calling it a win that she didn't bolt.

I run to change and when I come back, I place the board between us, so it's propped on the arms of our recliners.

She glances at me before I sit down and she still looks so concerned.

"It won't happen again, okay?" I say, smiling to soften my words.

She nods slightly, and we both eat and drink and watch the movie.

Well, *she's* watching the movie.

I'm still stuck on what happened between us and wondering how in the hell I'll be able to survive around her and not touch her again.

It's no wonder I've been able to walk away from everyone before now, and with absolutely no hesitation—I've never felt anything close to what I felt with Sadie tonight.

CHAPTER TWENTY-TWO

MIND-BLOWING

SADIE

Oh God. What did we just do?

I can't even focus on one of my favorite movies because…that *kiss*…the way he made me feel. We didn't even have sex, but it was the most intense experience I've ever had.

I'm not sure how I keep sitting here next to him because my whole body is feverish and I want nothing more than to rewind and jump back on his lap and get more of that. But I laugh quietly at the appropriate parts and absentmindedly grab things from the charcuterie board in a desperate attempt to pretend that this is normal.

I can do this. I can pretend like that was just a flash of hormones going haywire and not because I want Weston Shaw more than my next breath.

I'm sure it really was just hormones for him. He's said it himself—it's been a while for him. That's all this is.

We both know it can never happen again.

I try not to wallow in my sadness that this was a one-time thing.

Don't be so pathetic, I tell myself. It was a mind-blowing make-out session, but that's all it was.

And we will act like it never happened.

We clear off the tray and Weston refills our wine glasses. When the movie is over, my head feels muddled and I wish I hadn't eaten so much. I jump up and grab our glasses.

"I can take care of this," he says.

"I don't mind."

We carry everything upstairs and I wash the glasses and board while Weston dries.

"I think we should talk about it," Weston says softly.

"Mmm. I don't think so." I shake my head.

"What if I want to?"

"I think it's awkward now, but it'll be different in the morning. I say we just forget it ever happened and—"

"Sadie, I don't think I can forget it. And I don't want to."

I turn to look at him and he's staring down at me with what I can only describe as hunger.

"There's too much at stake for us to mess around with this," I whisper.

He runs his hand through his hair and looks away.

"What are you afraid of?" he asks, when his eyes meet mine again.

"I'm afraid of losing what we have…and I also feel like I am betraying my sister."

"Even if you put aside what we're building here together, what just happened between us is so much bigger, so much *more* than anything that happened with Sasha."

When I don't say anything, he nods.

"Okay, we won't do anything," he says. His head tilts when he looks at me again. "But it won't change the way I'm feeling. And that was…incredible."

My breath hitches and he stares at my mouth.

"Yes," I whisper.

I move past him and take the stairs two at a time.

After a restless night, I wake up early and get ready. No big plans today really—my mom is coming over in a while, that's it—but I've noticed it helps me feel better if I get dressed as if I'm going to work. I love sweats and leggings, but if I keep doing that every day, I won't have any idea when I'm unable to fit into my jeans anymore. I don't put as much makeup on as I would for work, but enough that I feel put together.

Not that I'm getting dressed for Weston's sake, but…

Okay, maybe a little bit.

All of this thought about clothes reminds me that I didn't make it to the apartment yesterday. Maybe I'll order a few things. I was right there too. It would've been good to knock that out while I was close.

Weston doesn't think he's paying me much, but it's more than I ever made at my waitressing job and I got decent tips there. Maybe I can order a few new things to wear, and I can worry about going through the stuff at the apartment another time.

My mom texts when I'm about to leave the room.

MOM

Does it still work for me to come later this morning?

Yes. Can't wait to see you.

MOM

Do you need anything?

I pause before texting her back.

I'd wanted to go by the apartment yesterday but didn't make it. Would you want to bring some of the boxes you took home with you? I could go through it here. I'm wanting to save anything meaningful for Caleb…

MOM

That's a great idea, sweetie. Sure, I'll bring them. I haven't had the heart to go through anything yet.

I don't mind doing it if you're not up to it.

MOM

It helps every time I see your face and Caleb's.

Love you, Mom.

MOM

I love you. I'll see you soon.

I step out of the room and nearly run into Weston. He's shirtless and sweaty and I want to lick his salty skin and—

I shake my head and force myself to focus on his eyes and not his body.

"Good morning," he says. He points toward Caleb's room. "I still haven't heard a peep out of him. Have you?"

"No. I've looked at the monitor every five minutes for the past hour and still nothing."

He laughs and pauses when his phone buzzes. He makes a face. "I've gotta take this."

I nod and he answers, moving down the hall. He leaves his door open though, so I can hear him curse. I turn and look back and see him pacing.

"I've needed time," he says. "I know. But it's a complicated situation."

He curses again and I'm relieved when I hear Caleb cooing so I can duck into his room and not keep eavesdropping.

I get Caleb cleaned up and take him downstairs in his jammies to get his bottle ready. He's happy this morning, all smiles and jabbering up a storm. Weston comes into the kitchen, still in his workout shorts but wearing a shirt now, and Caleb bounces and practically jumps toward Weston when he comes close.

"He sure does like you," I tease.

When he doesn't laugh like he normally would, I look at him. He kisses Caleb's forehead, but he looks distracted.

"What's wrong?" I ask.

He looks at me and my heart drops. He hasn't looked this serious since those first days in the hospital.

"Photographers were apparently snap-happy yesterday. There are pictures all over the place, some of us with Caleb and some of just you and me. My agent and publicist have been after me to make an announcement about Caleb long before now so we could control the narrative." He sighs and kisses Caleb's head again. "But I wanted time to get to know him myself before inviting the whole world into it." His eyes are pained when he looks at me. "It's important to me that I speak kindly about Sasha, and I was so angry at first, I was worried some of that might seep through. I've seen too many times how things turn on women, and I will do everything in my power to keep that from happening." He gives me a pointed look. "Okay?"

I nod. "Okay."

He lets out a relieved sigh. "Now that the news is out, I need to do damage control. Today."

"What can I do to help?"

His eyes are still full of concern, but his smile zeroes in on me. It warms me and I smile back, hoping he gets the same warmth in return.

"Thank you for even offering to help deal with my mess." He scoffs. "You've done more than that—I have a massive list of things to thank you for. I'm going to owe you forever, you know that, right?"

I laugh and his shoulders relax.

"You don't owe me anything," I tell him. "Get ready. I've got Caleb. My mom's coming over today, so we'll be busy."

"Okay. The press conference won't last long. Amy will be coming today to clean. And shit…I wanted to be here when the crib arrived. I'll call and see if they can come when I'm back this afternoon. Let me know if you need anything while I'm out."

"Will do."

"I'll go get my shower and then bolt."

"All right." I move to take Caleb from him, and Weston leans in closer than I expected, so our mouths are within an inch of each other.

My eyes lift to his and he's staring at my lips. I'm not

sure how long we stand there staring at each other, but my limbs feel weighed down when he takes a step away from me. He clears his throat and tousles Caleb's hair.

"I'll see you two in a little while," he says.

He walks away and it's only then that I can take a deep breath. My phone buzzes and it's Kim.

KIM

You didn't tell me you were dating WESTON SHAW! When did this happen?!

I'm not. Don't believe everything you read! <Laughing emoji>

KIM

Pictures are worth a thousand words and the pictures of you and Weston are worth WAY more than that. <Fire emoji>

I don't know what to say to that so I go quiet, and after I've fed Caleb his bottle and laid him down for a nap, I google Weston Shaw to see what photos come up. After seeing him with a steady barrage of models and celebrities in the past, it's unsettling to see myself next to him. I don't look bad, but I don't look anything like the women he dates…or hooks up with, I guess, since he doesn't really date.

When I stop critiquing myself and study Weston's face, I draw in a deep breath.

He looks really, *really* happy.

CHAPTER TWENTY-THREE

BEAUTIFUL THINGS

WESTON

The press conference is painful. I knew it would be.

I try to keep it short and simple.

“Due to tragic circumstances, I’ve kept the news of my son quiet. His mother died in a car accident in February, and out of respect for her family and this time of grieving, I’d ask that the attention be kept off of them. Becoming a dad is not without challenges, but my son has quickly become the light of my life. I never thought I could love anything more than my family and football, but this little boy has crept into my heart. Now I know what all my friends meant when they said having kids would change my life in the best way. It's a love like I've never known."

The questions start as soon as I pause.

"Who is the woman you've been seen with recently?"

"Were you in a relationship with your child's mother?"

I take a deep breath.

"No, I was not in a relationship with his mother. The woman I've been seen with recently is my child's aunt, his mom's sister. We're raising him together."

"Are you romantically involved with her?"

Joan lifts her hand and I've never been so grateful for my publicist. She flew in from California for this and to think I almost tried to talk her out of coming. She's about five feet and a hundred pounds soaking wet, and she can put the fear of God into even the most aggressive reporters.

"That's all we have time for today. Thank you," she says.

The questions keep coming as I walk out of the room and I don't relax until we're back in the car. Joan had her driver pick me up at the house so we could discuss what I could and couldn't say at the press conference.

"That went as well as it could possibly go," she says. "You know you just fueled everyone's curiosity by keeping it a secret."

"I'm just now starting to feel human again since finding out I had a son. The exhaustion is no joke, and I was in shock. Trust me, the last thing I was trying to do was fuel curiosity."

"I know." She sighs and pats my hand before lifting her huge black-framed glasses to peer at me. "Just listen to me next time, okay?"

"Okay."

"I'm not sure it was a good idea to say you weren't in a

relationship with Sasha," she says. "You went off the script there." She takes off her glasses and looks out the window. "Unless there's something you want to tell me about this other girl, her sister. What is her name?"

"Sadie."

She turns to face me. "And *are* you in a romantic relationship with her?"

I think about kissing her last night, watching her fall apart, and it just makes me crave more of her. "No."

She makes a face and points at me with her glasses. "That was too long of a pause for me to believe you."

My head falls back against the headrest and I groan. "We're not." It still sounds weak, so I add, "But she could be someone who makes me want to be."

I turn my head sideways when Joan nudges me in the arm. Her eyes are bright and she's smiling, which is rare. I roll my eyes and turn my head away from her again.

"This is a first, right?" she asks.

I don't respond.

"You definitely did the right thing with what you said then. Still a touchy situation but less so. People could even wonder if Sasha was a surrogate for you and Sadie if we stay quiet about the details."

I lift my head and glare at her. "No, we're not going to lie about it. I don't even know if anything more will develop with me and Sadie...but Sasha is Caleb's mother. It would hurt her family if I tried to make it seem like anything other than that."

"Okay, okay, got it," she says, raising her hands. "Just keep your mouth shut on the details, okay? And for God's sake, use protection."

"I did...I always do. Things can still happen, as we've

seen." I straighten my tie, ready to get this suit off and ready to be done with this conversation.

"Easy, big guy. I'm on your side," Joan says, patting my arm.

That's about as sweet as Joan gets, so most of my anger fizzles out and I smile at her.

"Thanks, Joan. I wouldn't want to try to navigate any of this without you."

"You're stuck with me, kid." Her loud, throaty laugh fills the car. "And I like the sound of this Sadie. I wasn't going to say anything until I heard how you felt, but the way you're looking at her in those pictures..." Her eyes widen and her hands mimics an explosion. "You deserve to be happy. Don't end up like me, old and alone, with nothing but work to warm your bed at night."

"You're timeless, Joan. And don't you know we're never too old to find love?"

"I don't know who fed you that crap, but it sounds good." She laughs.

We're quiet for a while and she perks up when we reach Silver Hills.

"You know…I really like this town. I'm only ever here to see you, but I could get used to this place."

"Do you have to hurry back to California? Stay and have dinner with us tonight."

"I wish I could." She pokes her lips out in a mock pout. "Maybe sometime soon, I'll plan a few days here. If things keep progressing with your girl, I may need to come do more damage control." She winks.

"She's not my girl, but yeah, come anytime. You need to meet my son too."

She waves her hand. "I'm sure he's beautiful with you as

his father, but me and babies go together like ice cream and bacon." She shudders.

"I've actually had that combo and it's not bad. You should give Caleb a try. Maybe he'll surprise you." I laugh at the expression on her face. "He's surprised me. I never knew I could get attached so quickly to a little human."

She sniffs and waves her glasses around right as we're pulling up to my gate. "Whew. Got here in just the nick of time. Thought you might convince me to join a cult next. You're persuasive, Weston Shaw." She grins at me. "Don't forget. Mouth shut. The fewer details said about…*anything*… the better. And you better not go falling in love without letting me know about it."

I shake my head. "No one's falling in love, slow your roll." I get out of the car and lean back down. "Unless it's you doing the love thing…then I'm all for it."

"Oh, go on." She laughs.

I shut the door and the car pulls away. I chat with the security guys for a few minutes before I walk inside. "Beautiful Things" by Benson Boone is playing through the sound system and when I round the corner, I see Sadie holding Caleb and twirling him around the living room. She's graceful and wearing the biggest smile as Caleb laughs. They twirl around and around until she falls back on the couch with Caleb on top of her. He has the hiccups from laughing and Sadie leans up and hugs him.

"You're making that poor boy laugh too hard."

It's not until I've heard Pam, Sadie's mother, speak that I even realize she's in the room too.

"It's good for him," I say.

They all turn to look at me, and Sadie pushes her hair back and sits up straighter. Caleb grins at me and bounces, and I go over and kiss the top of his head. I don't know when

I started this little ritual with him exactly…sometime during our long nights together, I think, but now I can't resist doing it whenever I see him.

"Hi, Pam, good to see you." I smile at her.

"You too," she says, returning my smile.

"That was faster than I expected. How did it go?" Sadie asks.

I make a face. "My publicist was happy, so I guess it went well. She suggested that we not share details about anything." I give Pam an apologetic look. "I'm sorry in advance if any of this comes back to you. I didn't share Sasha's name, but when asked about you," I look at Sadie, "I did say you're my child's aunt and that we're raising him together."

Sadie looks flustered and she starts bouncing Caleb when he gets restless. "I'm surprised you said anything about me at all."

"They asked about the woman with me in the photos…you."

"Ahh." Her cheeks are already flushed from dancing, but she fans her face as if she's just now feeling the heat.

"And since I'm sure we'll be seen together a lot more in the future, it seemed best that I be upfront about it."

"Maybe it's best if we're not?" She looks up at me and it's silent for a few beats while we stare at each other.

I can't tell if she's saying what she wants or asking me what I want.

"That wouldn't be realistic," I say finally. "We don't need to avoid living our lives just because of what might be said about us."

"Well, let me know if you change your mind," she says.

"I won't change my mind." My tone is sharper than I intended, but fuck, I don't even know what to say.

"Why don't I go lay Caleb down for his nap?" Pam says. "He's looking sleepy."

Sadie kisses Caleb's cheek and hands him to Pam. "Thanks, Mom."

I kiss him too and Pam takes him upstairs.

"I'm sorry I snapped at you. I feel like an ass. If you don't want to be seen with me, I'd understand."

"You're fine. It sounds like you've had a crazy day," she says.

"It's no excuse." I lean my hands on the back of the couch and lower my face until we're a foot apart. "There are parts of this life that aren't the easiest," I say.

She swallows hard.

"Offseason is like a summer vacation. It'll get busier than it's been the past month and a half before too long, but when I'm playing, I'll be gone a lot. It'll be a lot different than this."

She blinks and she looks so damn pretty, it's distracting. My eyes fall to her lips and she swallows again. I force myself to look in her eyes again.

"I guess I just want you to know what you're getting into…and that this isn't an accurate picture right now. The media can get intense. I've liked being in this bubble getting to know Caleb…and you. The people in the lives of the players…the women…can get hit pretty hard. I don't want that for you, but I'm selfish enough that I don't want you retreating either. At least not retreating from me."

I lean back and run my hands through my hair, too much energy coursing through me. I need to work out for a few hours.

"I like where we are now, Sadie. I don't want anything or anyone messing that up. I want to see…where it goes."

Shit. I didn't mean to say that last sentence, even though it's how I feel.

My hand slides off the back of my neck and I sigh, waiting for her to say something.

"I like where we are too," she says. "But don't you think it's normal that we'd get somewhat attached raising a baby together and living in the same house? We're new to this and we're relying on each other for a lot. We can't mistake that for…anything more."

"I've never felt anything close to what I felt last night when I kissed you," I tell her.

Her mouth parts and she blinks, stunned silent for a few seconds.

"Maybe it's best that I go stay in my apartment," she says. "I can drive back and forth during the day."

"What? No. Sadie, come on. I don't want you to go. If you tell me that what happened last night didn't mean anything to you, I'll let this go and we don't have to talk about it again."

"I don't want to talk about it again," she says.

Well, fuck.

I guess that's my answer.

CHAPTER TWENTY-FOUR

LANDMARK MOUNTAIN

SADIE

"What do you think we forgot?" Weston asks.

I laugh. "I'm sure several things, but hopefully nothing urgent."

It's Easter weekend and we're driving into Landmark Mountain. Felicity has been to see us a few times, but this will be the first time I've gone to see her. I'm excited to meet everyone.

It's been a little tense for the past few weeks, while

Weston and I navigate living in the same house, but we've both worked hard to get to a comfortable place with each other. After our kiss—I don't even know what to call what happened because he's right, it was so much more than that to me too—and the conversation the next day, I haven't brought up leaving again. Nothing was officially said, but after he looked so panicked when I suggested leaving, I decided then and there that I would stay, even if it was hard on me.

It's definitely been hard.

But I just want to do what's right for Caleb.

I think Weston was hurt, thinking we weren't on the same page, but the truth is, that kiss meant *too* much, and if anything, my feelings for him are growing stronger by the day.

I wonder, several times a day, if he's changed his mind about me. If he feels the same or if he's written it off to a weak moment. I don't think I'll ever know because we're both doing such a good job of *not going there.*

"Oh my goodness, this town is so cute," I say. "It's so festive. Look at the bunnies! Oh my God, Caleb is going to love the bunnies."

Weston looks over at me and grins. "They go all out for every holiday, even more than Silver Hills. You should see it around here at Christmastime."

We pull into the Landmark Mountain Lodge & Ski Resort parking lot and Weston gets Caleb out of his seat while I make sure everything is in the backpack.

"Should we change him before we meet everyone?" I ask.

"Yeah, probably."

"Just lay him on the seat, I can do it quick and no one will even see what we're doing."

"So bossy," he teases. "I'll change him, thank you very much."

I give him a pointed look. "Did you pack the tinkle tent?"

He makes a face. "Dammit. No, I didn't. Why doesn't he ever *tinkle* on you?"

"Because you're too fun to surprise."

He laughs and my stomach flutters. Yeah, I'm obviously an amazing actress because I don't think Weston has a clue how bad I've got it for him.

His phone starts going off like crazy and my eyebrows lift.

"Someone is desperate for you."

"At least someone is," he quips.

My cheeks heat and I motion for him to let me change Caleb. He checks his phone while I get to work. I hear him chuckling and I'm dying of curiosity. I guess he could be chatting with other women, but he's definitely not had time to go be with any. He's still with me and Caleb all the time.

I think that will all change when he's playing again.

I get Caleb snapped back up and lift him, smiling at my sweet boy. He's getting so big.

"Hey, listen to this," Weston says. "Penn volunteered to be a tutor for that mentorship program my mom told us about. And he has met his match with the kid." He laughs and shows me the text.

PENN

Okay. What the fuck do The Single Dad Players have to say about this? I showed up to tutor my dude Sam, and the first thing he asks is when should he expect to get armpit hair. The hell kind of question is that?

RHODES

Did you tell him you were fifteen before you got yours?

PENN

Very funny. He's freaking nine. Why does he want to know that? I tried to get him back on track with the math problems, but then he asked how old I was when I first kissed with tongue. I said, Crap, Sam, you're giving me all the heavy hitters right off the bat. And he said he had a lot more questions! <Cursing emoji>

BOWIE

This is payback in the purest form. I didn't know you as a nine-year-old, but this just feels so fitting.

PENN

You guys are supposed to have my back.

HENLEY

I haven't been able to text back because I've been laughing so hard.

I've got your back, man. And correction, Rhodes. He was fifteen with the armpit hair, nineteen when he first kissed with tongue.

PENN

I was a late bloomer!!!

Weston is laughing so hard, he's crying. I crack up too, and Caleb thinks we're laughing at him, so he joins in.

"What is so funny?" Felicity comes up behind us and puts her arms around me and Weston. We hug and she takes Caleb out of my arms, squeezing him.

"Penn," he says.

"Ah. That explains it," she says, laughing.

"He's tutoring a kid through that foundation Mom's a part

of and the kid is already making him work hard for it," Weston says.

"He needs to work hard for something," Felicity says, grinning. "I'm so excited you're here! The kids are hunting for Easter eggs right now, but I thought Caleb might like to see the bunnies."

"Yes!" I squeal. "He'll love them."

"And he can get his picture taken with the Easter bunny," Felicity adds.

"Cannot wait."

Weston gets a funny look on his face.

"What?" I ask.

"I'm fucking terrified of the Easter bunny," he whispers.

Felicity hears him and cracks up. "He's not lying. The one time our family went to Disney World, I tried to get West to go stand in line with me to get pictures with the characters, and he always ran away crying." She manages to kick the back of Weston's leg when we're walking and his leg buckles.

I cackle. I've seen her do this multiple times now and it never gets old.

"I did not run away crying," Weston argues. "I just wanted to stand in line for something else."

"Mm-hmm, as you sniffled behind Mom and watched me get my picture taken with Minnie Mouse."

"Whatever," he huffs.

He looks at me and grins, rolling his eyes.

I meet a ton of people when we get to the side of the lodge where all the activity is taking place. Sutton's brothers and sister are there and their spouses, and everyone is so lovely, both in how nice they are and in how attractive they are. I'm surrounded by beautiful people and if I weren't distracted with seeing how cute Caleb is with the bunnies, I'd be a little starstruck by everyone. Sutton's sister Scarlett and his sister-in-law Marlow probably talk to me the most, but they're all wonderful. Marlow has a little girl named Dakota who falls in love with Caleb and she stays with us while we play with the bunnies.

When Weston and I stand in line to get pictures with the Easter bunny, Weston gets fidgety.

"Are you seriously nervous?" I ask.

"You never know what's behind the suit," he whispers under his breath.

Owen pipes up. "I think Pappy was Santa Claus last year. He always keeps peppermints in his pocket and Santa was handing out candy canes." He looks at me with big eyes and I smile. He's adorable.

"That's a really good guess then. If I knew it was Pappy playing the Easter bunny, I wouldn't mind so much," Weston says.

"I don't think it's Pappy," Dakota says. "See? He's over there with Grinny."

I look over and see a striking elderly couple standing together near the Easter egg hunt. Weston has had to tell me several times who everyone is and I'm still having trouble keeping everyone straight. But I believe Grinny is the Landmarks' grandma, and Pappy is the Ledgers' grandpa…as in *Zac Ledger*, formerly my favorite quarterback until I met the one next to me.

We're next in line and when the helper motions for us to come close, I do and Weston stands back. I look at him and he makes a face and then moves forward with us. It's our turn for a picture and when I step closer to the bunny, Caleb starts wailing. He looks at the Easter bunny and cries his eyes out. I think pictures are still taken, but it can't be a good one.

"Let's go, let's go," Weston says, hustling us away from there as fast as he can.

Caleb's lower lip sticks out as he looks back at the bunny and cries a little more.

"It's okay, sweet boy. We won't go back there," I tell him.

"You never have to get your picture with a dressed-up character if you don't want to," Weston tells him solemnly.

I burst out laughing and he gives me a mock hurt look.

"No, you're right. He doesn't," I say, trying to get serious and failing.

Later, we take a ride up the highest mountain in a big gondola. It's full since it's a clear spring day and everyone is out for the festivities. April has been amazing this year, and I can't wait until the weather is even warmer so we can get in Weston's pool. When we reach the top of the mountain, we take a few selfies of the three of us, and Felicity takes a few of us too. I get some of her and Sutton and Owen, and while I'm busy with that, Weston gets mobbed.

"Oh my God, Weston Shaw," I hear the shriek and turn to see a bunch of hot girls in skintight jeans and boobs lifted up to heaven, surrounding him.

"Can we get a picture with you?" they ask, and he agrees.

I've never heard him say no to an autograph or a picture, and by now there have been a few occasions when it wasn't the best timing. Like last month at Caleb's doctor's appointment.

"Sure," he says.

They take no less than three dozen pictures, each of them wanting one-on-one shots and then multiple group shots, and then they want him to sign things. One girl lifts her shirt and flashes her boobs and points at her cleavage, asking him to sign there.

Felicity turns Owen away so he doesn't see too much.

"I'm here with my family," he says, shaking his head. "But you guys have a nice day, okay?" He starts to walk away and several of them stick pieces of paper in his pockets.

"Nerves of steel, these women," Felicity mutters. She looks at me and rolls her eyes. "Don't worry. He's not into that. He's grown up a lot."

"I'm not…he can do whatever he wants." I lift my shoulder.

Her eyes narrow and her lips poke out like she's trying to read me. "But you know he's into you, right?" she whispers.

I make a face. "No. It's just a weird situation. I don't think he really is at all—"

She snorts. "Uh, I've seen the way he looks at you…and I thought I was seeing something in the way you look at him too, but—" She shrugs. "Maybe I have it wrong?"

"I think so," I say.

"Hmm."

"What do you think?" Weston asks, coming up to us.

"I think you got a lot of girls' numbers just now," I say.

He groans. "If there was a trash can up here, I'd toss them."

"Mm-hmm," I say.

His eyebrows lift. "You don't believe me?"

I lean in and whisper in his ear. "I think it's been a while for you and you're probably ready to have sex just for the sake of having sex."

I said it playfully, recalling the conversation we had a while ago now about sex. But when I step back to look at him, grinning, the look on his face wipes it away. He looks hurt and maybe a little mad.

"Weston," I whisper.

He tugs on his hair, a gesture I know by now means that he's annoyed or anxious. Before I can say anything else, he moves closer to Felicity and asks Owen something about what he sees below.

The girls who took pictures with him say, "Bye, Weston Shaw," loudly as they walk toward the gondola station and I'm tempted to duck out and go with them.

If I think *this* is hard—it's going to be *really* hard to hide my feelings when he actually starts sleeping with someone. It's inevitable, and I can only hope I can get a handle on this before then. It's funny that I would hear Sasha's voice in my head about this now, but I do.

She'd be saying, "You know the best way to get over a man is to get under a new one, Sade," and in the past, I'd laugh and tell her she may have a point.

But that's the last thing I want to do, and I don't think it would help anyway.

CHAPTER TWENTY-FIVE

BACK IN MY FACE

WESTON

"We've missed you," Henley says, giving me a bro-hug. "You haven't been to the last two meetings."

"I know. I've missed you guys too. We went to Landmark Mountain for Easter and then last weekend Caleb got a cold."

"How's he doing now?" Bowie asks.

I sit down at the round table at Luminary and take a long drink of my flat white. "Better. Still not a hundred percent, but better. I think he's teething too."

They all groan.

"That's not for the faint of heart," Rhodes says.

"I'll tell you what's not for the faint of heart," Penn says. "Sam and the endless barrage of inappropriate questions. This week he wanted to know if I could tell him about sex because he said he's getting conflicting messages from the other foster kids in his house. One told him you could get a girl pregnant by hugging too long. Another said only if you're lying down and hugging at the same time." He puts his hands in his hair and tugs. "I just want to do math, man. I don't need all this other drama."

"Who knew you are such a nerd?" Henley says.

We all laugh and I feel lighter than I have in weeks. I've been in a funk for a while—a couple of weeks, I guess—and it's good to see my guys.

"He's a curious kid. Tell it to him straight," Bowie says.

"I agree. I was told so much shit when I was little, and I'm glad Bree and I still agree on this at least. We don't want to skirt around the sex talk. We've already talked with Cassidy and we will with Audrey when she's ten…unless she asks about it sooner than that."

"Okay," Penn says. "If you say so. I just don't want to do anything to mess him up. He's already dealing with a lot."

Rhodes puts his hand on Penn's shoulder and shakes him slightly. "Our boy here is getting attached. I think there might be some paternal strings in there after all."

Penn scoffs. "Right. Me? Nah."

I grin. "It happens to the worst of us."

They all turn and look at me and I cringe because it feels like they can see right through me.

"What?" I say.

"You gonna tell us what's going on with you?" Rhodes says. "Or are we gonna have to pull it out of you?"

"What? I'm fine."

"Yeah, I can tell you're keeping up with workouts because you're ripped as fuck, but your eyes look like this." Rhodes does puppy-dog eyes and pokes out his lower lip for good measure.

"I do not," I snort.

"He's not lying for once," Bowie says.

"How are things going with Sadie?" Henley asks.

"Fine." When they all look at me pointedly and I shake my head and focus on my coffee mug. "She has Caleb right now and they're at the apartment with her mom going through things."

"So, she's still staying with you?" Penn asks.

"Yeah, she hasn't threatened to leave again."

"Wait, she threatened to leave? You didn't tell us that." Henley frown.

"I…something happened. We kissed and…it's been a while ago now." I lift my hand when they start talking at once. "We didn't have sex, but we messed around and after…she said it couldn't happen again. I told her I'd keep my hands to myself…which I've done. It just—"

"Just what?" Rhodes prods.

"Don't leave us hanging there," Penn says.

"It was different for me," I say.

I glance up and see blank faces staring back at me before they start talking all at once again.

Finally Rhodes whistles between his teeth and it's quiet again.

"Explain thyself," he says, holding his hand out and nodding like I've got the floor.

"I've never felt anything like that from a kiss."

"In a good way?" Henley asks.

"In an incredible way."

They hoot and holler and carry on and Rhodes doesn't do anything to stop it this time because he's the main instigator.

I lean back in my seat, my head falling back as I stare at the ceiling, and their noise dies down.

"What's the problem then?" Bowie asks.

"*She said it couldn't happen again,*" I reiterate. "At first I thought it was because she didn't feel the same, but I don't know, the way she looks at me, the way she kissed me back before she let her head shut it down…" I lean forward and they all do too, completely invested in what I'm saying. "When we were in Landmark Mountain, a bunch of girls came up to me and they were flirting hard and gave me their numbers. At first, I thought she was a little bit jealous and it made me hopeful, you know? But then she brought up an old conversation we'd had and sorta threw something I'd said back in my face."

"That sounds like jealousy to me," Rhodes says, tilting his head.

"She said it'd been a while for me and that I'm probably ready to have sex just for the sake of having sex." I fling my palms out.

"Well, yeah," Penn says. "How long has it been anyway?"

"She was testing you," Henley says.

I frown. "She doesn't play games. She's not that way."

"Maybe not, but did you reassure her? Did you say *only if it's sex with you* or something like that?" he asks.

Penn snorts and the look I give him shuts him down.

"No, I didn't say that. Did you not hear me say she said it can't happen again? Why would I push it after that?"

"So she knows how you feel. That you're not just wanting to get laid. She might've thought that kiss was just you scratching an itch or that you're just horny…" Henley sighs.

"If it was just that, I'd have gone out and gotten laid by

now." I shove back from the table and put my hands in my hair. "Fuck yeah, I wanna get laid. But so what. I'm a grown-ass man. It's not the worst thing in the world. But what *is*, is the fact that I can't stop thinking about *her*. We say goodnight and I miss her the second I go to my room. I can't wait to see her every morning. When she sees Caleb for the first time every day, something weird happens in my chest. When she laughs at something Caleb does or something I say, my stomach does somersaults. I work out for hours and it doesn't do anything to lessen this—" I rub the place on my chest where it aches.

When I look at the guys again, they're staring at me in a combination of shock and amusement.

"You need to wine and dine her." Henley holds his arms out wide and announces, "Our boy is in love, guys."

"No," Penn gasps.

I point at him. "Agreed. I'm not in love. I'm just…I'd like her to take me seriously and maybe go out with me sometime and…oh, fuck. Am I?"

I lower my elbows to my knees and my head drops as I try to focus on breathing in and out.

"Are you hyperventilating?" Penn asks. "Who even are you right now?"

"I don't know," I moan. I point at them. "We keep this between us. Not another word about it."

Rhodes pats The Single Dad Playbook lying in the middle of the table and nods sagely.

"We are the vault. What happens with us, stays with us," he says.

Everyone piles their hands on the notebook and I put mine on top.

"What are you going to do?" Bowie asks.

"I'm going to pretend this isn't happening," I say.

Rhodes groans. "Didn't you hear Henley? You need to wine and dine her. Tell her you only want her. You're wasting valuable time. We'll be training soon. You won't have all day for this then. You'll be at practice wishing you could have sex with her and these mugs will not be staring back at you in sympathy." He points at his face and everyone else's. "No, we will look at you like, *why didn't you listen to us when we told you flat out what to do*?" He shakes his head. "Pretend this isn't happening. Shit. I'm with Penn on this. Who even are you right now?"

"I'm trying to be considerate of her feelings. To respect what she said…and give her time to heal," I say quietly.

Fuck. I am falling in love with her.

CHAPTER TWENTY-SIX

A BOOK THIS PRETTY

SADIE

"Hey, how's it going over there?" Weston asks.

"We've almost got everything boxed up," I say.

"Do you need me to come get a load?"

"No, my parents have been taking things to Goodwill all day and everything else will fit in my car for now. My dad just went to grab takeout for us and I think Caleb and I will get on the road in an hour or so."

"Okay, sounds good. I might go eat at Bowie's with the guys if you're taken care of."

My chest squeezes. I try not to make it mean anything more than what it is. Weston is a genuinely kind person. He looks out for people, and since I'm taking care of his son, he looks out for me now. He also drops In-N-Out off for the security team at the house if he's close to one because he knows they love it.

"They've been griping at me for ignoring them," he adds.

"Tell them I said hello."

I hear Rhodes in the background yelling, "You miss us, Sadie?"

I laugh. "Yes, I do actually."

"I'm not telling them that," Weston says, laughing. "They don't need their egos inflated any larger than they already are."

When I get off the phone, my mom's look has me shaking my head. "What?"

"I'd ask you the same question." She laughs. "How are things going with Weston?"

"They're…good. Really good."

Her eyebrows lift and I shake my head again.

"Not like that."

"Are you sure?" she asks.

I hesitate and her smile grows.

"Something did happen a few weeks ago. We kissed."

I'll spare my mom the details about what else we did.

"I've felt bad about it ever since." I bite the inside of my cheek. "He said he'd never felt like that from a kiss, and I shut him down."

"Why, honey?" My mom pulls me closer and tucks back a stray hair. "You deserve happiness, you know."

"I know. Just not with him." My lips tremble and I sigh, looking down.

My mom tilts my chin up to meet her eyes.

"Why not with him? Honey, as hard as it is to say out loud, Sasha isn't here. But you know what? If she was, do you think she would've been ready to settle down? I don't. I don't even know if she was going to be up to the full-time mom gig. When you weren't working and helping with Caleb, she'd drop Caleb off for me to watch him so she could go out shopping or see her friends or…I don't even know half the time what she was doing."

"I didn't know that." I stare at her, trying to process this new information.

"We all caved too easily with her. I'm not sure if it was because she'd been sick or if her personality was just always more forceful than the rest of ours, but if I could do things over again with her, I would. Maybe she wouldn't have been in the car that day if I had, driving when she shouldn't have been." Her voice breaks and I put my hand on her shoulder.

"Mom, you can't blame yourself for what happened. Sasha always did exactly what she wanted to do."

She nods. "You're right about that. She didn't want me and Dad to go on that trip because she didn't think she could take care of Caleb for that long without us, and we almost listened to her. I wish we had, but—"

"It wouldn't have mattered, Mom. I've blamed myself for not waking up before she left that morning, but it's…I don't know, it doesn't bring her back."

"No, it doesn't." We both wipe our tears away and she leans in to hug me. When we pull apart, she puts her hands on my cheeks. "I want you to be happy, Sadie. If Weston makes you happy, you should give him a chance. If it didn't work out, I trust that your love for Caleb would outweigh any of the possible negatives."

My dad comes in with the food then and I'm glad to set the subject aside.

When Caleb and I get back to the house, Weston still isn't home. Caleb wakes up from snoozing in the car just long enough for me to give him a bottle and change his diaper. I put him to bed and take a long shower, feeling grimy after the long day. When I get in bed, my hair still wet, I pull the box onto the bed that has Sasha's journals. I'm torn about reading them. I wouldn't want my journals read after I'm gone. I stopped writing in one because I caught Sasha reading all of mine. She wasn't ever apologetic when she got caught either.

She'd laughed and shrugged, saying, "Things written down are meant to be read."

"Not if *Private Property, DO NOT READ* is written in the front," I'd said.

"It's a book," she'd waved my journal around, "and you know how much I love to read. It's torture for you to write in a pretty book like that and not let me read it."

I think I threw something at her and she laughed. The next time I caught her, I yelled at her and she laughed, and the last time, I didn't speak to her for a day and then decided it was my own fault for continuing to write in one.

I never knew she even kept a journal because I didn't go digging through her things the way she dug through mine. Being two years younger than me, Sasha thought what was mine was hers, and for the most part, I was okay with that… except with my journals.

I smile now and pick up one of her journals and open it, laughing out loud when I see what's written inside the cover.

Sadie, if you ever read this, I am going to laugh so hard.

See? A book this pretty is meant to be read!

I look at the date of the first entry and it's probably a year after she found my first journal.

She would've been fifteen and I would've been seventeen.

Her first line gets right to the point.

I want to lose my virginity by fifteen since I found out from Sadie's journal that she lost hers at sixteen. She might be smarter and more mature than me, but I'm sexier. Right, Sadie? Wink, wink.

Sadie will probably never read this because she's a better person than I am, but I hope she does! Then she can get off her high horse about me reading hers. Mine is going to be so much more exciting than hers anyway. All she talks about is school and studying and grades and about Jake and Ian and Charlie. I'm glad she lost her virginity to Charlie though. He's the hottest guy in high school and loaded, so it shouldn't even matter that the sex wasn't better than it was. If she'd dated him a little longer, I bet he would've given her killer presents.

Okay, seriously, my journal isn't going to be about Sadie. It's going to be about MY exciting life.

So, anyway, if I'm going to lose my virginity while I'm fifteen, I only have like four months left to make it happen.

Here are the options and in the order I'd prefer:

1. Charlie—what? It's not like Sade's dating him anymore! And I want to see what kind of gifts he'd give me.

And as I said before, he's the hottest guy in high school. I bet he's learned a few things since last year.

2. Jon Paul. He has more acne than I'm comfortable with, but he's R-I-C-H. Good gifts, plus I've heard he has an amazing pool.

3. Aaron. He's hotter than Jon Paul but not as rich, so that's why he's last.

I groan, but I've laughed as I've been reading too. This is Sasha to a T. She was sassy and irreverent and so funny…and rotten.

God, I miss her.

There is a large stack of journals. I didn't look through any of them at the apartment, just stuck them in a big box. She wrote in more journals than I ever did, and I laugh and cry reading her thoughts. I read almost all of the first one and fall asleep, happy that I have a lot more to read once this is done.

CHAPTER TWENTY-SEVEN

MADLY

Four months later

WESTON

The night before our first game of the season, I stretch out on the bed and pick up my phone to call Sadie. Even though I live close to the stadium, we're required to stay in a hotel by ourselves the night before a game, whether it's a home game or an away game.

I went through withdrawals from Sadie and Caleb when I started training camp, but that was easier than this because I still went home to the two of them every night.

I was raw for a few weeks after I shared my feelings for Sadie with the guys, but it was also a relief to get it off of my chest, and it opened my eyes to how deep my feelings really went. It's only gotten harder to not cross any boundaries, to not let her see how she affects me, to not look at her too long, to not kiss her…damn, I deserve a gold medal for all my restraint.

We've gotten so much closer to each other than we were all those months ago. Not only are we in the trenches together with raising Caleb—never has it been more obvious than when he was sick for the first time. We were exhausted and Sadie didn't complain once about any of it. She tirelessly took care of him, rarely taking a break even when I tried to make her rest. She cried when she heard his awful cough, and I don't think she'd ever been more beautiful to me than in that moment. But her walls have come down with me too, not just when it comes to Caleb.

We discuss everything and she makes me laugh all the time.

She's the first person I want to tell anything, and the last voice I want to hear every night. I feel like part of me is missing whenever we're apart.

She's my best friend, and I'm madly in love with her.

It's going to be really hard to be away from her.

I FaceTimed earlier when Caleb was still up and that was fun. He says *Dada* and *Mama* now and *gog* for Felicity's dog Chewy. At first I could tell it concerned Sadie that he called her Mama. She said she'd read that that's a word that babies just start out saying.

"I didn't tell him to call me that," she said.

But her mom said something that put her at ease about it.

"You're the mama he knows, Sade, and Sasha would want him to have a mama on this earth. When he's old enough you can tell him all about her, but you're right here, and you're the one who's loving him like a mother would."

Sadie stopped repeating, "Sadie, Sadie, Sadie" to him and let him call her Mama.

I check the time again and FaceTime her. Caleb should be in bed by now and if he's not yet, she'll call me back.

"Hey," she says, grinning.

She's in a tank top and has her hair piled up in a messy bun, face clear of makeup. I love her like this. I love her dressed up. I love her however I see her.

"Hey. How's it going?"

"It's been a good night. Caleb went down easy. He did ask for Dada when it was time for stories. I don't do the sounds of the wild things as good as you."

I laugh and nod. "Yeah, I've heard you. Your roar is pretty weak."

She laughs and I just stare at her for a moment.

"I miss you guys," I say. "I don't like not being there for his bedtime."

"We miss you too. The FaceTime helped. He liked seeing your face."

I want to ask her if *she* misses me, but I don't.

"I liked seeing your faces too. Have you talked to Felicity yet? Are they coming by the house before the game?"

"Yes. She called right before you actually. We're going in one car, my parents too. They were worried they'd get lost trying to find the family parking lot." She laughs.

"Nice." I grin.

"You ready for the game?" she asks.

"I am. The team is looking great, feeling strong. Hopefully we crush tomorrow."

"You will. We'll be cheering you on. You'll probably be able to hear my dad from the field."

I grin. "I want to hear *you*."

Her cheeks flush and she presses her lips to the side. "I might do some cheering too."

"You better."

We look at each other for a minute, and it's nice to have an excuse to look at her and not worry that I'm gonna get caught staring.

"You'll meet me in the family area afterward?" I ask.

"Yeah, we'll come say hey and then probably hurry out so Felicity and Sutton can drop us off and get back to Landmark Mountain."

"You're not riding back with me?"

Her full lips part for a second and her head tilts slightly.

"Well, I wasn't sure if you go party after a game or what."

I snort. "Uh, no. I'll be wired, especially if we win, but I'm coming home. Did you not hear me say I miss you guys?"

She tries to hold back her smile, but it doesn't work. "Okay. Well, yeah, I guess we can ride home with you then. If my parents did too, that would save Felicity and Sutton some time."

"I'll try to get off the field as soon as I can, but it'll still be a little wait. Then I'll shower, and I'm all yours."

Her cheeks flush and she nods. Her teeth press against her lower lip for a second and I stare as her full lip pops back out. My dick swells in my shorts and I grip it tight to try to contain it, but it feels too good, especially when she's looking at me with those huge eyes and full lips.

One eyebrow lifts and her lips pucker slightly. "You okay?"

"Me? I'm good."

"Your cheeks look a little flushed. Is it hot in the hotel?"

I let go of my dick and nod. "Yes. It's definitely hot in here."

She adjusts the phone and shifts on the bed, enough for me to see that her nipples are straining against her tank. A small groan comes out of me and she lifts the phone back to where it was.

"I'll let you get some sleep," I tell her. "Call me if you need anything. I hate that I have to stay in a hotel when I'm so close to home. But if anything comes up, I want to know about it."

She smiles. "We'll be fine. Don't worry."

I smile back at her. "Sweet dreams, Chapman."

"Sweet dreams, Shaw."

"Oh, I already know I'm going to have the sweetest dreams."

She licks her lips and smiles again. My hand is back on my dick when we say goodnight, and I barely even give myself three long strokes before I'm coming.

CHAPTER TWENTY-EIGHT

A COLD SHOWER

SADIE

My phone rings as I get in my seat and I'm shocked to see that it's Weston.

I answer and his face fills the screen. He's grinning big and his eyes light up as he smiles at Caleb.

"Look at you, nice jersey," he says.

It's the first game of the season and I've got Caleb in a Weston Shaw jersey, number fourteen. Okay, I'm wearing one too.

"I didn't expect you to call us right now!" I laugh nervously. Players are already out on the field and I look everywhere but don't see him.

"Just wanted to see you guys before I go out," he says.

I can't do anything but beam at that.

"We're all here, cheering you on." I show the screen to my family and his and they all yell at him, telling him to play safe and win this game for us.

He's laughing when I point the screen back at myself. He does the sign for *I love you* with one hand, and my heart flutters. He does this all the time to Caleb and sometimes I wish he'd do it for me too. He pounds his fist against his chest, grinning.

"See you out there," he says.

I nod, overwhelmed all of a sudden, and we hang up.

My heart is pounding so hard.

Caleb tugs on my hair and it's enough to distract me. He's crawling everywhere now, so I'm nervous that it'll be hard to keep him occupied through an entire game, but Weston assured me I could take him to the Mustangs childcare for the players, as long as I pick him up by the third quarter.

We're here with both sets of grandparents and Felicity and Sutton though, so between the exciting sounds of the game and him being passed between the seven of us—the grandpas sneaking him bites of hot dog when they think I'm not looking—Caleb is having the time of his life.

We cheer our heads off when Weston and the rest of the team file out. I can't believe I'm here. I've been to some of the practices and have loved seeing the players behind the scenes, but it's different being in the stadium for an actual game. The adrenaline is sky-high.

I watch number fourteen like a hawk. It isn't hard to do, I feel like I already spend my days watching him like it's my job. He is *not* hard to look at. His body is my favorite work of art. It's become harder and harder hiding how much I want to study him up close and personal, but I'm doing my best.

Weston wasn't exaggerating about the change in his schedule. Once training camp started in late July, we went from seeing each other all day, every day, to seeing him for a few hours in the evening. And now that the season has started, I think it's just going to get more hectic.

I've missed him so much. I didn't realize how spoiled I was, having him around all the time. He did most of the cooking for us and we got into a regular routine of watching a movie with a glass of wine, or spending time out by the pool, or watching the stars out on the deck. When he started training, I put more effort into making dinner for him, carefully following the meal plan the team's nutritionist put together for him. My cooking isn't great, but it's getting better, and he acts like it's delicious, no matter what I make. And we still watch a movie—me with a glass of wine, him with plain water or electrolyte water—but he usually falls asleep before it's over. I nudge him awake, loving the way his sleepy eyes open up and then he grins like he's so happy to see me.

I've gotten to know some of the players' girlfriends and wives, but not very well yet. I still feel out of place because I'm not the girlfriend or the wife. I'm more like the nanny, I guess. And I also feel like I'm Weston's best friend. He's, without question, mine.

We talk endlessly now, about our days, about our thoughts and dreams, about everything and nothing. I know where all his scars came from, at least the ones that I can see when he's wearing a swimsuit, and he knows that I once dreamed of being a famous singer, even though I can't sing well at all. I know about when he lost his virginity at sixteen and was proud that he lasted three minutes. He knows that my first time, also at sixteen, was more like one minute, so we high-fived that he really had accomplished something at three.

Our life is fun and wonderful, and I didn't think I'd ever say this, but I don't want it to change. I've never been happy like this, and it's all because of Weston and Caleb.

I'm scared about what will happen when Weston's on the road. Multiple times now, I've watched what happens when his adoring fans see him. They don't care whether I'm next to him or not, they nudge me out of the way and demand his attention. He always checks to make sure Caleb and I are okay and then is politely distant with them, taking photos and signing what they hand him to sign and declining when it's in an inappropriate place.

I won't be able to blame him for anything he chooses to do. He's been a perfect gentleman with me since we kissed all those months ago, and I've given him absolutely no sign that I want anything more.

But I do.

I want it all with him.

I did then too, but everything was still too new. I'm still grieving my sister, but it's not as fresh as it was. She's been gone seven months and I don't think I'll ever get over losing her, but I can get through some days without crying now. I can talk about her without feeling guilty that I'm here and she's not.

I'm still reading her journals, savoring them one at a time, and taking a break between them. It's too much if I try to read too much at once and I find myself slipping back into the despair. But most of the time, reading them helps me. It's like hearing her voice next to me, and half the time, her words in her journals are directed at me like she hopes I'm reading them.

Sometimes I wonder if she knew she wouldn't live long

and that I might be reading them. Her diabetes was a constant struggle, and in her journals, I learn that it concerned her more than she ever let on. I can smile more when I think about her since finding these books and reading her thoughts.

Once halftime is over, the game flies by. They play an incredible game, winning by fourteen. We hang around until the stadium clears a little bit and then head to the family area. There are meals boxed up for the players and some are already digging into their food. I'm full from the food I ate during the game, but my nerves wouldn't let me eat now if I wanted to. Now that I personally know Weston, it's a lot different watching him play than it used to be on the screen. There's a constant underlying panic that he will get hurt.

When he comes out, he rushes toward us, coming for me and Caleb first. He puts his arms around us and hugs us to him.

"My good luck charms," he says. His smile is so sweet when he pulls away. "Did you have fun?"

I feel tongue-tied all of a sudden. "It was the best. You were amazing."

His smirk is cocky when he looks at me. "I love hearing you say that," he says under his breath.

Did I hear him right?

Penn and Rhodes stride through the door next and they hug us and hang out while they eat their food.

"Aren't you going to eat?" I ask Weston.

"Are you hungry?"

I shake my head. "I ate during the game and got too excited." I clutch my stomach. "I might still be recovering."

He laughs and grabs a meal and waves Henley and Bowie over when they come into the room.

They wolf down their food and before I know it, we're grabbing the extra car seat from Sutton and Felicity's vehicle so they don't take it back to Landmark Mountain, and we're heading home. My parents are chatty all the way back, and Weston keeps glancing over at me and smiling.

I don't know if I'm imagining it or if he's looking at me differently.

Once my parents leave and we have Caleb tucked in, Weston leans against the wall outside Caleb's room.

"You need a glass of wine?" he asks.

"I might do a hot tea tonight. Aren't you exhausted?"

"Yes and no. It's hard to come down after a game."

"What sounds good? Do you need another shower? A glass of wine yourself?"

"A cold shower, maybe," he says, laughing. "You look hot as hell in my jersey, Chapman."

I flush. "You like it?" I ask, my voice husky.

"I fucking love it."

My mouth drops open and he stalks toward me until he's in front of me, his hands on the wall, caging me in. He leans in and I gasp, and he stops within an inch of my mouth.

"I'm trying to do the honorable thing here, Chapman," he whispers. "You're making it really hard to do so. I don't know if I can keep showing so much restraint." He lowers his head and his nose trails from my jawline to my ear, and then his lips are against my ear. "And then you showed up in my jersey, and you smell good enough to eat." He inhales and lets out a soft moan and I shiver. "I know what I'm going to be dreaming of tonight."

"What?" I ask shakily.

"My mouth between your legs, devouring you."

I gasp and he moves past me, walking to his room. When he shuts the door behind him, I second-guess that it even happened.

CHAPTER TWENTY-NINE

JELLY AND NOODLES

WESTON

I take another shower—I wasn't kidding about needing a cold one after seeing Sadie in my jersey. I take care of matters in there and when I step out and dry off, I feel ready to go again. I'm always too amped up after a game, but living with Sadie already has me feeling this way most of the time.

I towel-dry my hair a little more before I head into my bedroom and get in bed, not bothering to put anything on. Since tonight was opening day and we won, we've got a lighter schedule tomorrow, so I don't set my alarm. Grabbing my iPad, I turn on the game to watch a few times, something we do after every game, and I think I hear a soft knock on the door. When it's a little louder the second time, I sit up.

"Come in," I call, heart thundering in my chest.

Sadie steps into my room and it looks like she's showered too. Her hair's wet, and she's taken off her long-sleeve shirt and skintight jeans and is only in the jersey now, her long, bare legs on display. I curse under my breath. She looks nervous.

"This look is even better," I tell her.

"I…I couldn't stop thinking about what you said," she says softly.

"Which part?" I can't help but smirk and she shakes her head at me, pressing her lips to the side.

"The part where you said you'd dream about your mouth between my legs, devouring me…"

"Yeah," my voice rasps. "I haven't stopped thinking about that either. I'm naked under this blanket or I'd be standing in front of you by now."

"That's no excuse."

I throw off the covers and she gasps when she sees me. My dick is straining to get to her, and she lifts her hand up to her lips. I don't know if she even realizes it, but she bites down on her thumb, and it's the sexiest fucking thing I've ever seen.

"It wouldn't be the first time I've thought it," I tell her, reaching out to touch her cheek when I'm close enough. "Just the first time I've told you."

"I'm glad you told me." She takes a step forward and I hum when my dick comes in contact with her stomach. "I wasn't sure we were on the same page anymore."

"Anymore? We've been on the same page all along?" I

bring my other hand to her face and hold her cheeks, staring intently in her eyes. "How is that possible? You've played it so cool."

She laughs. "There is no part of me that's been *playing it cool*. I stopped that kiss, but I never wanted to. It's been torturous living under the same roof, close enough to touch, but not..." Her fingers trace their way up my stomach and my muscles jump beneath her.

I'm ready to pounce, so I take another fortifying breath, trying to steady myself.

My forehead touches hers and I drop my hands around her waist, groaning. "I've been desperate for you for months," I whisper. "Did you really not see it?"

Her hands reach my chest and then my shoulders and I tug her against me tighter and her mouth parts. "I was too blinded by my own feelings, too caught up in all that could go wrong."

"Sadie?" I whisper.

She blinks up at me.

"I don't just want one night with you. This isn't just sex for me. You're my best friend. I love the life we've created together. I'm falling in love with you," I tell her.

Her eyes get glassy. "You are?" she whispers. "Are you sure?"

I laugh. "*Yes*, I'm sure. I knew it months ago, I was just trying to give you time to find out what you wanted. And trying to find a way to be okay if you don't feel the same. So, if you don't think you want a relationship with me, we probably shouldn't do this."

"I feel the same," she says. "I'm falling in love with you too, Weston." She leans up on her tiptoes. "Can we talk about it more later?"

I laugh. "Yes, please."

She leans in and gives me the softest, sweetest kiss. My insides are jelly, and when our kiss deepens, it's like a million nerve endings come alive inside my body.

I lift her, my hands closing around her ass as she wraps her legs around my waist, and she whimpers when she feels me against her core. My mouth doesn't leave hers as I turn toward the bed and lay her reverently in the center. I have to break away from her to lift the jersey over her head, cursing when I see her tits for the first time.

"I love you in my jersey, but this is so much better," I say, reaching out to touch her pebbled nipples one at a time. "Let's get these off too." I pull her white lacy panties down and curse again, seeing her bare and wet for me. "I knew you were beautiful, but God, you're so beautiful, it hurts."

She reaches out and wraps her fist around me. "So are you," she says, gripping me tight.

"Mmm, you feel too good," I tell her. I gently remove her hand and bring it to my lips. "I've got somewhere to be first." I grin and kiss my way down her body, stopping between her legs.

She leans up on her elbows to watch and I glance down, taking my time to get a good look at her. My fingers spread her lips apart and I whisper, "So fucking pretty," against her skin.

She gasps and I look up at her when I swipe my tongue across her slit for the first time. I hum as I do it again and again, loving the way she tastes, and her head falls back.

"So good," I whisper.

She arches into me when I flick my tongue against her clit, and I stay there playing with her, finding the rhythm she likes best—and bringing her to the edge until she's begging.

It's the best thing I've ever experienced. When she rides my face like she can't wait for another second and falls apart, I watch her squeeze her eyes shut as she trembles and pulses against my tongue. I kiss her once more and then her thighs and wipe my mouth as I reach in my drawer for a condom. It's a new box. I haven't had any action for a long time, but that doesn't mean I haven't been hoping this day would come.

I rip open that box and tear the wrapper, sliding it over my length. She watches me, her eyes greedy, and when I get in place, she guides me inside, wrapping her legs around me like she can't wait for more.

I close my eyes when I feel her around me. The aftershocks of her orgasm are still going and it's fucking heaven.

"You feel so good," she gasps. "I don't know if I can be still," she says, thrusting up. "I want all of you."

I groan and fill her completely, and she goes still then.

"I'm sorry. Too much?" I ask.

She takes a deep breath and slowly exhales. "You're way bigger than my vibrator," she says, taking another breath.

I laugh in her neck and pull out slightly. "How did I not know you had a vibrator? These walls are too soundproof if I've been missing out on that."

"I made sure to order the quietest one," she says, laughing.

Her breath hitches when I rock back in and ease out, back in with shallow thrusts and out, in deeper and out, rubbing against her clit with every slide back in until she's taking me easier, and then I'm all the way in. We both groan, our mouths colliding in a kiss so hot, I never want to come up for air. Our tempo picks up until it's frantic. I stop kissing her so I can fuck her better. She grips my ass as I slam into her and she meets me with every thrust.

"God, Sadie," I chant.

Her head shakes side to side as she starts coming hard, gripping my dick inside so hard that I see stars.

It's insane and a spiritual experience, the way we come together. I think I black out for a few seconds, and when I open my eyes, she looks as blissed out as I feel.

I lean down and kiss her and when I pull back, her eyes flutter open.

"Are you okay?" I ask.

"That was…incredible," she whispers.

"It was." I move her hair out of her eyes. "*You* are incredible. I've never come that hard in my life." I grin at her smug expression. "Yep, that was all you."

I ease slowly out of her, pausing when she flinches.

"Did I hurt you?" I ask.

"No, I just don't want to let you go."

"I'll be back, I promise."

I go to the bathroom to take care of the condom and after I've washed up and brushed my teeth, she comes into the bathroom and goes into the room with the toilet, closing the door behind her.

"You need privacy after we just did all that?" I call.

"One hundred percent, yes," she says.

I chuckle. When she steps out, I'm still in the bathroom and she stares at me while she washes her hands.

"We're naked," she says, laughing.

"It's about fucking time," I tell her, moving behind her.

My dick gets too happy near her ass, and her eyes widen. "That was fast."

"We don't have to if you're too sore. But yeah, I've lived in this state around you for a long time now."

"I don't know how you kept it so well-hidden." She laughs, leaning her head back against my shoulder.

I reach around and put my hands on her tits, squeezing and loving the way they fill my hands. Her breath hitches when I start playing with her nipples.

"I'm not too sore," she whispers.

"Yeah? Hold on one sec." I grab a condom from the other room and come back, squeezing her ass cheeks before I slide it down my length.

I bend my knees and position myself so I'm rubbing her clit, and we both watch my fingers glide over her in the mirror. She bites her lower lip and sucks in a breath when I tap against her.

"You want to see me go in?" I ask.

She nods, and I turn us to the side, and slowly inch inside of her.

"We look so good together," I whisper in her ear. "Play with yourself."

Her cheeks flame, but she does it, her fingers rubbing small circles, her movements getting wilder when I pull out and thrust back in faster this time.

"Ahh, I can feel that. Don't stop," I tell her.

She whimpers and doesn't stop and the combination of me pistoning inside of her and her fingers on the outside and the clenching around me on the inside…it's heaven.

"Sadie," I groan. "I'm not going to last."

"I'm close," she says, and when her head falls back against my chest and she spasms around me, I lose control.

I come with a loud moan, and she does too. She collapses against me and I try to keep us both standing.

"I'm a noodle," she says weakly.

I laugh and scoop her up.

"Stick me in your shower?" she asks.

"Want me in there too?"

"Yes, please. I might be too weak to wash myself." She laughs over her shoulder and I put my hands on her hips, leaning in to kiss the back of her neck.

Best night of my life.

CHAPTER THIRTY

SIDEWAYS

SADIE

After we wash each other and he licks me to make sure he hasn't missed a spot and washes me again after I come all over his face…and I sit on the shower bench and take him in my mouth and gaze up at him while I suck and bob over his stunning dick until he comes all over my face and chest…we wash up one final time and get out of the shower.

We get in his bed and he pulls me to him, my head on his shoulder.

"You weren't kidding about being amped up after a game," I say.

His chuckle is deep and I love hearing it rumble underneath my ear.

"I would've been like that for our first night together no matter what," he says. "I've been dying for this to happen and now that it has, I can't believe it. And you're here in bed with me right now too, which is even better. I thought you might…"

"Bolt?" I fill in.

"Yeah." He gazes down at me and I reach up and put my hand on his cheek.

"I'm not going to run." I pause for a second. "Are you?"

"Hell, no."

"Should we talk more about all of this or wait until morning?" I ask.

"I'm good with now if you are."

"I—" My hand wanders down his chest. "I'm surprised by how right it feels. I thought I might be second-guessing it more, but—I'm more peaceful than I've been in a long time."

"I'm glad," he says. "I knew we would be amazing together. We are in every other area, and I've been living off of that make-out session when we watched the movie for a long time." We both laugh. "But making love with you far surpasses everything I imagined."

"I never thought I'd hear Weston Shaw say *making love*," I giggle.

He tickles my side and I wiggle, trying to get away, but he pulls me back in, one hand on my bum and the other holding my breast.

"That was the first time I've ever said it, and if the guys

ever found out, they'd really revoke my man card. They already think I'm a pussy when it comes to you. And after I've tasted your pussy, I will be the first to admit that I am addicted to it."

I lean my face into his chest and laugh so hard at that.

"They thought I should wine and dine you months ago."

"I think I would've for sure bolted back then."

"I know." He squeezes me and groans when I hike my leg over his thigh. His dick bobs against his stomach. "Just ignore it. I promise I'm gonna let you sleep."

I reach out and run my hand over his velvety hardness. His cock pulses in my hand and he lets out a ragged exhale.

"One more time and then we sleep," I whisper, climbing on top of him.

He watches intently when I slide the condom over him and hisses when I lower myself on top of him. I hover, taking him in slowly. He's huge and even when I'm completely ready for him, it takes a minute to adjust. His hands grip my hips and he leans in and sucks my nipple, first one and then the other. I arch into him and lower another couple of inches and then the rest of the way, feeling so incredibly full.

He looks up at me as he tongues my nipple and his fingers move between my legs, rubbing me at the perfect tempo. I lean forward and feel like a wave undulating over him. He doesn't stop his fingers and my movements cause even more friction. When I feel close, I lie flush against him and kiss him, our tongues tangling as I keep rocking on top of him. The intensity of my orgasm takes me by surprise, our slow and leisurely thrusts pausing as I take him as deep as I can and shatter around him.

He chokes out my name seconds later and we arch into each other, frozen on the outside, but inside, our bodies are doing their own dance. I feel every pulse he makes and my squeezes in return make him curse. It feels endless and when the tremors finally slow, I collapse on his chest, spent.

He moves me next to him and takes care of the condom, and when he's back, he lifts me like I weigh nothing and places me on top of him again.

"What are you doing to me?" he asks. "*Sadie*..."

I grin against his skin and then lean my chin on his chest. "If we wake up in the morning and you decide you just want to stay friends, I'm going to kick your ass."

I laugh at his expression and he smacks my backside and then squeezes it.

"I'm over here wondering if we can stay in this bed forever and you're talking about staying friends?" He laughs and leans in to kiss me, stopping when he sees the expression on my face. "I guess that was too soon, huh?" He looks so worried, I close the distance and kiss him.

"Yeah." I giggle and when he still looks worried, I reach up and smooth the space between his eyebrows. "Let's see what it's like when you're on the road." *With all that temptation*, I think, but don't say. "And during the day when we haven't just had sex for the first...or fourth time."

"So oral sex does count as one," he says, smirking.

I pause like I'm thinking about it and then nod. "I'm counting it. Or we could say three and a half if you feel that would be more accurate?"

He tilts his head back and forth. "Since we both came, I'm okay with counting it."

He squeezes my backside with both hands this time, and I swear, the guy's hard again.

"Sadie," he says, his voice husky. "I wouldn't have done any of this tonight if I wasn't sure about my feelings for you. I know relationships can go sideways—I've seen it go both ways, awful and amazing—but I've waited to give my heart to someone until I was certain. Besides my family, I haven't told a woman I love her…ever. If you need time to be sure, I understand, but I'm not going anywhere."

I look at him for a long moment before I kiss him, trying to convey everything I'm feeling in that kiss. When it builds between us, he turns so he's on top of me, his lower half on the bed, and we kiss for a long time. I turn sideways and pull his mouth back to mine. This time, we face each other as he slides on a condom and we rock into each other, our movements slow and lazy. After we've both come and keep staring at each other in the moonlit room, I whisper, "I've waited to give my heart to someone too, but it's yours now. It's all yours."

He smiles and my eyelids get heavy. The last thing I remember seeing is him smiling at me.

And the first thing that I see the next morning is his head between my legs.

What is this life?

CHAPTER THIRTY-ONE

TROLLS

WESTON

I arrive to practice Monday afternoon on a cloud.

After the coaches assess our performance from yesterday's game, the team spreads out, getting various medical treatments throughout the facility. I do an ice bath and head back to the locker room to call it a day. The guys are in there already, and Henley takes one look at me and starts laughing. Rhodes perks up to see what has him laughing and he gets the biggest shit-eating grin. Bowie grabs my arm and turns me around so he can see my face and then he's laughing too.

"What?" Penn asks. "What'd I miss?"

"Take another look at Loverboy," Henley says, tilting his face toward me. He leans in and whispers, "Those bee-stung lips, pretty sure I see a hickey or two on your neck, and—"

"Take a look at his elbows," Bowie says, laughing.

He turns me around so they can look at my elbows and when they start cracking up, I frown.

"What's wrong with my elbows?"

"Looking a little chafed," Rhodes says in a British accent.

I make a face. They do feel a little raw after all our sessions. We went until the wee hours of the morning and then I started the day out right, between her legs, my new favorite place to be, and she wanted more, so I happily obliged.

I guess I'll have to make her take the top more often. I grin and they laugh again.

"You're going to need to fill us in," Henley says. "Impromptu meeting in an hour?"

I act like I'm thinking about it for a second and shake my head. "I need to get home to my girl."

"*My girl*," Rhodes repeats.

"I heard that too," Bowie chimes in.

"It was bad enough when you stopped going out with me to find women. Now you're going home to your girl? Fuck my life," Penn says.

Rhodes puts his arm around Penn. "I'll be your wingman, pretty boy."

Penn glances over at him and tilts his head up. "You'll do." He smirks.

"So easily replaceable," I yell as I leave the locker room

"No one can ever replace you, Shaw," Henley yells back, and I laugh as I walk to my SUV.

I call Sadie like I do all the time before I head home. She's grinning when she answers, holding Caleb.

"Hey," she says.

"Hey, beautiful."

I wave when Caleb looks at the screen. He grins, but he's distracted by something else.

Sadie's eyes widen. "I'm liking these new perks. Some fun times in bed, being greeted with *hello, beautiful…*"

"I'm just getting started," I tell her, grinning.

"If that was you *just getting started* last night and today… I'm gonna need to start taking more vitamins." She laughs.

"I can hook you up."

We stare at each other for a minute, cheesing pretty hard.

"How's that boy been today?"

"He's extra tired from his late night too. He's been a little grump. I'm putting him down for his nap earlier today. Like, right away."

"Aw, you being a grump, little guy? You ready for some sleep?" I ask.

Caleb's lower lip pokes out and he leans his head on Sadie's shoulder.

"That lower lip says it all," she says.

"Poor guy. And poor you. Maybe you can take a nap too. Do you need anything while I'm out?"

"Are you coming home already?" She lifts her eyebrows.

"Yes. Usually when we win and we're home, we don't have to come in the next day, but they wanted to start out the season with a bang. I'm already in the parking lot."

"Amazing. Well, hurry home and maybe you can catch some of that nap with us."

"I can't get there fast enough."

I pull into my gate forty-five minutes later and the house is quiet when I walk inside. Sadie did fast work if she's already got Caleb in bed. When I reach his room, I peek inside and he's already out. Sadie's door is cracked, so I take a look and she's in bed, sound asleep too. I undress quietly and when I'm down to my boxer briefs, I climb under the covers and scoot next to her, spooning her. I've heard people talk about spooning, but I've never done it with anyone, and damn, there's something about it. She sighs and nestles her ass deeper into my crotch and I will my dick to forget about it. Persistence is one of my strengths, so it takes a while, but I'm determined to let her sleep, and I'm tired too. When I finally crash, it's a fucking amazing sleep.

Caleb's jibber-jabbering wakes me up, and when I open my eyes, Sadie is already going through the door to get Caleb. I sit up and stretch and get up, walking into the other room. Sadie turns, holding Caleb up and kissing him on the cheek, and she freezes when she sees me.

"So we're walking around in our underwear now, huh?" She grins and nods.

Her eyes do a long sweep down my body and she gets stuck on my junk. She licks her lips and points, and I look down, groaning when I see my tip is hanging out quite a bit.

"Obscene," she whispers.

"Sorry. Not awake yet. I learned the joys of spooning and," I point to my dick, "loves it. But I can go back to wearing pants so you'll have something to look forward to when you undress me at night."

"Don't you dare ruin my fun. I'm just..." She continues to stare at me and I get harder.

I growl at her and cover myself so I don't scar Caleb. "Just what? And stop staring. You'll worsen the condition."

"I'm just wondering how you can run or do anything else with all that going on," she finishes, laughing.

I turn and walk into the other room to get my pants. "Not helping."

Once I'm dressed, I walk back in there and walk over to them, kissing Sadie first. Caleb leans in to kiss her after he sees me doing it, and we start laughing. I kiss his cheek and he slobbers all over me too.

"He seems happier now," Sadie says when we get downstairs. "I guess he just needed a nap."

"It's a great day out there. Feel like getting in the pool? Might be one of the last days for it."

"I think we will," she says.

My phone rings as we're giving Caleb a snack and I try to swallow my bite of apple before I answer. "It's my agent. I should take this."

Sadie nods and I walk out onto the patio as I answer.

"Hey, Joan."

"Helluva game last night," she says.

"Aw, you watched? Thank you."

"Of course, I watched, big guy. You're my bread and butter."

I chuckle. "It was a good game. Nice to get back out there."

"I bet. So I'm sorry that I'm not only calling to congratulate you about the game," she says.

I pause mid-walk. "Your tone doesn't sound great."

"It's probably nothing serious, but there have been some rumblings online…surmisings about your relationship with Sadie, and things about Sasha too. I just wanted to touch base with you again about all of it. You're not dating Sadie, right?"

"Well…as of last night, I am, yes."

I hear her say *shit* under her breath.

"Why does it matter? What's this about?"

"It's just getting ugly online. You know how the trolls can get. I'd maybe avoid taking it public for a while. Let this die down a little first."

"What are they saying?"

"Are you sure you want to know? I wouldn't recommend you going to look for yourself, so if me telling you keeps you from doing that, then I will."

"I try not to read what everyone's saying, good or bad."

"Smart boy."

"But I'd like to know what we're dealing with here."

She sighs. "Okay. They're saying things like Sadie and Sasha are both gold diggers and that Sadie should be ashamed for going after her sister's man…and the worst…are we sure Sasha's car accident was really an accident? And it's the way it usually is with athletes and the media—they're going after Sadie the hardest." She pauses and I can hear a car honking in the background. "You want my two cents? I'd recommend you give it at least another…how long has it been? Seven months? I'd give it a good five months before I'd be seen with her publicly, and—"

"That's the rest of the season," I interrupt, heated.

"I'm just telling you what I think you should do. You don't have to take my advice, but if you don't, I hope Sadie has thick skin."

"*Fuck.*" I tug my hair hard and walk to the pool, pacing around it. "Sasha was a one-night stand. I only met her the one time. I was drinking too much and she came on to me at a party and I went with it. I can't regret that night because I have Caleb, but there was *never* going to be anything else between me and Sasha. If I'd met her even a few months later, when I wasn't being so reckless and stupid, I would've turned her down like I have the hundreds of other women who have offered to sleep with me since then."

I hear Caleb and turn to see Sadie and Caleb in their swimsuits. Sadie's pale and I don't know how much she heard, but enough to upset her.

"I have to go, Joan. I'll talk to you later, okay?"

"All right. Let me know if you want me to do anything in the meantime."

"Thanks."

I hang up and look at Sadie carefully. "How much of that did you hear?"

"From *fuck* on. I wasn't trying to eavesdrop, but you sounded so upset, I rushed to see if you were hurt or something and then I sort of froze when I heard the rest," she says.

"I'm sorry. I was angry and I shouldn't have said any of that. You look really upset and rightfully so. Which part is upsetting you most?" I move toward her and pause when she takes a step back.

"All of it?" She laughs and her eyes fill with tears. "And no, I don't. I have no right to be upset about any of it." She shakes her head and wipes her face quickly when the tears start falling. "The way you talked about Sasha. You've never said any of it quite that way to me before, and it makes me wonder what you really thought of her. It's like I'm torn in two with how to feel about it. I want you to have liked my sister as a person, but I'm in love with you and I don't want you to have ever liked her…but you have a baby together!"

She takes a deep breath and a choked sob comes out of her. I want to put my arms around her and make this go away, but I also feel warm inside because she said she's in love with me.

"And hundreds of women? Hundreds? How am I supposed to ever compete with that?"

Caleb looks at her solemnly and pats her cheek. "Mama."

She hugs him closer and cries harder.

"There's no competition. I only want you," I say.

"Why would you even say all of that to Joan? What's going on?"

I exhale and move toward her, wiping the tears from her cheeks. "I'll tell you, but I want to make sure you heard me. You don't have to compete with anyone. I love *you*."

"We'll see how you feel when you're traveling and all amped up the way you were last night, only I'm not there to fuck all night."

It stings a little that she'd think she was only a body for me last night, but I know she's just hurt right now.

"I've never had a night with anyone like ours last night," I tell her. "Nothing even close. This is crass, but I was a one-and-done kind of guy. And I hope this doesn't sound negative about Sasha, but we were both only there for a good time that night. I know I've said this before, but I want you to understand that even if I met Sasha today, I don't think she would be what I would look for in a partner. There has been no one that I've wanted anything more with…no one, Sadie, until you."

She takes a deep breath and sits down on one of the loungers. I sit on the one across from her and tell her about the rest of my conversation with Joan.

And fuck my life, she agrees with Joan and wants to keep our relationship a secret.

CHAPTER THIRTY-TWO

COASTING

SADIE

The next week and a half goes by quickly. I've had a really hard time with this whole online business. I haven't looked any of it up, knowing it'll make me spiral too hard. After we had sex that first time, I wanted to shout it from the rooftops that we were together. Joan's call put a huge damper on that, but thank goodness, she caught it in time and warned us.

Weston doesn't want to keep our relationship a secret at all, but I think because I already feel guilty about loving the father of my sister's baby, I've jumped on Joan's advice and welcomed the pause. It's not like I need to go anywhere with him anyway. I can get my social interactions with other people in when he's at practices or traveling, and we'll spend time together at home.

It's better this way.

But I'm going to have a hard time missing out on the games.

I wanted to see how the two of us did while Weston was traveling anyway, so we'll see how it goes. This weekend is his first away game. If we survive this season, keeping our relationship a secret…well, I'm scared to even hope right now. He'll be leaving in just a little while, and I'm trying to not show any nerves. Since Weston's call with Joan, I've just been coasting. I can't keep my hands off of him, so that hasn't changed, but I'm uneasy. I don't have the same lightness that I had for that small window of time.

I think he senses my uneasiness, trying to make me laugh as we walk outside for a picnic with Caleb. We cross the bridge over the lake and once we're past it, he pauses and sets down our things, tugging my hand in his and pulling me toward him. He leans in for a kiss and before I know it, he's tilting me back, dipping me low as we kiss. We're both laughing as he lifts me back up, Caleb clapping his hands at us.

"You look so beautiful," Weston whispers, his eyes still on me.

We kiss once more before he lifts me back up. We put a blanket on the grass, and Weston runs back into the house, saying he needs to grab something. He takes Caleb with him and when they come back, Weston's carrying a huge bouquet of flowers and Caleb's holding a peony that's almost as big as he is.

Weston hands me the flowers and nudges Caleb. "Go ahead, give it to Mama."

Caleb holds it out for me and I take it, my heart melting.

"Thank you. These are beautiful. I've never seen such pretty flowers." Peonies and dahlias and hydrangeas with silver threads woven throughout the flowers. It's stunning.

"That's Calliope from The Enchanted Florist. She's fun and a little eccentric, and her flower shop is an experience. I'll take you there sometime," Weston says.

He jogs off to steer Caleb back in our direction before he sits on the blanket next to me. Caleb's crawling everywhere these days and he crawls up to get a bite of strawberry or cheese and then crawls off. Weston's up and down, chasing after him. Every time Weston catches up with him, swooping him up and kissing his neck, Caleb throws his head back and cackles.

I love how happy he is.

"God, he's cute," Weston says. He sits down beside me with Caleb in his lap and leans in for a kiss. "And so are you."

I laugh when Caleb gives me an open mouth kiss.

"Just like his daddy," I say.

Weston pokes my side and I yelp.

"He better not walk while I'm gone," he says.

"He's not going to yet…at least I hope not. I'm not ready for that." I laugh. "No walking yet," I tell Caleb, bopping his nose. He blinks with each bop and grins.

"Nonono," he says. His head falls back on Weston's chest and his eyelids are heavy.

"Hey, little sleepyhead. Should I put you to bed?" Weston says in Caleb's ear.

Caleb's eyes drift closed and Weston chuckles.

"There's my answer," he says. "I'll be back."

"You don't have much longer. I'll take this in while you're putting him down."

He pokes out his lips and stands. "I was enjoying the picnic."

"There will be more," I promise.

Later, I'm in the bathroom, and he comes up behind me and puts his hands on my hips, kissing my neck.

"I'm going to miss you so much," he says against my skin.

He props his head on my shoulder and looks at me in the mirror. We've had a lot of sex in front of this mirror and it's like a Pavlovian response now when we're looking at each other in it.

"I'm going to miss you too," I tell him, leaning my head back when he palms my breasts. "You all packed and ready to go?"

"I've got a few minutes." He thrusts against my backside and kisses his way up to my ear.

My eyes close and when I open them, they look hooded as he tweaks my nipples.

"So beautiful," he whispers.

I'm in a tank top and leggings, and my hair is in a messy bun. I don't feel very beautiful at the moment, but he always seems to think I am.

"Do you feel like playing before I go?"

"Yes." I lift my hands behind me and grab his hair.

He stares at me for a second, and then he tugs my panties and leggings off and turns me around, lifting me onto the bathroom countertop. We have condoms all over the house now, tucked in couches and in every drawer for easy access.

He grabs one now from the top drawer and slides it on, always ready. He fingers me, grinning when he lifts the wet to his lips and licks them. And then he bends down and flicks his tongue over my clit until I'm squirming.

"Hurry up and get in me." I tug on his hair. "We don't have long."

"I want you to come first," he says.

"I want to come with you in me," I tell him.

"In a minute." He grins and goes back to sucking on me, and it takes less than a minute for me to be moaning his name.

When he stands up, he doesn't take the time he usually does to ease into me slowly. He buries himself in me, and I scream into his neck, nearly coming again right then. His hands squeeze my ass, tugging me to him in time with his thrusts. He starts hitting a spot inside that makes me dizzy and I clamp down hard on him, my insides clenching him. He rides through it and then when I feel another wave of my orgasm, he comes with a shout, tucking his head into my neck as he jerks into me and then finally stills.

He's sheepish when he looks up. "Was I too rough?"

"No, I loved it. Couldn't you tell?"

He grins. "It sure felt like you were loving it." He puts his hand on my cheek and kisses me, his tongue making my heart pound all over again. "I love you, Sadie."

My throat hitches. "I love you too," I whisper.

His eyes gleam. "God, I love hearing you say that." He kisses me again. My lips, my cheeks, back to my lips.

"I'll be home late Sunday night…well, more like early Monday morning. Warm our bed up for me, okay, beautiful? I want you naked in our bed when I get home. I'll let you sleep, but I'm gonna feel you up."

I laugh and roll my eyes.

He takes care of the condom and tucks himself back in his pants before washing his hands.

"You're gonna smell like sex," I tell him.

He wiggles his tongue at me. "I hope your taste lingers on my tongue all night."

My face flames and he kisses my cheek and puts his hands on my face.

"I'll FaceTime you when we get there and probably a dozen other times. Message or call me about anything, okay?" He kisses me again. "I don't want to leave you."

I kiss him and get off the counter, pulling my panties and leggings up.

"Go. Don't be late. I'll be here."

I put on my brave face and we walk out of the bathroom. He checks to see if Caleb is still sleeping and he is, so we walk downstairs and he grabs his bag.

"Why don't you move the rest of your things into my bedroom while I'm gone…our bedroom…"

"Awfully bossy." I roll my eyes and he growls.

"I mean it."

I stand on my tiptoes and kiss him one more time and watch out the window while he pulls away.

He doesn't seem concerned at all about what will happen while he's on the road, but I am.

Could I be one of those progressive women who's like, *as long as he comes home to me, he can have his flings while he's away*?

No. I could not.

This will be the true test.

CHAPTER THIRTY-THREE

WHAT WAS LOVE BEFORE?

WESTON

I slept some on the plane ride home, so I'm not quite as exhausted as I was when we finished playing. We beat the Jaguars 17 - 9, a little too close for comfort, as far as I'm concerned. But we got through our analyzing on the plane and have the day off tomorrow. Tuesday, we're off too, and I can't wait to get home to Sadie and Caleb.

Joey and Seth are on security detail when I get home, and they cheer me on when they open the gate.

"Great game tonight," Seth says.

"Thanks, man. Everything good around here?"

"It's been quiet," Joey says.

I nod. "I like quiet. Goodnight."

I get a couple of bottled waters when I'm in the kitchen and hurry upstairs, peeking into Caleb's room first. He's on his back, both arms spread out, and he looks so sweet, I can't take it. Did I even know what love was before him? Certainly not to this extent.

Sadie's sound asleep when I walk into the bedroom, and I smile when I see that she listened to at least part of what I asked. And her arms are spread out just like Caleb's were. Again, I think, what was love before her? This is a whole different kind of love that is all new to me. One of her nipples is showing and my mouth waters, but I quietly walk into the bathroom and leave my suitcase in my closet before going back to the sink and brushing my teeth. By the time I strip and get in bed next to her, the exhaustion has returned, but I put my hand on her stomach and my dick stirs to life. I don't want to wake her, but I want to taste her more than anything. It really is my favorite place to be, whether it's my tongue, my fingers, or my dick.

She surprises me by turning toward me and opening her eyes.

"Hey," she says.

"Hey." I brush her hair away from her face and kiss her.

She hitches her leg over my thigh and groans when she feels how hard I am. Her heat feels so good against me, I clutch her hips and rub her up and down over me. She gasps.

"I was dreaming about you," she says. "And when I woke up, you were here."

"What were you dreaming?" Up and down, slick against me.

"We were facing each other like this and you were inside me, your eyes never leaving mine."

"Is that what you'd like right now?"

"Mm-hmm," she says, her hips starting to swivel as she rubs against me.

"Use me," I whisper.

Her mouth parts and she rubs faster, her mouth dropping open and when she's coming, she grabs my fingers and presses them against her so I can feel the flutters. Her head falls back and she lets out a long, shuddering sigh.

"You weren't wearing a condom in my dream," she whispers.

"I wasn't?"

I've been nervous to bring this up with her for some reason, but it's worth a conversation. I'm glad she's the one to bring it up.

"Did it feel different?" I ask.

She giggles. "Well, in my dream, it was amazing. I woke up so ready for you."

"I've wondered so many times what it would be like to be inside you bare. I've never done that."

"You know I'm on the pill," she says.

"I know. I didn't know how you'd feel about ditching the condoms. We haven't talked about it, and I'm in no rush. I want you to be comfortable."

"I've never done it without one either," she says, leaning forward to kiss my chest. "I want to with you."

"Are you sure?" I ask.

"Yes," she says softly.

We start kissing, and I get lost in her as I always do. Her mouth is like a drug. It's calming and home, and it's a fire inside of me that never goes out.

I put the tip in and it's already a different experience. She was telling the truth, she's ready for me, and feeling her slick heat surrounding me is sensory overload.

"Oh," I shudder. "I feel everything."

"I love this." Her hand moves to my hip and then my ass as she starts to thrust faster than I'm going. "Faster," she says.

I go faster and moan.

She does too.

"I'm not going to last long," I tell her.

I slide out and thrust back in, faster and faster and faster. Her leg opens wider and I put it over my hip, going deeper. The second she starts coming, I let go and spill into her. It feels like it lasts forever but is over before I want it to be.

"That was…so good," she says breathlessly.

"Sorry about the mess." I make a face and she grins.

"Worth it," she says.

She gets up and goes to the bathroom and comes back a few minutes later. I take my turn in the bathroom and when I get back in bed, she turns into me, her head finding its place on my chest. We talked no less than ten times while I was gone, but I still feel like I missed so much.

"I missed you," I tell her. I probably said that at least ten times too, but every time was true.

"I missed you too. Caleb asked for you a lot too. I thought he might not think it was any different than you going to a long day of training, but he definitely knew this was different."

"I think you should come to the game next week. Fuck what anyone thinks."

She sighs and her hands continue tickling my chest. "I'm not ready yet."

I kiss the top of her head. "The second you are, you'll let me know?"

"Yes."

"Okay. I'll try to be patient. But just so you know, I'm ready to tell the whole world I'm in love with you."

She kisses my chest and lays her head back down, quiet.

We fall asleep that way.

CHAPTER THIRTY-FOUR

OFF DAYS

SADIE

The first time I second-guess my decision about keeping my relationship with Weston a secret is the following week when it's a home game and everyone's going but me. My family, his family, and even some of Sutton's family from Landmark Mountain will be there. I'd told Weston I wasn't going, but he got me a ticket anyway, in case I changed my mind.

I never knew how pricey the tickets were for the players. Before I knew Weston, I assumed there was a family section of seats that were free or that the suites were reserved for family and also free. So naive. Those excellent seats and beautiful suites are a fortune. Weston's making more than enough to pay for the tickets, but a lot of the players don't make anything close to that, and I feel bad for all those wives and girlfriends who don't get to go to the games.

"Just come, Sadie. I don't give a fuck what everyone thinks about us."

He's leaning against the bathroom counter watching me comb my hair after our shower. He's already dressed, about to leave for the team's hotel the day before the game. Since I've moved all my things into his bedroom and bathroom, I have to say, I haven't minded sharing space with him one bit.

"Give my ticket to someone who needs it. What about that one wife I met at practices this summer? I think she was married to that defensive lineman who didn't get to play last year. I can't remember their names. Scott? Trisha Scott? Give it to her."

His jaw tightens and I hate the disappointment I see in his eyes. I turn and put my hands on his waist, leaning up to kiss him.

"Caleb and I will be watching every second, I promise." I kiss him between words. "You're gonna kill it out there."

He tugs me closer and deepens our kiss, growling at the end. "I don't want to give your ticket away in case you change your mind."

"Joan's right. It's too soon."

"I disagree."

Our foreheads touch and he sighs.

"I love you," I whisper.

His eyes soften and he kisses me again, melding my body against his and leaving me breathless when he pulls away. "I love you, beautiful. You're not changing your mind, are you."

I shake my head, and he rubs my cheek with his hand one more time before he steps back.

"You better answer my call before I go on the field," he says from the doorway. "You're my good luck charm now."

"I always answer your calls." I narrow my eyes and put my hands on his waist, pushing him out of the bathroom. "And you played just fine before you ever met me."

"You're my pre-game ritual now," he says with puppy-dog eyes.

I groan. "Go. You have so many pre-game rituals I don't know how you make it onto the field."

When he first told me all the things he does before a game, I didn't believe him at first, and then I laughed my head off.

He wears the same pair of—clean, thankfully— socks every game. This is the pre-game ritual I'm most concerned about because what happens when those socks disintegrate? He has an order of how he puts on his clothing. He kisses a picture of his family and now one of Caleb and me that he keeps in his locker. When he closes his locker, he taps the ceiling above three times. He calls me after this, and we talk for maybe two minutes. When he hangs up, the team huddles together and says a prayer and a team chant. As they walk down the tunnel, he taps the side of the wall once when he enters and one more time before he's out.

Once he's on the field, he's all focus.

"I'll be at away games the next two weeks," he says when we get downstairs. "It'll be three weeks before I have another home game. Think about that one at least, okay? We'll be into mid-October by then."

He's persistent, I'll give him that.

I kiss him instead of answering. I don't plan on going to

any games this season, but he doesn't want to hear that. It's the closest we've come to arguing.

"Tell Caleb I love him when he wakes up," he says.

"I will."

"I'll see you tomorrow night," he says.

I smile. "Give 'em hell, Shaw."

"You know I will, Chapman." He grins and goes out the door.

I start a load of laundry and sit down and read Sasha's journal. I'm up to her twenty-first birthday now and I've been curious to see what she'd say about it. We got a hotel with two of her friends in Denver and went to a club where we drank too much and danced until we closed the place down. She ended up going home with a guy despite her friends and me trying to tell her that was a bad idea. She came home the next afternoon, giddy about her night out, and I was so mad at her about all of it—the way she bailed on us, going home with a stranger, and not letting me know if she was okay—I didn't speak to her for at least a day after that.

It's official! I'm twenty-one! Last night was amazing. Sadie splurged on a hotel for us. Jessie and Claire were there too, and we went to this club that was so fun. No more fake IDs, baby! Free drinks all night. Honestly, I think Sade's been saving for my birthday for at least a year. She's been cheap all year, never wanting to go out, but she made up for it last night. Lol

I met this guy. Dillon. So hot. He danced with me for a long time, and when he said he lived in Hilltop and asked me to go home with him, I didn't hesitate. I've always wanted to see what the houses are like there, and his place was NICE. The sex was sub-par, but I'd be willing to overlook it to live in that house. We had sex twice and slept really late. I thought we'd hang out a little—I didn't even have time to explore his whole house! But the ass called an Uber for me without even feeding me lunch. I was pissed.

And now Sadie's pissed at me. I honestly don't know why she's so mad at me. It's not like I bailed on everyone the whole night. We danced until two this morning. And it's not like she'd gotten us a room in the Four Seasons or something. The room was nice, but not that *nice. And last but not least, it was my fucking birthday! I thought the whole point of a birthday was to do what I wanted, and that's what I did.*

Ugh. Anyway, I'm gonna let her pout it out. I love her more than anyone on earth, but she's so self-righteous sometimes.

The page blurs together after I've stopped reading. The hurt stings like it's happening for the first time. I thought I'd worked through my anger about that weekend with her a long time ago, but it blooms fresh. My heart thuds in my chest and I fling the journal across the couch. Why would I be angrier now than I was when it happened? Makes no sense.

Through this grieving process, I thought I'd managed to bypass the anger stage, but it smacks me across the face now. I shake out my clenched hands when I hear Caleb on the monitor and walk to his bedroom, the whole time trying to shut off the noise in my brain.

Why did I put up with her selfishness?

Talk about the ultimate gaslighting. She was so good at it and I always just put up with it.

But what I keep coming back to is: Was she right? *Am I self-righteous?*

I hug Caleb and change his diaper, trying to focus on him.

We go downstairs and I pull out leftovers and heat them up. I feed him little bites at a time while I pick at the food too and then fix his bottle. He clangs it on the high chair and then slugs it back, gulping it fast. He's breathless when he pulls it away.

"Slow down there, little guy."

Low on diapers and needing some fresh air, we run to the store, but while we're out, I can't wait to get back to the house.

Weston's texted a few times and then it's quiet when he's in the meeting they have the night before a game. He Face-Timed us after we'd eaten and then again after I put Caleb to bed. I'm leaning against the headboard when I answer and he frowns when he sees me.

"Why aren't you in our bed?"

"I don't know. I'll probably end up back in there, but I was just missing you too much in that room. It feels weird when you're not here. The last time you were gone, I was so exhausted, I crashed late, but today's been a chill day and I'm awake, so I just went in there and—" I make a face.

"You don't want to watch a movie or anything?"

"The house feels extra big. And I don't want to be all the way down there when Caleb's up here."

He nods. We've been watching movies in the living room more often for that very reason. He looks sad and I feel bad that I said all of this.

"I wish you'd asked your parents to stay over," he says.

He mentioned that this morning and I blew it off because I thought I'd be okay.

"Don't worry. I'm fine. It'll just take some getting used to, that's all."

"I don't want you to get used to it there without me," he says. He makes a face. "Ignore me. That's super selfish of me to say. What can we do to make it easier when I'm not there? Is it too late for your mom to come over?"

"Yeah, I think so. And I'll have to get used to it at some point. I think the problem with tonight was that I ran to the store to get diapers and came back after it was dark, and then everything felt weird." I laugh. "I didn't know I was afraid of the dark, but apparently I am a little bit. I'll be running my errands during the day from now on."

"Don't forget you can order anything you need, and one of the guards will bring it to the house, or Amy would be happy to pick things up and bring them over too. She offers to do it all the time."

"No, it's fine. I don't want to bother them."

"Chapman, they're happy to do it, I swear."

I still can't believe I'm living in a house this luxurious, so remembering that Weston has a small staff on salary that could help me is not something I ever consider. It feels wrong to ask them for anything. I'm not Weston. It's not my house. They don't work for me.

"You're my family now, Sadie."

I glance at him, surprised and feeling all airy inside with his words.

"Am I yours?" he whispers.

I lick my lips and don't hesitate. "Yes, you are."

He takes a deep breath and smiles, but he still looks worried.

"You're not unsure of my feelings for you, right?" I ask. "They're stronger than ever."

His eyes soften and his lips quirk up. "I know this career is a lot to ask of you. I love what I do, but there are certain aspects of it that are so hard. We've had a lot of obstacles in our way from the very beginning. I don't want my job to come between us too."

"It doesn't have to," I tell him.

"We haven't left this house together since Joan's call. You don't want to be seen publicly with me for the next five months. It already is."

"If we can get through the next five months, I feel like we're in this for the long haul."

"I love you, Sadie. I'm already in this for the long haul. That's where I'm not sure you're hearing me or if you're on the same page as I am."

"I'm in for the long haul too." My eyes fill with tears and I groan. "This is not the kind of conversation you need to be having the night before a game. You should go to bed, sleep, and focus on the game."

"I'll stay on here all night long if that's what you need."

"I'm okay. *We're* okay. I love you. I'm getting sleepy and I'm gonna go get in your bed."

"Our bed," he whispers.

I smile. "Our bed."

"Call me anytime, okay? And if you're feeling nervous, one of the guards can come to the house and stay."

"I'm feeling much better now."

We hang up and I move into the other room and cry when I get into our bed. The day suddenly feels like it's been endless; I've been feeling off for most of it.

Everything will be better tomorrow

CHAPTER THIRTY-FIVE

THE BIRD

WESTON

Joan calls the day after our home game. I'm chatting with Blake and Ed at the gate after a long workout and lift my hand in apology.

"I've gotta take this, sorry."

They wave and go back to talking about yesterday's game. We beat the Bears 41 - 10, and it felt great.

"Hello?"

"Have you seen the magazines?" She gets right to it.

"Uh, no. What magazines?"

"You name it, Sadie's in them."

"What? Why? She's hardly even leaving the house."

"Well, apparently she and Caleb were out buying diapers the other night, and a few days before that, they were at lunch with her parents. It's caused a lot of commotion that she wasn't at your game yesterday and her parents were."

"You said it was best for her not to go, and she's taking your word for it, believe me."

"I still believe that's for the best. Unless you want to do another statement of some sort, but I feel like that could backfire on you. Bottom line, I don't want this interfering with your game."

"It's not. I want her at my games, but she's convinced you're right about that."

"Can I have a stylist send her some clothes that she can wear when she goes out? Send her measurements and we'll overnight it."

"Are you serious right now?"

"Well, yes, that athletic wear she wore on Saturday looked like it could fit three people. It was horrendous."

"Joan, come on. Sadie hasn't looked horrendous a day in her life. She's fucking stunning." I pause, my head dropping. "*Shit.* She and Caleb are out right now with her mom while I worked out. I need to make sure she doesn't see those magazines."

"If she goes anywhere that has periodicals, she will see them," Joan says primly.

"Fuck."

"Think about what I said about a stylist," she says.

I growl and hang up.

I've never growled at Joan and I half expect her to call me back and chew me out, but she doesn't.

I call Sadie and it goes to voicemail. I'm too agitated to leave her a message, so I try again, and hang up a second time when she doesn't answer.

I pace around the living room for an hour and finally go take a shower when I still haven't heard from her. When I get out, I put on gym shorts and a tee and think I might hear something downstairs. I jog down there and Sadie and Caleb are in the kitchen…next to the kitchen table covered with a slew of magazines. Fuck.

I look at Sadie tentatively and her eyes are red-rimmed, but her face is dry and her shoulders are squared.

"Hey, beautiful," I say, moving toward her and lean in to kiss her. It's what I would say to her any other day, but today she looks at me suspiciously.

It's only then that I realize her mom is also in the room. I drop my hands from Sadie's waist, unsure of what to do. "Hey, Pam."

She smiles at me. "Hi, Weston. Sadie told me about the two of you a few days ago. I'm happy for you guys."

I sag in relief and put my hands back on Sadie, grinning. I told my family about us right away, but Sadie didn't, and it was starting to concern me a little bit that she hadn't.

"Haven't you heard? I'm not beautiful." Sadie kisses me back and picks up a gossip magazine. She's on the cover, and I've honestly never seen the face she's making on the cover. It's the worst angle, and she looks like she's about to say something but is going to be sick first.

I study it.

"I've never seen you look like that, not one time, and I live with you."

"Well, I don't believe you because look…" She holds up five other magazines. "I look equally terrible in all of them."

"I swear, you don't," I tell her. I lower my eyes to hers

and put my hands on her cheeks. "Every day I'm in awe of how beautiful you are. I love every way you look, whether you're just waking up, or you're all dressed up, or Caleb has just spit up on you." I lower my voice, "Or you're in my jersey. But I swear to you, I've never seen you making those faces."

"I told her the same thing," Pam says. "Some of those magazines are just trying to make people look bad…"

"I've been avoiding looking at anything online, but we drove into Denver to go to Whole Foods and Target, and I was everywhere I looked, *at both places*. And they're saying such mean things." Her cheeks are splotchy as she gets angrier. "I've hardly been anywhere in weeks, months really, but both times I was out the past week, they've captured it. And wouldn't you know, both times I've looked like a gross blob." Her eyes fill with tears. "At least *Us Weekly* has a shot of me at that one game, so I look better there, but then they also show this awful one…like a before and after downgrade. And then I went online on the way home, and the things they're saying on there are so much worse. I can see why they'd think I'm a gold digger when I'm out looking like that. I *need* some money to help that mess." She waves her hand at the mound of magazines and her mom giggles.

"You'd never be a gold digger. They don't know how much you love a good sale," Pam says.

"Yeah, there's a whole other group of people who are mad that I'm not wearing designer clothes. I never even shopped at Whole Foods until I met your sorry ass, and I went today to get something for *you*," Sadie says, glaring up at me. "I'm sure there will be a bunch of pictures of that too." She points at her outfit and then lifts both hands up, giving the magazines the bird.

I press my lips together, trying to hold back my laugh, but

it bursts out. Her eyes narrow, but there's a hint of a grin on her face.

"I'm sorry this is so stupid," I tell her. "And I'm glad your mom was with you today. I actually think it'd be best if you'd have someone with you every time you go out, if I'm not with you."

"Is there something more that you're not telling me?" she asks. "You've never said you wanted someone with me when I go out. Has Joan said something else?"

I look down and she reaches up and smooths the crease between my brows.

"People can be so hateful." I take her hand, weaving our fingers together. "I hate it, but it seems like it comes with any high-profile job. We'll get through this. It'll all die down. Joan called right before you came home, so I'd just heard there were some periodicals, as Joan put it, featuring you."

She snorts when I say *periodicals*.

"What did she say? Tell me everything." She looks at me expectantly.

I hesitate and she pins me with her stare.

"Tell me."

"She still thinks we're doing the right things…unless we did some kind of a statement, but she said that could backfire on me. And that she doesn't want any of this interfering with my playing, which I assured her it won't."

She nods. "What else?"

"That was…it."

"No, what did she say about me being in the periodicals?"

"Just that you were in a lot of them…"

"And?"

I raise my head to the ceiling and groan. "She offered to hire a stylist for you and she'd overnight the clothes. But Joan is a snob and I wouldn't pay any attention to that. I like the way you dress."

She holds up the magazine with the baggy sweat suit. "Gross. Blob."

"You wear comfy clothes sometimes. Everyone does." I point at myself and what I'm wearing. "If you want to go shopping, you should buy things you like…unless…do you *want* a stylist?" I frown, trying to get a read on her mood.

"I don't really trust my sense of fashion, but the press would really have a heyday with that if I suddenly turn up everywhere looking all done up."

My phone buzzes and I check it. Felicity.

"It's my sister. *Hey*—she'd love to go shopping with you."

She's shaking her head, but I grin and answer the call.

"Hello?"

"Hey. You guys okay over there?" Felicity says.

"You saw the magazines."

Sadie makes a face.

"Yeah. I saw them at Cecil's this afternoon and was going to call then, but my phone has been going crazy with all of my sisters-in law calling to check on Sadie. They really loved her and we all want you guys to come back soon."

"That's sweet. Maybe we can on one of my Mondays off." I put my hand over the receiver and whisper to Sadie, "She's checking on you and the female Landmark crew have been calling her to see how you're doing too."

"Aw," she says softly.

"Tell her she does not look like that," Felicity's saying when I start listening again.

"I've told her. I'm not sure she believes me yet."

Sadie's eyes widen.

"Can I put you on speakerphone?" I say, laughing. "Here, tell her."

Felicity laughs and says it again, "You do not look like that." And then softer, she whispers, "Those motherfuckers are messing with the wrong family."

"Whoa, sis," I laugh. "Better hope Owen doesn't hear that potty mouth."

"He's almost got me trained, but not quite," she says, laughing. "Seriously, Sadie, I'm sorry they're going after you so hard. It's ridiculous."

"Thanks. I've laughed and cried and spewed curses about it. It's just weird. I'm used to minding my own business and staying under the radar."

"Yeah, no one should have to get used to this kind of garbage," she says. "If you need to get away for a few days… or weeks, come anytime."

"I might take you up on a visit sometime," Sadie says. "And…the next time you're visiting your parents or coming to a game, if it's convenient…would you ever be interested in going shopping and helping me pick out cuter clothes?"

"Hell, yeah," Felicity says. "Dangit, hi, Owen. Yep, go ahead and stick it in the jar for me. You're bleeding me dry, Ace." She laughs. "I'd love to go shopping with you. I don't think you need me to pick out cute clothes, but it'd be fun to hang out."

"No, I definitely need you," Sadie says.

"You know who would be better at it than me and would love to come along too? Scarlett and Ruby. My clothes are all right and Marlow and Sofie always look great too, but Scarlett and Ruby have that eye for fashion. I swear, I can look at something and not see the potential at all, and they'll look at it and pair it with another piece that makes it *amazing*."

"I do not have that gift," Sadie says.

"I've only seen you look fabulous," Felicity says.

"Except for the sweat suit on most of the covers right now…" Sadie laughs and Felicity joins in.

"Except for that," she says.

"I was having cramps. I wanted something loose."

"See? I get that. Women everywhere get that. One sec, I'm just gonna look at the calendar real quick. Weston's leaving Saturday, right? I don't know what time he's leaving, so it might depend on that whether you want to go Saturday or Sunday. But if I can get the girls together this fast, what if we come pick you up Saturday and go to Boulder? Maybe there'd be fewer photographers there, and there are cute shops, great food. Ooo, we could spend the night Saturday and then shop all day Sunday…what do you think?"

"That sounds so fun. I don't want anyone to feel like they have to go...only if—"

"Are you kidding? They'll all want to go. We need a girls' trip desperately and I need my Caleb fix."

"Well, that would be…amazing." Sadie looks at me with wide eyes and I smile, squeezing her hand.

"I'll call or text later tonight once I've heard back from everyone, okay?"

"Okay. Thank you." She clears her throat and I think she might cry. "This is really great of you, Felicity."

"Sadie, I can't wait to spend time with you," she says.

"Love you, sis. Thanks for checking on my girl," I add.

"*My girl*, heehee, I love the sound of that," Felicity says. "Talk later. Bye."

When we hang up, I put my arms around Sadie and hug her. She melts into me, and we stay like that for a long time.

"Does this mean you'll come to a game?"

She smacks my arm, but it got a laugh out of her.

"I may as well, since they're gonna be like this," she says eventually, but I don't think she's convinced.

CHAPTER THIRTY-SIX

CONFIRMATION

SADIE

I don't know if I'm a glutton for punishment or what, but when Weston goes to practice a few days later, I pull out the journal again. My anger has dwindled, as it always did with Sasha, and when I read the passage following the birthday, I'm reminded why.

. . .

Sadie's not mad at me anymore. THANK GOD. I hate it when I disappoint her. But even when I do, she loves me no matter what. We're so different from one another, but she's the one person I trust more than anyone. I know she'll never let me down. I'll let her down plenty, but she will always have my back.

I haven't decided if I'll tell her about the party I'm going to on Friday night. Claire said she heard that after the Nuggets games, the players go to this one bar downtown, and I think we're gonna go see if that's true. Sadie would try to talk me out of it, or she'd want to go to look out for me, and that would be fine except...Sadie doesn't realize how hot she is. All those basketball players would take one look at her and those long legs and forget about me. Lol I can't let that happen!

Anyway, Claire's loaning me a dress and I'll get ready over there. I'll report back if I land a sexy player.

I'm almost scared to keep reading, but I read enough to know that she does indeed land a sexy player and she probably never told me about this one because they had sex in the men's bathroom at the club. I put my head in my hands, the sister worry I carried with me from as early as I can remember stirred back up. Part of me was always in awe of her impulsiveness, while it also made me a nervous wreck.

I think about how she changed when Caleb was born. It surprised both of us that she didn't mind being pregnant, and by the time he came, she'd settled some. Well, I thought she had. I've thought a lot about my mom saying Sasha would drop Caleb off with her all the time when I wasn't around to help, and I wonder for the hundredth time since she's been gone, how well I really knew my sister. Or maybe more accurately, I did know her, but I just always made excuses for her.

I close the journal and tuck it away. That's enough for today.

On Saturday morning, Weston and I have a lazy morning in bed and a big breakfast once Caleb's awake. We go to his parents' house for lunch, taking separate cars, and I kiss him goodbye before I walk out of their house. He still comes outside to put Caleb in the car, and when he leans in to kiss me again, I put my hand on his chest, looking around.

"Seriously?" He laughs.

"I didn't know photographers were around the other times. What if they're lurking in the bushes?"

"I don't think they are," he says, smirking. "The security is great in this neighborhood. I think we'd be safe to kiss."

"You would," I snort. "We're not kissing in public until I come back cuted up…and maybe not then." I point at him and get in the car.

He leans down, his muscled arms distracting me when he leans them against the roof of my car. "If you get any cuter, we won't be coming up for air."

"We barely do now," I whisper and he laughs. "I'll miss you, but I might need a night to recover from last night."

He smirks, his eyes heated. "I'm going to be replaying last night in my head for a long time to come."

I grin. "Me too."

"Are you sure I can't kiss you out here?"

"I'm sure. But I'll make it up to you when you get back."

"I'm counting on that. Love you, Chapman."

"I love you, Shaw."

He looks back at Caleb in his car seat and grins, closing my door. I watch from the rearview mirror as he nuzzles Caleb's neck until they're both laughing.

He meets my eyes in the mirror. "Have fun. Let me know how you're doing. I don't want to bug you when you're with the girls, but call me anytime."

I nod. "Have a good trip. Stay safe."

"I will."

I miss him the second I drive away, but the excitement over my weekend with the girls helps. I drive back to the house and make sure Caleb and I have everything we'll need for our overnight. Ed lets me know when Felicity pulls up to the gate, and everyone piles out of the SUV. After hugs all around, they go to the bathroom and meet back in the kitchen to refill their water bottles.

Felicity takes Caleb from me and covers his face with kisses until he's laughing. He loves her so much.

I lift the bags of snacks from the island. "Okay, how is this? I've got Reese's popcorn, M&M'S in plain, peanut, and peanut butter, Snickers, Heath, and Butterfinger…sour gummies, Cheez-Its, barbeque corn nuts, jalapeno kettle chips, sea salt kettle chips…" I look again to make sure I'm not forgetting anything. "There's probably more in my hidden stash if you want to take a look for anything else. I keep it in the laundry room cabinet behind a few things." When they all stare at me, I add, "I try not to keep all this junk around in plain sight when Weston's on a more regimented diet. He spots all the things on the high shelves, but rarely notices anything down low." I laugh nervously.

"Can we keep her?" Marlow says and everyone laughs.

"I already knew I loved you," Scarlett says, "but that list of snacks just solidified it."

"Same!" Ruby says.

"I didn't even know Reese's popcorn existed, so you had me right from the start," Sofie says.

I laugh and Felicity puts her arm around my shoulder and leans her head against mine.

"This is gonna be the best weekend. I don't think we need to add anything to the stash. You thought of everything," she says.

"It's the very least I can do. You guys put this trip together so fast, and I could not be more grateful. Besides sounding like the exact kind of fun I need, hanging out with all of you, you're helping me out with the whole wardrobe thing." I make a face, and they laugh and Ruby shakes her head.

"Your clothes are fine. It's impossible to not be caught at a bad angle occasionally, but I've got some tips I'll be sharing to avoid that," she says, grinning.

"Should we get on the road?" Felicity says. "Oh, wait." She pauses and pulls a black American Express out of her purse, waving it in the air. "Weston says this weekend is his treat, and I have specific instructions that *you* are not to pay for a thing." She grins, pointing at me.

Everyone cheers and I stare at her in shock. I start to shake my head and she mimics me.

"Nope, there's no getting out of it." She laughs.

"That's a good man right there," Scarlett yells. "Let's get this party started."

"Woohoo," I say weakly, and Caleb tries to say it afterward, which makes everyone so happy that he keeps repeating it. I record him saying it and send it to Weston, and when we're in the SUV on our way to Boulder, he texts back.

WESTON

He did not just say woohoo perfectly!

There's no telling what he'll be saying after a weekend with six women.

WESTON

<meme of Steve Carell shouting, NOOOO! GOD! No, God, please no!>

You know you wish you were here too.

WESTON

You're so right about that, Chapman. I'd much rather be with you. I'm surrounded by a bunch of grumpy-ass dudes who are pouting because there's no caffeine on this flight.

Ooo, harsh.

Hey. I can't believe you sent your fancy card with Felicity.

WESTON

You deserve this and so much more.

My eyes gloss over and I stare at the screen.

Thank you. You didn't have to do this, but it's really sweet.

WESTON

I only wish I was there seeing you try everything on like they do in all those movies my sisters made me watch growing up.

I bite my lip to keep from laughing, imagining teenage Weston enduring rom-coms.

Caleb gets a short nap in while we drive to Boulder and

wakes up as we're checking out our Airbnb. It's a gorgeous house, and there's even a full-size crib for Caleb. The place is massive and each room is stunning. The kitchen and living room are perfect for a group, and once we've all put our things away and met back in the kitchen, Scarlett pulls out a page that she's printed out with places for us to go.

"Sofie and I have been to Boulder the most, but Ruby had heard of great places too, so we put this list together. Should we start with what's closest and see how many shops we can hit before they close?" She points at the two at the top. "These two are closed tomorrow, so we should definitely hit those today."

Everyone looks at me, and I hold up both thumbs.

"I am just along for the ride," I say, laughing.

We get back in the SUV and I try a couple of things on at the first place, but don't love anything, so we move on to the next shop. I find so much there that I have a hard time choosing. While I try things on, Caleb is being passed around to everyone and in his element. Felicity insists that I step out of the dressing room to show off each new outfit.

"My brother is going to die when he sees you in that," she whispers after the salesperson walks away. "Just so you know, I have neither confirmed nor denied about you and Weston with them." She tilts her head back to the girls. "I thought I'd leave that to you, but believe me, they *all* have plenty of thoughts about it." She laughs and I do too, my cheeks flaming.

"Let's see this one," Ruby calls. "Oh, you have to get that. All of it."

I nod. "I think so too." The jeans fit perfectly and the light sweater is the perfect amount of sexy without being too revealing.

There's a dress that I almost don't try on, but they insist

on it, and I can't resist it. It's cute in the front, but the back amps up the look with the low V and the material beneath that ties into a big bow.

"I wouldn't have thought I like this, but I love it," I say.

I get a few cute blouses from there too, and then we hit one more shop. This place has the best loungewear I've ever seen. The sweats and sweatshirts have cute detailing and I get comfortable sizes that still aren't over-the-top baggy.

"One more thing for you to try," Scarlett says, tossing some leggings and tanks my way. "Your butt will thank you for wearing those." She laughs when she sees my expression. "Trust me."

I try them on and when I turn, I gasp. "Holy hell," I say, looking at my backside in the mirror.

"Let's see!" Felicity says.

I step out and my cheeks are red, but I turn around and they clap. I face them quickly, laughing, my hands reaching up to cool my face.

"I want them in every color," I say.

They crack up at that, and I think we all leave the place with at least three pairs of the peach-lift leggings.

We go out to dinner and never struggle for things to talk about. When we get back to the house, Scarlett's the one who brings up Weston and me first.

"So, am I right to have picked up on a vibe between the two of you?" she asks, lifting an eyebrow.

"You're not wrong," I say, grinning. "His agent thinks we should keep quiet about it because of my sister, and I agree with her. Weston doesn't love it, but I don't know…me being on those covers might convince him she's right."

"I get that it's a complicated situation, but no one knows the details like you do," Marlow says. "You're not doing anything wrong, and it's no one else's business anyway."

"Those articles were harsh," Sofie says, shooting me an apologetic expression. "I'd probably be doing the same thing as you to avoid more of that..."

"But they're not openly dating and it still happened," Felicity says. "I say you live your life openly and let the chips fall where they may."

"That's easy for us to say, but I agree," Ruby says. "Hopefully, it'll die down soon. I hate the idea of you and Weston avoiding being out together. This is such an incredible time when you're first falling for each other." She covers her mouth. "That is what's happening, right?"

"My brother is so gone over her," Felicity says, grinning at me. "And I could not be happier about it."

"And judging by that spark in your eyes every time you talk about him, I think it's safe to say you feel the same," Marlow says.

I nod and they all chatter excitedly about it for the next half hour. Felicity and Ruby make cocktails, while I put Caleb to bed. We stay up talking until late, and before we go to bed, I thank them again for this trip.

"I haven't laughed like this since...my sister. Maybe ever, honestly," I add. "You're all incredible and have made me feel so special."

"You're one of us now," Felicity says. "And we're here for you, Sadie. This whole paparazzi thing feels huge, but the important thing is you and Weston. Don't let them, or Weston's agent, or anything else detract from what's happening with the two of you."

I nod, thinking about what she's saying and wishing I could just take the leap.

CHAPTER THIRTY-SEVEN

THE FINE MERITS

WESTON

On the plane ride home, we're exhausted after our win against the Jets. 23 - 20, entirely too close for me, but we won. Penn is next to me, and his eyes narrow as he lifts his head from the back of the seat.

"We haven't talked about the photos," he says, as quiet as he can.

I groan and hold up my cell phone so he'll text instead of

talking. He starts typing away and a message from our group chat with the guys comes up.

PENN

We haven't talked about the photos of Sadie everywhere, but seriously, what the fuck? She's hot as fuck and those pictures make her look like…I can't even say. It'd be too mean and it's not true.

HENLEY

I'm sorry. I've been meaning to bring that up. I've been preoccupied with some things going on at home with Cassidy. Pissed me off so bad when I saw them. I hope Sadie's okay.

RHODES

What pictures? I have no idea what you guys are talking about. Not nudes, right?

BOWIE

Of course, they're not nudes. That's not Sadie.

RHODES

Hey, even the most appropriate women are capable of sending a nude every now and again. We don't judge.

BOWIE

I'm not judging. I'm just saying that's not Sadie.

No, it wasn't nudes. She's been on multiple covers and in various magazines not looking her best.

PENN

I wouldn't have even recognized her if it hadn't had your name in big letters next to her. You can tell her I said that.

I'm bummed because it just makes her less likely to come to a game now…or to go anywhere in public with me, for that matter. Joan doesn't think the press is good for us, and Sadie is taking it as gospel. It's okay for now, but thinking about her holing up at home for the next five months is just sad.

RHODES

Yeah, if anything, she needs to strut her shit around everywhere, looking sexy as hell.

HENLEY

Tell her we've got her back.

I will. Thanks, guys. Is everything okay with Cassidy?

HENLEY

She's having trouble at school, and she doesn't want me to get involved, but if it doesn't get better, I'm going to have to.

BOWIE

Hate that.

RHODES

I hate school, period.

PENN

Hey, so I saw Sam this week, and he was quiet. That's not like him. I mean, he doesn't always talk about things I'm comfortable talking about, but he's always talking. He was NOT that way this week, and when I tried to ask what was up, he said he didn't want to talk about it. What am I supposed to do with that?

HENLEY

Are you able to call and check on him?

PENN

He doesn't have a phone and we do all our scheduling through the program. I guess I could ask if they'd give me the number to his foster home.

BOWIE

You could ask if anyone's heard anything about him. Maybe the people from the program have talked with his social worker or something. They probably wouldn't tell you anything though.

It's quiet as I think about it. I assume everyone else is too.

RHODES

Can you set up appointments to see him?

PENN

I've never done that. I've just shown up when it's set up for us. I know he'd like to meet more than once a week though.

RHODES

You could try that. And ask if you could get him a phone so he could connect with you if he wanted.

HENLEY

Sometimes you have to ask specific questions for kids to start talking. And sometimes that doesn't work either, and they just have to come to you when they're ready.

PENN

I don't know why I ever thought I could help the kid. I obviously don't know what I'm doing.

HENLEY

Just be there for him, Penn. You're doing more for him than you think you are. But for the record, I still feel like I don't know what I'm doing most of the time with my kids.

RHODES

Same.

BOWIE

Yes.

I'm glad it's not just me.

When I climb into bed a few hours later, Sadie is sound asleep. My hands roam down her side and pause when I feel the soft lace. When I reach her ass, I feel her bare cheeks beneath the lace, and I inhale, trying to rein myself in. I know she was exhausted from her trip with the girls, but it sounded like she had a great time. Instead of waking her up, I pull her back against my chest and rest my hand around her tit. I ignore the way my dick tries to jump its way into her and force myself to think quiet thoughts. It eventually works and I fall asleep.

I'm in for the most amazing surprise when I wake up the next morning and she's standing over me in a blue lacy thing that matches her eyes. The swell of her breasts between the plunging neckline makes my mouth water and I press my thumbs to my eyes, thinking I might be dreaming.

"Am I awake?" I ask.

She giggles. "I was just checking to see if you were."

"The way you look right now makes me…speechless."

Her smile grows. "Seems like you're talking just fine to me. It's a teddy. You like?"

"I like you in whatever you wear, Chapman, but yes, I really like this."

"Scarlett made it for me, and you know I don't normally wear stuff like this, but I kinda like it." She turns around and flashes her backside, looking at me over her shoulder.

"Oh, the view is outstanding on either side," I tell her.

I reach out to squeeze her perfect heart-shaped ass, and she sighs when my hands make contact with her.

"I missed you," she says.

"Not as much as I missed you. You know what I like best?"

She turns and I tug her over until she's straddling me. "What?"

I undo the ribbons at the shoulder and grin when her breasts are bared. "When you're *out* of whatever you're wearing…"

We spend a considerable amount of time in bed and in the shower, going over the fine merits of her not wearing anything.

I'm in the living room later, playing with Caleb when she walks by, and I do a double take. I reach out and grab her waist, pulling her toward me and turning her around so I can get another look. She laughs when I curse under my breath.

"You didn't tell me you were going away to buy things like this," I say reverently. "I'm already in a constant tortured state around you. That will be the case whether you're in the baggiest sweats known to man, which are also fine by me, or these…what are these amazing things called?"

"Leggings," she says, cracking up.

"These are not just any leggings. They are the goddesses of leggings. They are one of the next best things to you being naked. They are—"

She skirts away from me when I start to feel her up. "Ahem. Little eyes are present."

"You are feeling very sleepy," I coo to Caleb.

She laughs. "Don't wish away his awake time!"

"I'm not. I just want him to rest his eyes for a minute while I do very naughty things to you."

She ducks out of my reach again and I sigh when she walks into the kitchen.

"I think she enjoys torturing me," I tell Caleb.

CHAPTER THIRTY-EIGHT

THE TRUTH

SADIE

My favorite days of the week have become Mondays and Tuesdays because that's when I see Weston the most now. And on Wednesdays, he goes back to work and the long days, so it's usually a little bit of a letdown when Caleb and I get up and Weston is already gone.

After such a fun weekend with Felicity and the girls, and then a fun couple of days with Weston and Caleb, I'm restless when the mid-week hits. I wash all my new things and hang them up, catch up on all the laundry, and when I've done all the chores that need to be done and Caleb is sleeping, I pull out Sadie's journal.

I start reading and then check the outside of the journal and go back to the entry. It looks the same on the outside as the last one I read, but it's more recent. I keep reading.

Claire and Jessie get mad if they don't meet a guy when we go out and I still go home with someone, so I've started to go out without them. It's become a thing I enjoy doing by myself. Sadie's not into one-night stands, and I've realized it's more exciting anyway when I go out by myself and find someone. I love the thrill of it. The slight danger. The freedom in knowing I won't ever see that person again. Everything about it gets me off. It's a little something I keep to myself because I know I'd be judged for it. Guys do it all the time and it's accepted. Why should women always be held to a different standard?

I've done my homework and learned about a bar the Mustangs frequent often, and that will be where I go next. Maybe in a month or two. I've been working up my nerve to build up to this one. I want Weston Shaw. He's one of the ultimate unattainables, as I like to call them. The men who have reached an insane level of success and could have anyone. The other athletes I've had sex with haven't been in Weston Shaw's league. And most of them are older than Weston. He's only a few years older than I am.

If I play it right, I can use that to my advantage.

I exhale and close the book, holding my finger in place and torn about whether I can keep going.

I don't like this, but I can't stop.

And when I turn the page, my heart pounds faster when I realize it's the entry I've been dreading.

I haven't written in a while. I got sick for a few weeks. Feels like I've been on antibiotics forever…I'm still on them actually, but I'm feeling much better. The doctor just wants me on them for another couple of days, more as an extra precautionary measure than a necessity.

I am DYING TO GET OUT OF THE HOUSE. My parents have been at our apartment a ton, and Sadie has been hovering over me nonstop. I can't wait to go out this week after the Mustangs game. I hope Weston will be there. I went once last month and he wasn't, so we'll see. The timing, if he is there, will be perfect because I'm so desperate to have a night out, I don't think I'll even have a problem with nerves at all.

Maybe by the next time I write, I will have had an amazing night with THE Weston Shaw. The next one on the list is Zac Ledger, but he's married, so I'll have to catch him when he's playing in Denver, away from his wife. Weston will be the perfect practice.

I put my head in my hands, mortified that my sister would even *consider* going after Zac Ledger. Oh God, I can't imagine if she'd tried anything with Zac, and then I find out that his wife, who's amazing, decorated this house. From what I've heard about Zac, nothing my sister tried would've worked on him. He loves his wife so much. And I've got to hope that when it came down to it, Sasha wouldn't have gone there, but everything else has been surprisingly strategic.

She mentioned the term *ultimate unattainables* to me, but

I didn't know it was an actual checklist she was trying to check off.

I'm scared to turn the page, but I do it.

I did it! I slept with Weston Shaw!!! I went in knowing as many stats as I could about him, and he thought that was funny. He bought a few rounds of drinks for me and a few others at the bar, and we danced for a while. When I thought he might be losing interest, I put my arms around his neck and swiveled my hips against him, nice and slow, and then said, "Why don't we go someplace a little more private and I can make you feel a lot better than this..." I'm sad to say he hesitated, but when I did my sad eyes and a slight pout, he said, "Sure, why not."

It was pretty dark in the hotel room, but I could tell the guy has an amazing body. And he knows what he's doing in bed, but I'd hoped we'd do it more than once, and that didn't happen. He fell asleep afterward, and the next morning, he was polite, but didn't want to linger. I started to ride him after I woke up, but he rolled me off of him and said he was too tired.

My favorite part of it all might have been when he said bye. His eyes met mine, and he just smiled at me and said, "You take care, okay?"

I thought that was really sweet.

The way she's talking about this is nothing like the swooning she did after the fact. I don't know if she built it up in her mind the more time that passed, or if she was just expounding on it for my benefit.

Caleb wakes up, and I have to work at not just going

through the motions as I fix him a bottle and feed him a little snack. My mind is on the journal and what really happened when she found out she was pregnant. A couple hours later when I put Caleb down for another nap, I hurry to grab it and keep reading.

I skim over a few sections that are more mundane and then I get to it. The words, *I can't believe it—I'm pregnant* standing out to me even though they're written the same as everything else.

Now I know why I've been so exhausted. It's not because I'm still sick. I can't believe it—I'm pregnant. And there's only one possible father—Weston. What am I going to do with a baby?

It's a few weeks before she posts again.

I've been so sick. Haven't felt like doing much of anything, but I'm making peace with the thought of having a baby. I want to have it. No idea whether I will be a good mom or not, but it seems miraculous that I'm pregnant, right? I have no idea how this even happened. He used a condom, and well... I've never been great at taking the pill regularly, but the antibiotics must have really made it not work. But also...I wasn't supposed to have a baby. I figure if I can carry this baby to term, it'll be a miracle baby, and I might suck at being a mom, but I have enough people in my life who will love it.

I told Sadie. I think she's in shock. She really wants me to tell Weston, but the more I think about it, the more I think he'd just take the baby away from me. My health isn't the best, my apartment with Sadie is a dump, and I don't have the best track record with jobs. His parents are lawyers and they could get Weston custody in a heartbeat.

I skim over the next few passages that are more of the same, and then it's months later when she writes again.

The baby kicks nonstop. He's probably going to be athletic like his dad. I found out it's a boy a few months ago, and I like the thought of bringing another little Weston Shaw into the world. I'm as big as a house. Sadie's been after me to tell Weston from the beginning, and I finally got serious about it today.

I've known where he lives for a while, and I went and parked a few houses down. He lives in a big, pretty house, but it's not in the most exclusive section of Silver Hills. That kind of surprised me.

It took time, but I finally got the nerve and went up to his door and rang the doorbell.

A woman answered. She was beautiful. Light brown hair and big eyes, a little taller than me, a few years older than me too, and wearing flawless designer clothes. She looked me up and down, and I felt like she could rip me to shreds with just a few more seconds of these looks.

Finally, she said, "This is really pathetic, you know."

When I didn't say anything, she shut the door in my face.

I realized I didn't want to have to deal with any possible girlfriends or future wives. I've let Sadie think I've tried to tell Weston so she'll get off my back, but today is the first day I truly have no desire to try again.

. . .

I sit there for a few minutes, shaken up about this passage. She definitely never told me she went to his house. Who was this woman? Instead of feeling clearer about things where Sasha is concerned, I'm only becoming more uncertain.

The next few entries are more details about her pregnancy. She wasn't shy whatsoever about talking those things over, so I knew a lot of this. By the time I reach the last page, she's had Caleb and feels like she's barely surviving due to the lack of sleep. I think nothing else could surprise me, but taped to the inside of the back cover, is a letter addressed to Caleb.

My hands are shaking as I unfold the flap and read.

Dear Caleb,

If you're reading this, it's because I've decided the time is finally right to tell you something.

You're the best decision I've ever made. From the moment you were born, I've loved you more than another soul. You're only a couple of months old when I'm writing this, but even on my hardest days, when I don't think I'm cut out to be a mom, you will look up at me while you're nursing or clutch my finger in your fist, and I feel like you love me. I never want to lose that.

I decided not to let your dad know about you before now because, selfishly, I was afraid you'd never love me once you met him. He's incredibly talented and successful and has way more money than I'll ever have, and he seems like a good person. But it's because of the way I love you that I'm going to tell you who your father is and give you that choice. You deserve to have two loving parents, and I hope that once he finds out the truth, he'll trust me to stay in your life. I'll fight for that as best I can. And I hope you'll forgive me and still love me, no matter what.

Your dad is Weston Shaw. When we met, he played for the Colorado Mustangs, and he'd just brought our team to the Super Bowl two years in a row. You look like him already, and if you're lucky, you'll be a lot like him too. Your Aunt Sadie says you'll be the best parts of me and him, and I'd really love that. I trust your Aunt Sadie more than another person on earth, so if she says it, I'm going to believe it.

When you're ready, we can tell your dad and see how it goes. I'm okay if you choose to never tell him, too, it's up to you. But I suspect you will because every little boy needs a dad, and I've kept you to myself long enough.

I love you always.

Mommy

The tears are running down my face when I'm done, and I sit staring into space, thinking about my sister long after I've stopped reading.

CHAPTER THIRTY-NINE

WAKE ME UP

WESTON

It's been a hectic week at work with the coaches riding us extra hard because of how close we came to losing on Sunday. Coach Evans points at me and a few others before he lets us go.

"I want your head in the game next week. Got it?"

"Yes, sir," echoes through the room as we all say it.

Afterward, he pulls me aside. "Everything okay, Shaw?"

"Things are going well, sir."

"Okay, because I'm seeing a lot more of your social life than I'd like in the news. Some are saying you're not playing your best game." He lifts his eyebrows.

I try to tamp down the anger and look at him with more calm than I feel. "We're still winning, aren't we?"

He gives me his signature cocky grin and pounds me on the back. "Damn right, we are. Just checking to see if you still have that fire in you or if it's been consumed by that pretty lady friend I've seen on your arm."

"My fire is still burning hot," I tell him, smirking now.

"That's what I like to hear. Let's keep it that way and win another Super Bowl…"

"Yes, sir."

The next afternoon, an emergency Single Dad Players meeting is called for Penn about Sam. He hasn't gotten to the bottom of it, unfortunately, but he's still concerned about the kid and feels like his hands are tied when it comes to helping him. I pull into the driveway late Friday night, worn out and anxious to see Sadie and Caleb. We're flying out earlier in the day than I'd like tomorrow, heading to Minnesota to play the Vikings on Sunday.

"Hello," I call when I come in the door.

"We're in the kitchen," Sadie says.

She's sitting in front of Caleb's high chair feeding him two of his favorite foods, carrots and pears. He is pounding the tray each time she gives him a bite, and she manages to keep him from grabbing the baby food himself, which saves us all from a huge mess.

I kiss her and Caleb, and my eyes go back to Sadie. She's been quiet the past few days. I've asked her if anything is up, but she hasn't said anything but that she's tired and has a lot on her mind.

"You okay?" I ask, my hand trailing down her cheek.

"I have something to talk to you about, but I haven't known if I should tell you right before a game. But it's kind of always right before a game, so…"

"You should definitely tell me." My apprehension doubles when she looks up at me and sighs, looking like she's carrying the weight of the world.

She nods. "I will. Let's get him fed and bathed and when I put him to bed, I'll show you."

"You're scaring me, Chapman."

Her eyes soften. "Don't be scared. It has nothing to do with me or how I feel about you."

That puts me at ease, but my mind also goes to a hundred other possibilities. It's hard to imagine what could be upsetting her like this if it isn't about us.

She relaxes a bit when we're giving Caleb a bath, and after I've read a book and put him to bed, I go down to the wine cellar and bring up a bottle that she likes.

She smiles when she sees it and says, "Yes, please. I didn't make much for dinner."

I look at the grilled chicken breasts, broccoli, and huge salad full of vegetables and fruit and nuts.

"Are you kidding? This looks perfect."

We sit at the table and I wait for her to say something. When she does, I exhale, not realizing how long I'd been holding my breath.

"I've been reading Sasha's journals…for a while now. In bits and pieces, when I could take it. It's been a lot to process."

This isn't an option I was even expecting and the dread in me builds. What kinds of things did Sasha say about me in her journals?

"Some of it is things I remember and the way I remember

it happening. A lot of it is things I didn't know. I thought I knew my sister really well, that she was an open book, but there was a lot she kept inside. I'm conflicted by a lot of it. There were things in there I'd rather not have known." She takes a deep breath. "I don't know how much of it you want to know when it comes to what she wrote about you—she doesn't say anything bad, so don't worry about that. And I believed you before reading this, once I got to know you, but it's clear from the journals that she didn't tell you about Caleb. But…I thought you should know…she did try to tell you once. Not long before Caleb was born."

I've been sweating since she started talking, but when she gets to the last couple of sentences, I gulp down the wine and wipe my forehead with my napkin.

"It would've been at your other house…before you had so much security, because she went right up to your front door."

I frown. "No. I would've remembered that."

"You didn't answer the door. She said a beautiful woman did. A few years older than her, and a bit taller, light brown hair, designer clothes. And nothing was said for a few moments until the woman spoke and said, "This is really pathetic, you know."

I stare at her in shock. Someone knew a pregnant woman showed up at my house and didn't tell me? I have no idea who that could've been. Around the time before Caleb was born, I wasn't having women over all the time, but it still happened often enough. I rack my brain for who it could've been.

"I can't believe it," I say. "She came to my house?"

For reasons I can't fully put into words, this news shatters me. I've tried to work through the resentment I've held against Sasha, and to know that she did try and was spoken to that way…everything would be so different if I'd known. I would've been there when my son was born. I would have had those early moments with him. I would've assured Sasha that they'd be taken care of.

I blink back tears and Sadie reaches out and takes my hand.

"I know. It helps me to know she did try to let you know, even though I don't think she planned on trying again anytime soon after that. But there was also a letter for Caleb where she tells him about you."

I nod and a tear runs down my cheek. I swipe it away quickly.

"I'm glad," I say. It's all I can get out.

"I'm sorry," Sadie whispers.

She reaches out and hugs me, and we hold each other for a long time.

After a while, she pulls back. "There's something I want to tell you. It didn't take reading Sasha's journals for me to trust you. In my heart of hearts, I've known for a long time that you would've moved heaven and earth to take care of Caleb the second you heard about him. I've seen the kind of dad you are."

My eyes well up again. "Thank you," I whisper.

I can't say more than that, but I think she knows it means everything to hear her say that.

Later, we reheat the food and try again with dinner, but we still don't manage to eat much.

We go to bed early, and I feel raw and numb at the same time. Sadie kisses me and tucks her head against my chest. When my body responds to her, but I'm too weighed down to move yet, she kisses down my body and wakes me back up, one kiss at a time.

When I sink into her, it's with a sharp, relieved cry.

I'll never like the way it happened, the time I missed out on with my son, but all of this brought me to Sadie.

She's my safe place and the love of my life.

CHAPTER FORTY

THESE SMALL AND MASSIVE WAYS

SADIE

I don't know how it's possible, but things have been even better between Weston and me since I told him about the journals. He's been so vulnerable and sweet. It's broken my heart while also healing it, as we navigate knowing more of the story together.

The mystery of who the woman Sasha saw remains, but it seems like we may never know. And I guess that has to be okay. We can't change any of it anyway.

It's the week before Thanksgiving and I haven't been to a game yet. I had two chances last month, and I lost my nerve. I didn't tell Weston I'd thought about going, and he hasn't asked since the magazine debacle. I've been in them again occasionally, but being aware that photographers are out there now has helped me up my game. I don't necessarily go out looking completely put together, but I don't look scraggly and like I haven't slept in months either.

Balance.

But it's getting harder to stay away.

Being with Weston has changed my life. Not because I live in this beautiful home and don't struggle to make ends meet anymore—although that has been a huge improvement, I won't lie—but it's because I never thought I could have a love like this. When I think back to how I didn't trust anything Weston said, it's like another lifetime ago. It doesn't compute that I wouldn't trust him now.

When he looks at me, it's with the most genuine, heart-wrenching adoration.

I feel his love down to my bones.

It isn't just in the way he tends to my body like a man at the altar he worships, even though I do feel his love there, each and every day.

It goes far deeper than that. It's in the things he says, the way his eyes warm when he sees me, the way he checks to see if I'm content in the littlest ways. It's in the way he laughs at the things I say, the way he tries to make me laugh, the way he makes sure I have some time to myself when he gets home from a long day, the way he jumps up to get Caleb out of bed when he knows I didn't get much sleep…in every way, Weston proves his love for me.

That's why when we lose ourselves in each other's bodies, it's transcendent…because the foreplay is never-ending. It's been going on from the time we get out of bed and just never stops. When he shows me all the ways he cares in all these small and massive ways, it shouldn't surprise me that the sex would be a revelation each time, but it is.

I can't deprive him of the one thing he still wants from me for another second longer.

He told me he'd always have a ticket for me, and two weeks before each game, like clockwork, I get an email with my digital ticket. Not just the home games either. I haven't even ventured into considering away games yet; that will come later. But since September, I've gotten tickets for every single game. I suspect once Caleb needs his own seat, Weston will also make sure he has one.

I kiss him when he leaves just like all the other weekends, and we have our usual FaceTimes throughout the day. Same with the next day. As soon as we have our last conversation before I have to leave, I jump into action.

The doorbell makes me pause and I run to let Felicity in.

"Perfect timing. I just hung up with Weston!" I laugh, hugging her.

Her eyes are bright when we pull away, and she squeezes my arm. "I'm so happy you're doing this." She looks around for Caleb and frowns when she doesn't see him. "Where's my boy?" She pouts.

"He's still sleeping and I'm hoping he sleeps as long as possible. He's teething and didn't sleep well last night."

"Aw, poor guy. He's going with us, though, right?"

"Yes. I didn't want him to miss out. He'll probably be a handful though. Since he's started walking, he's going *nonstop*."

We go upstairs and Felicity helps me decide on which outfit to wear. We've been shopping a few times since the girls' trip and we've become even closer. I've seen Olivia here and there at Lane and David's house, but she's not around as much as Felicity, even though she lives near us. Felicity and Weston have both mentioned that they wish they were closer to their older sister, but she's busy with work. They don't agree with me, but I think she wishes she had what they do. A loving relationship, and a family of her own.

"Will Olivia be at the game tonight?" I ask.

Felicity frowns. "I think so. I'm not sure, though. She's been trying to make it to more games. I know my parents and yours will be." She grins. "And I couldn't believe it when Weston told me Romeo Knight would be there tonight."

"I know." I fan my face. "I'm already nervous about going, but knowing he's in the suite with us—eek! Did you see his fight against Leo Burns? It was epic."

"No, but I heard about it for days afterward. Sutton and his brothers couldn't stop talking about it. Neither could Weston."

I nod.

"The guys will be awestruck over Romeo tonight." She laughs. "Sutton is meeting us there with…I think Theo, Callum, and Jamison. I believe Wyatt had to work tonight." She makes a sad face and then it brightens. "But…I might've told the girls you were thinking about coming." She holds up her hands at my raised eyebrows. "Don't worry, they won't say a word. There's no way Weston will find out until it's time. But they're coming too, and we'll be in a suite." She does a little shimmy.

"Ahh. That's so great. I've missed them. I wish everyone lived closer."

She lifts a shoulder. She reminds me so much of Weston when she's being playful. "Or you could, I don't know… move to Landmark Mountain when Weston retires. Football players don't play forever, you know."

"If I could talk my parents into it...and your parents." We both laugh. "It might be a while. I hope Weston can play for as long as he wants. He loves it so much."

Felicity smiles at me in the mirror as we do our makeup. "This is why you're so good for him. Not everyone is cut out for this lifestyle. And it's only going to get better now that you'll be at the games."

I focus on getting my eyeliner right. "It makes me nervous to think of anything beyond today. It's ridiculous, I know. I don't know when I became such a coward."

She turns to look at me, mascara wand in mid-air. "You can't possibly think you're a coward. There's no way. You have raised your sister's baby as your own. You've made peace with the guy you thought wanted nothing to do with the baby and have set aside your feelings to take care of Caleb. You're dating a professional athlete! You've gotten hounded by the press and handled it with grace..."

"I don't know if it's grace as much as hiding out..."

She levels me with a look. "You've handled it with grace," she continues like she never stopped. "If you were a coward and not the strongest person ever, none of this would have happened. My brother wouldn't be happier than I've *ever* seen him, Caleb wouldn't have a healthy environment with two loving parents, and we wouldn't get to hang out like this right now." She winks at me in the mirror and goes back to applying the mascara.

When I get to the game, I feel good about the way I look. My hair is in loose waves down my back, my makeup is on point, and I love the dress I'm wearing. It's the color of the Mustangs teal to show my support, and it's short but not too short. I've tried to straddle the line between appropriate and sexy and hope that I've succeeded.

But the nerves are *intense.*

Caleb is in the same jersey Weston will be wearing tonight, and he's a lot more excited about being here than he was the last time we came. He runs around the suite, hugging all his favorite people and loving being the center of attention. And my nerves about meeting Romeo Knight were for nothing—he's the nicest guy and Caleb warms right up to him.

When Weston Facetimes, I hold up the phone and Jamison whistles so everyone turns to look at me.

"He's calling," I say, waving the phone.

They move out of the way, waiting for my signal.

I answer, my smile a little wobbly. "Hey!"

"Damn, Chapman." He whistles. "Should I be jealous? You look hot as fuck. What are you doing tonight?"

I flush and hear a few people trying not to laugh.

"You have nothing to be jealous about." I grin. "I'm cheering you on, Shaw. Stay safe and play your ass off."

He lifts his eyebrows, his smile huge. "All right, I will." He chuckles. "Where's Caleb? Can I see him before I go out?"

"Who has Caleb?" I call, switching the camera to face out, so he sees everyone else in the suite. My dad holds Caleb up high. "Caleb, tell Daddy to play good," I say.

"Dada, pay goo," Caleb says, bopping his head in a little dance when everyone cheers.

I turn the camera back to face me, and Weston's got tears in his eyes and looks so happy.

"You're *here*? Sadie." He sniffs. "God, I'm turning into fucking mush and I'm not even mad about it," he says. "I have such mad love for you, Chapman."

"I love you, Shaw. More than I can even say."

He lifts up his hand in the *I love you* sign and when I return it, he puts his fist on his heart, and we hang up.

They're undefeated so far this year, in spite of coming close to losing several times. But tonight they win big. *41 - 7.* Everyone's talking about it—will the Mustangs continue their winning streak? Could they win out? There's only been one team, the Miami Dolphins, who've had a perfect season and that was in *1972*.

Weston and I celebrate like we've never celebrated before. If it weren't for Caleb, I don't think we'd come up for air.

If I'm all over every magazine cover for weeks to come, going to that game was worth it.

CHAPTER FORTY-ONE

SCORCHED EARTH

WESTON

The doorbell rings and I open the door wide, grinning when I see my parents *and* Sadie's parents. Clara pops her head around my dad.

"Got room for some stragglers?" my dad asks.

"Clara! I was hoping you'd make it. So happy you're all here. Come on in." I hug everyone and Caleb toddles his way toward his grandparents, laughing when he's scooped up. "Happy Thanksgiving!"

Caleb repeats his version of it in gibberish and we all go on over him like he's really said it. Everyone carries the dishes they brought into the kitchen and then hugs Sadie. She's been cooking for days and keeps adding one more item to the menu. It'll be our parents and Olivia for the main meal, and then later, Felicity, Sutton, and Owen will come, and Penn, Rhodes and Levi, Bowie and Becca, and I think even Henley and the girls might stop by.

Olivia arrives a few minutes later and when Caleb sees her, he runs over and hugs her legs. She looks down in surprise and then bends down and hugs him.

"Hi," she says.

"Hi," he says back.

She looks up at me in delight, and I don't remember ever seeing that expression on my sister's face.

"I heard he was running all over the place at the game on Sunday," she says. "Sorry, I didn't make it." She looks at Caleb again. "It's been so long since I've seen you, I wasn't sure if you'd remember me."

He smiles at her and does a long string of jabbering that cracks us all up. When she stands, he holds his arms out for her to pick him up, and I watch her physically melt. It makes me so fucking happy. I chuckle under my breath and she gives me a withering look. My sister is still in there, but when it comes to Caleb, she's whipped.

He points at something on the counter and Olivia walks over there. When he sees the jar of his cubed peaches, he starts bouncing.

"Is this what you want?" Olivia asks, holding up the little jar.

He can only use one hand since he's holding onto Olivia, but he does the sign for *want* with his free hand.

"He's doing sign language for *want*," I tell Olivia when he does it again.

Her eyes widen. "Why is he learning sign language?"

"It helps babies communicate before they can speak. He only knows a few words. Please, more, want."

"Hungry," Sadie adds. "Most are all related to food when he uses them." She laughs.

"Impressive," Olivia says. "Can I give him these peaches?"

"Sure," Sadie says. "We're eating soon, but he's probably so hungry by now…so yes, if you don't mind." She looks at me. "I think we're ready for you to cut the turkey."

"Let me at that thing." I get out the new electric knife we bought for the occasion and start slicing. "I've never felt more domestic than I do right now." I laugh.

Olivia yelps and I turn to see Caleb holding the now empty jar of peaches, a few peaches stuck to his soaking wet shirt. Olivia looks mortified.

"I'm so sorry. He grabbed it before I could—" she starts.

"It's fine," Sadie and I both tell her.

"He's handsy when we're trying to feed him. Quick as lightning," I say in the voice I use with Caleb. He smiles like he's being praised.

"I'll go change him," Olivia says, still looking uncertain, but everyone else is busy with something, so she nods like she's convincing herself.

I laugh. "Thanks. I don't think you've been up there since I moved in. His room is next to ours, and his closet is full of clothes, so take your pick."

She nods and carries him upstairs, holding him out so he doesn't get her wet. He laughs like they're playing a game together and I shake my head as I get back to the turkey.

Once everything is ready, Sadie moves next to me and I put my arm around her.

"We thought everyone could fill their plates here," Sadie motions to the island, "and then we'll take it to the dining room. The drinks are set up in there."

"This looks incredible, you guys," my mom says. She reaches up and pats my face. "I can't tell you how happy it makes me to see you so happy." She looks at the ceiling. "I am not gonna cry," she says, laughing. "My boy is all grown up and entertaining us in his beautiful home with his beautiful family." She waves her face. "Okay, I am gonna cry." She looks at Sadie. "Thank you. Thank you for having us today. Thank you for loving our son and grandson the way you do. I don't know what we did before you came into our lives."

Sadie's eyes are glossy as she hugs my mom and they both sniffle afterwards. I smile when she walks back toward me and I tuck her back against my chest.

"We're so glad you're with us today," I say. "I'm beyond thankful for my family and the way my family has expanded this year." I shake my head. "Jeez, there's something in the air. Where are the waterworks coming from? My heart is full." I take a deep breath. "Everyone help yourself. Let's *eat*!"

I'm moderate with my plate. It's full of things I wouldn't normally be eating, but in smaller portions, and I avoid the food that triggers me to eat too much. My mom's broccoli rice casserole, for example—I can't just have a little and be satisfied. I'll still be sluggish in my workouts later, but nothing I'm eating should affect the game on Sunday.

I'm getting ready to sit at the table when I realize I haven't seen Olivia in a while. I go into the kitchen expecting to see her there, and when I don't, I ask, "Have Olivia and Caleb come back yet?"

"I haven't seen them," Sadie says.

"I'll go check on them."

I take the stairs two at a time and when I reach Caleb's room, I find Caleb dressed and pulling out all his books from the shelves, and Olivia is sitting in the chair where we read to him.

"What's going on in here?" I ask and Caleb jumps. I try to give him a stern look, but he holds out a book like he's excited for me to see it, and I can't resist. I'll work on getting firmer pretty soon, but so far nothing he does seems too naughty.

"Clean up, clean up," I sing.

He bobs his head back and forth with the song and tries to put the books back. I help him and turn, grinning at Olivia, but when I get a good look at her face, I'm in front of her in seconds.

"What's wrong? What happened?" I bend down until we're at eye level, and when her eyes meet mine, I'm shocked to see them full of tears.

I don't think I've ever seen Olivia cry in my whole life.

"Olivia, what is it?"

She points to the picture of Sasha and Caleb hanging on the wall next to us.

"This is his mother?" she asks, her voice breaking.

I nod once. "Yes, that's Sasha."

She closes her eyes and the tears spill over. "Weston, I have something to tell you and I don't think you'll ever forgive me for it. I can't forgive myself for it."

I clasp her hand and look at her for a second, and then the realization hits me like a huge, hard stone.

"It was you, wasn't it? You were the one who saw her?"

Her eyes flicker back to the picture and she nods reluctantly.

"She showed up at the other house and I thought it was just another crazed fan coming to tell you she was having your baby. You had just had that other woman who wouldn't stop stalking you, so I guess I went into big sister protective mode. I didn't even buy that there really was a baby." She lets out a choked sound. "How did you know?"

"Sadie read about it in Sasha's journals."

"I was so rude to her." Her face crumbles and she starts crying harder. "Weston, I'm so sorry. If it hadn't been for me, everything would be so different. You would've known your son from the very beginning. I can't—you must hate me."

I put my arms around her and hug her. I shed a few tears, but not many. I don't want to spend this day looking backward. When Olivia stills, I pull back and get a tissue from the side table, handing it to her. She blows her nose and gets another tissue to work on her eye makeup. Caleb barrels over to us when he sees that Olivia's crying and stares at her in concern. I pat his back and he comes over and leans on me.

"I don't hate you, Olivia," I say. "It's time to put this to rest. There's a lot that could've been handled differently. I'd give anything to have been there when Caleb was born, but I'm just so grateful he's in my life now. I can't be angry at anyone anymore because I'm living this beautiful life with my son and Sadie."

"That's a generous way of looking at everything. You and Felicity have always been so much better than me," she snorts.

"Not true."

She gives me a pointed look. "So true. If this had happened to me, I would have scorched the earth to make everyone pay."

I chuckle. "This would've never happened to you. It's not part of your life plan."

She rolls her eyes. "Damn straight, it wouldn't."

Her expression softens when I laugh.

"Can we not tell Sadie about this?" she asks.

I give her a pointed look. "I'm going to tell Sadie. We don't keep secrets, and she'll work through any feelings she has about it. We've both learned to do that this year."

"Thanks for not tossing me out of your house forever," she says.

I stand and hold out my hand and she takes it, standing up. "You're welcome. Thanks for coming today and for changing your nephew into a cute outfit after he demolished his other one."

"You're welcome," she says, her smile growing. "Thanks for not forcing me to make anything for Thanksgiving."

"We *all* thank you for not making anything for Thanksgiving," I snark.

She whacks me across the chest, and I laugh, lifting my shoulders.

"I'll never live down that Jell-O mold," she says.

"It was lime and had chunks of *carrots* inside."

Just thinking about it makes me shudder.

She laughs. "It was supposed to be Thanksgiving-y."

"More like Thanks-go-away."

She rolls her eyes again. "*Oh-kay*, Weston," she says in the snide tone that I'm far more used to than the teary one from a few minutes ago.

I pick up Caleb and grin at my sister.

"Come on, let's go eat."

The party is in full swing when we get downstairs. I put Caleb in his high chair and sit down to the feast. Sadie glances at me and I squeeze her thigh under the table, as we share a smile.

Life is so sweet, and it goes by in a flash. We never know what a day will bring.

I don't want to waste another minute regretting anything.

CHAPTER FORTY-TWO

BOXES AND FEET

SADIE

"Can we leave this tree up forever?" Weston asks.

We're standing in front of the huge Christmas tree we put up right after Thanksgiving, and it's Christmas Eve. Weston's arms are around me, and I lean my head back on his chest. We're pretending like today's Christmas because Weston has to play at noon tomorrow, so that means an early day for him, and not in front of this tree.

"Oh, no." I laugh. "Caleb is wearing me out. He's

obsessed with the ornaments, and he's almost pulled the tree down on himself no less than five times."

"And you have a coronary every time," he says, laughing as he leans in to kiss my temple.

"Exactly." I grin up at him and he gives me a soft kiss on the lips.

"Can we wake him up from his nap now?" he asks.

"You're such a kid." I turn and tickle his side and he grabs my hips and throws me over his shoulder, smacking my backside.

I smack him back, laughing as all the blood rushes to my head.

"You're proving my point," I yelp when he gives me another smack.

"I just love Christmas." He tosses me on the couch and hovers over me, grinning before he kisses down my neck. "Aren't you ready to see him open his presents?"

"Yes." I arch into him when he moves my sweater aside and tongues my nipple through my bra. "So why are you trying to distract me?" I moan.

"Because this feels like Christmas too." His eyes are bright as he looks up at me. He moves lower, until he's between my legs. "Let me just unwrap this first," he says, unzipping my jeans and tugging them down my thighs.

He gives me his undivided attention and I get lost in the sensations, losing all track of time. He makes me see stars, and I hold onto his hair for dear life while I shatter. But I still want more when I come down from that high, and I pull him up and hurriedly free him from his pants. When he lowers his weight on top of me and his tip nudges me right where I want him, we both moan. He slides in a few inches and back out, going in deeper the next time. When he bottoms out, I grip his hair in both my fists and tug his mouth to mine.

"I'm already so close again," I say against his lips.

Just then I hear Caleb singing in the monitor.

Weston and I freeze and stare at each other.

"Please, don't stop," I whisper.

That's all the encouragement he needed. He's a man on a mission, his tempo punishing and perfect.

"Are you still close?" he asks.

"Yes," I gasp.

He grins at me and tilts my hips up, the angle he hits inside when he does this move, never failing to make me fall over the edge. He's groaning in the next second when I start pulsing around him. His head falls back and he swells inside of me, making my orgasm even better.

"Best Christmas ever," he says into my neck.

"Mama," Caleb calls.

We both laugh, and Weston slowly pulls out of me. He stands up, tucking himself back in his pants.

"I can get him," he says.

I nod and move toward the downstairs bathroom to clean up while he rushes to the kitchen to wash his hands.

"Coming, little guy," he yells as he goes up the stairs.

When I come out of the bathroom, I hear Caleb's enthusiastic, "Daddy!"

"Aw," I say in the empty kitchen.

That's the first time Caleb's said it like that. I bet Weston is beaming right now.

When he brings Caleb down, freshly changed, I was right. He's got the happiest smile on his face.

"Did you hear him call me Daddy?"

"Cutest thing ever," I say.

We sit under the tree, and I look at my two favorite people.

"You guys make me so happy. Merry Christmas," I tell Weston.

He meets me in the middle for a kiss.

"Merry Christmas, baby," I tell Caleb, leaning over to kiss his cheek.

He pats my face.

"Look, did you see what's over there?" I ask, pointing to the little bike that he can sit on but also move around with his feet.

Weston picks him up and sets him on it and it takes a minute for him to realize he can make it move. When he runs into the tree and the massive thing wobbles, Weston hurriedly pulls him off and shows him another present.

"Yeah, that thing's gotta go," Weston teases.

"I never knew a Christmas tree was full of such danger," I add.

When Caleb just looks at his present, Weston tears a little of the paper to show him how it's done. Caleb grins and rips the paper and flings it into the air. When he sees the little tool set inside to go with the little workbench we got for him, he tosses the box. Weston takes the tools out of the box, laughing when Caleb tries to put his feet inside the box.

"Look, did you see the workbench?" Weston asks, pointing to the toy sitting next to the tree. He takes Caleb's hand and grabs the hammer from the tool kit and walks over there, trying to show him everything.

Caleb points at the box behind him and does the *want* sign, which makes us laugh so hard.

"I guess it's true that you only need to give kids boxes at this age," I say.

"Well, let me give you a present then," Weston says, "but first, you have to find your stocking."

I look around, seeing his stuffed stocking still hanging,

but mine is gone. I lift my eyebrows. "Is that a thing? Hiding the stockings?"

He laughs. "It is now?" He says it like it's a question.

"I love how we just keep winging it."

We both crack up at that.

"Makes life an adventure," he says.

"Well, next year, I will make sure Santa hides your stocking."

"Santa's part of the stockings?" he asks.

"I think. I mean, I never really believed, but…"

He looks affronted. "Sacrilege!"

"Hmm. I didn't know you felt so passionately about believing."

"Believing is everything," he says. "I just wasn't sure which part Santa was involved in."

"Well, now you have me questioning everything."

He grins and stands to pull me to my feet, and when I move around the living room, he says if I'm hot or cold or warm. I finally find my stocking sitting between books on the built-in bookshelves.

It's like a treasure trove of amazingness. Delicious-smelling bath scrub and perfume, cozy socks, individually wrapped truffles, cute earrings that I'm shocked he picked out, and at the bottom I freeze when I feel a long jewelry box that fills the whole foot of the stocking.

I open the box and my mouth parts when I see the white gold pendant on a beautiful chain. In the center is **W+S.** Above the plus sign is a **C,** and below the plus sign is a small heart with a diamond in the center.

"I love it so much," I tell him, my voice trembling. "Thank you." I lift it out of the box and turn so he'll put it on me.

"If you like wearing it and we ever need to update it

with…I don't know, new initials or something…I'll make sure to put in a word with the Claus family."

"Oh, you will?" I grin, leaning up to kiss him. "I'm not sure why we'd need new initials, but…"

His hands squeeze my backside as he gives me a longer kiss. "One thing at a time, Chapman. It's all part of my master plan."

"I see. Very interesting."

He looks over my shoulder and laughs when he sees Caleb pounding on the box for the tool set with another present.

"I hope that box didn't have something breakable," he says.

"It's those cute little boots we got him," I whisper.

"Oh, perfect," he whispers back.

"Are you ready to see what's in your stocking?" I ask.

"I thought you'd never ask."

He's pure mischief as he goes over to his stocking and shakes it like a box. When it doesn't make a sound, he frowns. "No clue."

He puts his hand in there and pulls out a huge bar of soap that says Lump of Coal.

"But I've been very good," he insists.

"Yes, you have." I laugh.

He pulls out *The Book of Terribly Awesome Dad Jokes* next and laughs as he flips through it. "I'm totally going to use these."

"I have no doubt."

Socks with Caleb's face on them are next, and he acts like it's the greatest thing he's ever gotten. When he pulls out another pair with us making goofy faces, he laughs so hard.

"This is perfect," he says.

At the bottom is a tobacco vanilla candle that says Sadie's

Sidepiece. His laugh reverberates off of the high ceilings and makes Caleb and me laugh too.

"You're the best thing that ever happened to me," he says when he's stopped laughing. He pulls me to him and gives me a lingering kiss.

When we move to sit under the tree, there are still mostly presents for Caleb under there, which is funny, because he couldn't care less about opening them. He's still happy with his box, and it's just as well, there are a few books and a singing toy left to open and a few things in his stocking that he can discover later.

Weston and I take our time opening the gifts. I get a pretty sweater and a sexy nightie that I recognize as Scarlett's brand. He gets a sweater too, and his last present is his favorite of all. It's an album of Caleb from the day he was born, until his first birthday earlier this month. We threw a huge party with our family and friends. He got more presents than he's gotten this Christmas, and the biggest was from Penn—an outrageously large ball pit. The pictures from that day are at the end and the very last picture is one I took as Weston was reading his bedtime story that night.

"I don't know how I got so lucky," he says, choked up when he closes the album.

"That's how I feel too," I tell him.

He pulls me onto his lap so I'm straddling him and hugs me. We look over at Caleb.

"He finally likes his workbench," Weston says.

"Yay."

"Oh…he's using it to fall asleep under."

We try not to laugh as we crawl toward him and move the workbench so Caleb's not stuck under there. When Weston picks him up, his eyes open and then roll back.

"Is that enough Christmas cheer for you, little guy?" Weston asks. "I hear you. Let's get you to bed."

He holds Caleb in front of me and I kiss his cheeks.

"I love you," I whisper.

I'm still sitting under the tree when Weston comes back a few minutes later. He moves me onto his lap again, but this time, both of us face the tree.

"Oh, wait. I think you forgot one thing," he says. He looks back at the tree and nods. "Yeah, you definitely forgot something."

He lifts me off of him and when he sets me on my feet, he says, "Warm."

I laugh. "I've barely moved."

He waves his hand like *get moving*.

I inch closer to the tree.

"Warmer."

I take a step to the left.

"Cold."

I take a step to the right.

"Hot!"

I look at the floor and bend down to see if I missed anything.

"Cold."

I stand back up.

"Hot."

I giggle. I look at the ornaments and notice something new tucked in the tree. I pull out the envelope and wave it.

"You're so hot," he says, with his sexiest voice.

I grin and open the envelope and squeal when I see the tickets for Turks and Caicos, leaving when his football season is over. I look at the departure date again and then up at him, my eyes filling with tears.

"If it's not the way you want to spend those days, we

don't have to go. And if you want your parents there with you, they'll be on the same flight," he says.

"Thank you," I whisper.

Losing my sister will always hurt, but as with everything else in my life with Weston, the anniversary of her leaving this earth is tempered with something good too, even if it didn't seem like it at the time.

It's the day I met Weston, and the day Weston met his son.

Sometimes lately, I've wondered if I gained a guardian angel who's been watching over me since the day I lost Sasha, giving me extra doses of happiness. I like to think so.

"I think this is a perfect way to spend the anniversary," I tell him. "You sure did change my life, Shaw."

He grins. "Not as much as you changed mine, Chapman. You turned me upside down and I don't think I'm right side up yet. I'm exactly where I want to be."

He sweeps me up into his arms, and his lips never leave mine as he carries me upstairs.

EPILOGUE

NUGGETS

Two and a half months later

WESTON

We're at Bowie's house and the chatter of all of our kids in the connecting room is at a dull roar. Cassidy is carrying Caleb everywhere and he's putting up with it, a sure sign that he adores her because my boy loves to be on the move.

"I cannot believe you're engaged, man," Rhodes says.

"But what I *really* can't believe is that you went to Turks and Caicos for two weeks but didn't propose to her until you got home. What happened there?"

They all laugh and I shrug, grinning and not giving a single shit that they're making fun of me.

"I wanted us to have our own day to celebrate. It didn't feel right for it to be the day we met, on a trip where we were honoring her sister."

"Oh shit," Rhodes says, his head falling back.

"I swear, Rhodes," Bowie says, shaking his head.

"You're telling me you thought of that already?" Rhodes looks at Bowie incredulously.

"Uh, yeah." Bowie's hands fly up. "It's kind of hard to forget."

"Well, congratulations. We're so happy for you," Henley says.

"I can't believe you're gonna be the only married one out of all of us," Penn says, shaking his head. "I love Sadie, but I do *not* know how to feel about this."

"Be happy for me." I reach out and shake his shoulder until his eyes look a little less crazed.

"First a baby, then a wife," he keeps going. "Next thing you know, you'll be having more babies."

"I cannot wait for that day." I get caught in a daydream, envisioning Sadie with a baby bump, smiling up at me with her radiant smile.

She's made my house a home, and the thought of us filling it up with more kids makes me happier than I thought possible. She says she's getting her interior design urges out of her system by making our house less of a bachelor pad. She's done some decorating for the guys too, but for now, her priority is Caleb. I'll support whatever she chooses to do in the future. I'm just so glad she's going to be my wife. And my family could not be happier for us—even Olivia. It might be a while before Sadie and Olivia are as close as Sadie and Felicity are, but they're headed in the right direction.

Rhodes dropping The Single Dad Playbook in the middle of the table pulls me out of my sweet thoughts.

"It's time for you to take a look at this if you're already thinking of having another baby," Rhodes says.

I grin good-naturedly. "Bring it."

I flip the pages, laughing when it stops on:

Being a dad is like constipation. You think you're backed up because you don't eat enough fiber, but there's also the water and the vegetables and the exercise, and maybe a weird twist in your intestines that you didn't even consider.
~Rhodes

"These nuggets of wisdom, I tell ya." I shake my head and keep flipping, stopping next on a diagram Rhodes drew of the levels of agitation a dad can reach in a single day.

I keep going.

Becca taught me to stop and appreciate the little things. She noticed the simplest things that my eyes had learned to skim over, and once I tried to pay attention the way she did, it opened a whole new world for me.
~Bowie

"Keep going," Rhodes says.

When I keep lingering on all the sentimental ones, Rhodes gets impatient and flips it to the page he wants, pointing at a passage I haven't seen yet.

"Read this one," he says.

When we found out we were pregnant with our second baby, everyone said, "It'll actually help keep Cassidy entertained. You'll see, it'll be great." And Audrey was *great, but our precious little Cassidy turned into a hellion because she wanted to be "only one girl." And when we were pregnant with our third, everyone said, "Two kids and two parents is a man-to-man defense, but three, you'll be like: WHAT THE FUCK WERE WE THINKING?"*

And that was true.

But I wouldn't have it any other way.

~Henley

I exhale. It is a lot to think about.

"And this one," Rhodes points to the next page.

When you have your first baby, you've never been so tired in your life. You can barely function, you're so blindly exhausted.

When you have your second baby, you've never been so tired in your life. When the new baby finally sleeps after being up all night, you have to gird up your loins and take care of your first child and just pray that you don't fall asleep while you're driving home from the grocery store.

When you have your third baby, you've never been so tired in your life. When the new baby finally sleeps after being up all night, the second child also doesn't sleep at night OR during the day, and the first child wakes you up every time your eyes drift closed because she's finally ready for her turn to have attention.

But I wouldn't change a thing.

~Henley

"Fuck," I whisper.

Henley gives me an apologetic look and then brightens, flipping through the sweet things Bowie says about not being afraid to sing princess songs or wear pink nail polish if it makes your kid happy. And Rhodes even has some sweet things to say about the first time you toss a football to your son. Even if it's the tiny one for newborns, there's just nothing like it.

"Here, this one is better," Henley says.

We were having a hard stretch with Gracie. She was teething and miserable. One night we were so exhausted from being up with her several nights in a row, and she'd been crying off and on for hours. She finally fell asleep only to wake up again, but she was quiet before we reached her room, and when we walked inside, Audrey had crawled into the crib with Gracie. She held her hand and sang to her and it was the sweetest thing I've ever seen.

Siblings might fight like crazy, but their love for each other is

like no other relationship. Best friends, co-conspirators, the next generation of memory keepers…
~Henley

He smiles when I look up at him.

"You really don't regret having three kids, do you?" I ask.

"Not for even a millisecond," he says.

"You could always enjoy being married first," Penn says.

"Have you set a date?" Bowie asks.

"I'd marry her tomorrow if she said yes…I'll keep you posted on that," I say.

"When are you gonna start adding to the book?" Henley asks, pointing to the notebook on the table.

"Me? You think I'm ready?"

"You've been in the trenches for over a year. Hell, yeah, you're ready," Rhodes says.

"I've convinced Sam to stop drinking Cokes every chance he gets, and his stomach and dentist are a lot happier," Penn says, leaning his elbows on his knees.

We all look at Penn and grin.

"That's great, man. When are we gonna meet this guy? I feel like I know him already," I say.

Penn looks shy for a second. "He's seemed happier lately. He's in a different foster home and likes it a lot better. I actually got permission to bring him to the family event Easter weekend."

"That's less than a month away," Henley says, pounding Penn's back. "Can't wait to meet him."

"I can't either," the rest of us chime in.

I take a sip of my now-cold coffee and stretch before

standing. "All this talk about babies has made me want to go have sex with my fiancée..."

"Everything makes you want to have sex with your fiancée." Rhodes points at me.

I point back. "You're not wrong."

I tap the table. "Thanks for all the words of wisdom."

"The constipation one is what's gonna stick though, isn't it?" Rhodes asks.

I snort. "It's right up there, yeah."

He grins, entirely too pleased with my answer.

I put my hand in the center of the table and they pile their hands on top.

When we pull back and I start to walk away, Henley holds up the notebook.

"Don't forget this," he says.

I take it from him and return his smirk. "You guys have set the bar high."

"You know that's right," Rhodes agrees.

I lift my hand and move into the other room, grinning at the way our kids are all playing together. Henley's girls have everyone doing crafts. It's actually a sight to behold, watching the little guys try to keep up with the girls.

"Hi, Weston," Becca calls. "Do you like my picture?"

She holds up her picture and I grin. "I love it."

Everyone else shows me their pictures and Caleb runs over to show me his scribbles.

"Great job," I say, ruffling his hair. "It's time to go home, son."

"See Mama?" he asks.

"Yeah, let's go see your mama. Should we pick up some flowers for her on the way?"

"Flowers!" he yells.

"Good plan. I like the way you think."

. . .

Want more Weston and Sadie? Click here!
https://dl.bookfunnel.com/ygwticrcko

For Henley's story
pre order Secret Love Here!
https://geni.us/SecretLove

SECRET LOVE COMING SOON!

Chapter 1

Wallowing

HENLEY

I hate it when the alarm goes off during a sex dream.

Lately, that's the only place I'm getting any.

Rumor has it that professional athletes have pussy falling from the sky day and night, and while I've had my share of offers, they do me little good since I've always been a one-woman kind of guy. For years, that woman was my ex-wife Bree, but when she decided she didn't want to be married to me anymore, I tested out the casual-hookup waters.

Not for me.

Most of the time.

Between football and kids, there's hardly time anyway.

But on mornings like today, when the blue balls are doing me in, I think maybe I should make time.

I'm not suffering from a broken heart. Bree and I are actually good friends. There's just no time to go out and find my soulmate while I'm at the height of my career as the wide receiver for the Colorado Mustangs and raising my three daughters.

There's also no time to wallow.

I take care of my situation in the shower and get dressed quickly. I made the mistake of not stopping by the store yesterday to get my daughters' favorite bagels and cream cheese and I want to make sure they have it before school. They're usually at their mom's during the week, but Bree went out of town, so they're with me.

I knock lightly on each door, making sure everyone's awake.

Cassidy groans when I knock on her door, until I remind her that I need to run to the store.

"Okay, I'll make sure we're all ready by the time you get back," she says.

We set this up last night before bed, and there is nothing my girl loves more than being in charge of her sisters. Lately, she's been a grump of sizable proportions, so I'm celebrating the wins.

"Thanks, Cass," I tell her. "Get up, girls. I'll be back with bagels soon. Love you."

They mutter their sleepy affection and agreement, and I hurry out the door. The parking lot of Aurora's grocery store is nearly empty when I pull in, and I rush inside, hoping I can avoid anyone I know. For the most part, in the small town of Silver Hills, people are respectful of my privacy. The past three Super Bowl wins have changed that somewhat, with people coming up to congratulate me or to talk about certain plays, but it's not too bad.

With the cream cheese in hand, I reach out to grab the bag of bagels and a pretty hand with white nail polish bumps into mine.

"Oh, sorry!" a soft voice says, and I turn to look.

The greenest eyes stare up at me from behind black-rimmed glasses, and for a moment I'm quiet as I take in her dark hair pulled back in a bun, those eyes, and her full pink lips. She's wearing a white button-down shirt, tan dress pants, and a matching jacket…accountant maybe? Something very buttoned up. Sexy librarian comes to mind. Her face is compelling and friendly, a smile playing at the corner of her lips.

"Looks like there's only one bag left of the cinnamon raisin bagels," she says.

"Go ahead. You take it," I say.

"No, I think you were here first. I wasn't paying attention. Those cinnamon rolls up there were distracting me." She points up a few shelves, and I spot the tantalizing cinnamon rolls.

My eyes narrow on them. "Oh, those look dangerous."

She laughs and picks up the package of rolls. "I like to live on the dangerous side." Her eyes are laughing and my heart does a little stutter-step.

Wait—is she flirting with me? I think she might be flirting with me.

God, I'm horrible at this.

I chuckle. "For someone who lives on the dangerous side, you look awfully—" I clear my throat as I wave my hand over her conservative ensemble.

She puts her hand on her hip in mock offense. "Awfully what?"

"Awfully proper," I say, grinning.

"Don't you know you can't judge a book by its cover?" She laughs and my heart does that weird thing again.

She's really pretty when she laughs. And when she doesn't.

"So, what are you…banker by day and cinnamon roll assassin by night?"

She winks and starts walking away, looking back at me over her shoulder. "Something like that."

"Do you have a name?" I call.

"Tru," she calls back.

Tru. I like that.

I'm still smiling, enjoying those long legs and the way her hips are mesmerizing me with that sway, as she rounds the corner.

She peeks her head back down the aisle and I'm caught standing there drooling after her. Shit, that sex dream must have messed with me more than I realized.

"And you are?" she asks.

I blink, loving that she doesn't have any idea who I am. That's rare, especially in this town.

"I'm Henley."

She lifts her hand in a wave. "Bye, Henley."

I stand there for another minute until I remember that I'm in a hurry. I told the girls I wouldn't be long at all, and here I am, dilly-dallying in the grocery aisle and lusting after a stranger.

Not a stranger…Tru.

When I get home, I catch myself whistling, pausing when I hear a racket upstairs.

"Girls. Everything okay? I'm back from the store. Come eat."

Footsteps stampede down the stairs and through the hall,

and when they reach the kitchen, all three girls start talking at once.

"Dad, Cassidy took so long in the bathroom, I almost wet my pants," Gracie whines.

"Audrey was in there just as long," Cassidy says, rolling her eyes.

"No, I wasn't!" Audrey glares at Cassidy.

Damn. I know an argument's been brewing for a while when Audrey snaps back. She recently turned nine and hates confrontation. I think Gracie came out of the womb ready to rumble. At six and with two older sisters, she's already a skilled opponent. And my thirteen-year-old Cassidy, who used to initiate fun games with her little sisters with a sweet smile on her face, is now in the throes of teen hell.

"I don't know why you all insist on using that one bathroom when we have five," I mutter. "You each have your own bathroom."

"It's the pretty one, Daddy," Gracie says.

"And the biggest," Audrey adds.

"I want to move my bedroom just so that can be *my* bathroom," Cassidy says. "*Alone*."

"Daddy, could you braid my hair?" Gracie asks.

I glance down at her and she looks like she just crawled out of bed. Her light brown hair is sticking up everywhere.

"What have you been doing all this time?" I frown.

"Waiting to go to the bathroom." She holds her hand toward Cassidy like *duh*.

I grumble, pulling out a brush that we keep in the junk drawer, along with some hair ties, and motion for her to stand in front of me. She beams up at me.

"Thanks, Daddy."

"You're welcome, peanut."

I hurriedly brush her hair out and start braiding, while Cassidy and Audrey put their homework in their backpacks.

The braids aren't my finest work, but they'll do. I squeeze Gracie's shoulder and unload the grocery bag quickly.

"How about we eat?" I set the food on the table and turn to grab the plates so they can get started. "We don't have much time this morning—"

The sound of glass breaking and a shriek is followed by more arguing. The hell? I glance back to see what happened, and the pitcher filled with orange juice is now on the floor and on Cassidy's clothes.

Cassidy starts crying and runs up the stairs, and Gracie folds her arms over her chest.

"Stay put, I don't want either of you to get cut on this glass." I get a towel and broom and start cleaning up the mess. "Want to tell me what's going on?"

"Cassidy's mean," Gracie says. "All the time."

I make a face. "Not all the time. She was nice at dinner last night."

Audrey snorts, and again, I look at her in surprise.

"Noted," I say.

Cassidy was just barely tolerable at dinner last night, and we all know it.

Audrey grins at me, and I tug on her ponytail.

"Mom says Cassidy's got big feelings right now," Gracie says, around a mouthful of bagel.

I nod. Bree and I are in agreement about this. I don't know what it's like to deal with the hormones girls do, but my life between the ages of eleven and fifteen were torturous, and Bree assures me it's worse for girls.

"Your mom's right. Cassidy does have big feelings right now. I'll talk with your sister, but let's try to be extra kind to her, okay? When we're struggling with something, it helps when the people we love are gentle with us."

"*She's* not being very gentle," Gracie says, her lips going out in a pout.

Audrey nods in agreement, but when I look at her, her expression turns sheepish.

"We treat people how we want to be treated, even if they don't do the same. Okay?" I wait and there's a long pause before both girls reluctantly agree. "All right. Finish up with breakfast and then go brush your teeth. We need to be out the door in ten minutes."

I get a bagel ready for Cassidy and take it upstairs, knocking on her door.

"Come in," she says quietly.

When I open the door, she's sitting on the edge of the bed in her changed outfit. She wipes her face with the back of her hand and lets out a shaky breath.

"You okay, bunny?"

She stares down at the floor and shakes her head, and I'm ready to fight an army and whoever else stands in my way to make my girl feel better.

"Talk to me. What's going on?" I reach out and take her hand and she clasps it hard.

"I don't want to go to school," she says.

She's usually trying to grow up way too fast and sounds like a teenager most of the time, but now, she sounds like my little girl. The one that used to run and jump into my arms every time I got home, yelling, *"Daddy!"* like I was the best dad ever.

"Why not?"

"Mrs. Carboni hates me. She's so mean. She says I'm wasting her time."

"What? Why would she say that?"

She swallows hard. “I didn’t turn in my project.”

I gape at her. “Mrs. Carboni is your *English* teacher, right? You’re talking about the project you worked on all last week?”

She nods, and a few more tears drip from her brown eyes that are just like mine. I can hardly take it. I put my arm around her, holding her as she sobs, just as Gracie yells up the stairs, “Audrey says we’re going to be late if we don’t leave now!”

“We’ll be right there,” I call back. “Cassidy, I don’t understand why you didn’t turn it in. I looked over that project. Your mom did too. It was good work.”

She doesn’t say anything and I hand her a tissue from her bedside table. She wipes her face and nose and takes another shaky breath.

“I’ll have a talk with her, okay? But you need to turn your project in. Turn it in today and I’ll call and set something up.”

She shakes her head and says in a much lighter tone, “It’s okay, Dad. I’ll be okay. You don’t need to talk to her. I was just having a freak-out. I feel better now.”

I frown, the mental whiplash too much for me this early in the morning. I’m much better at getting whiplash on the field than I am with the mental gymnastics my girls put me through every day.

“You’ll turn in your project?” I ask.

She nods and even musters a grin.

“Okay?” I say, reluctantly.

“We should really get going, Dad. Mom will be so annoyed with you if you make us late.”

I stand and stare after her as she hurries out of the room.

“I’m not the one making you late,” I call.

She pokes her head back in the door and I see the mischief in her eyes.

"Hurry up," she mouths.

"Trying my patience this morning," I say, shaking my head.

She grins then and I'm happy to see that smile on my girl's face.

We hustle down the stairs.

"Let's go, kiddos." I grab the keys and help Gracie with her backpack. The girls start thumb wars to see who gets the front seat in the Suburban. Audrey wins today, causing a new round of complaints.

I have the cure. No matter how much they argue, when I turn on Taylor Swift, they start singing "Cruel Summer" at the top of their lungs, and all is well.

I drop them off and drive to the gym, still humming to Taylor.

Damn, my daughters keep me hopping.

It felt good to have that small interaction with that woman at the store. Really good. The way she looked me over makes me think I've still got it.

I wonder what she'd think if she knew how chaotic my life is.

Too bad I'll never find out.

Pre Order Secret Love Here!

https://geni.us/SecretLove

ACKNOWLEDGMENTS

I'm especially grateful to everyone who helped me pull off getting this book (and the next!) out. I got a concussion during the editing process of this one and then everything went haywire for a few months...hopefully by the time this comes out, I'll be through the worst of it!

But I needed more help than ever, and I'm so grateful for those of you who stepped in!

To my family, first and foremost, you are everything to me and I love you with all my heart.

Kira, Kess, and Greyley, see the family section above... but also, I can't thank you enough for the beauty you've given my books and swag with your artwork. I'm in awe of your talents and the things you each contribute. Love you SO MUCH.

Laura and Catherine, thank you for all the love and encouragement, the sprints, the pet reels that make me laugh, the check-ins. You make this solitary process not so solitary and a lot more fun. I love you both dearly.

Christine, thank you for holding my hand through all the steps with all the things. I love you and I'm so grateful for you!

Natalie, thank you for ALL you do! And for laughing with me when I go sideways. I love you and am so happy you're doing this with me.

Georgie Grinstead, I love you madly, and I love working

on these books with you. Thank you for making them and me better.

To the entire VPR team, I cannot thank you enough for all you do for me. Kim, Christine, Sarah, Kelley, Valentine, Josette, Meagan, Daisy, Ratula, Amy, Megan, Charlie, and Nina, I love you all dearly and am so grateful for each one of you!

Katie, thank you for coming in at the ninth hour and helping/saving me!

Claire, our voxes are life.

Tarryn, I took *live like an animal* to a whole new level with this one. Thanks for being my safe place.

Christine Maree, so grateful for everything you are in my life.

Tosha, Courtney, Savita, the ones who are always and forever in my corner.

To every reader and blogger and bookstagrammer and booktoker who has read and reviewed my books—thank you from the bottom of my heart!

I know I'm forgetting people. Please know that I'm so grateful for the love and friendship and support of all my author and reader (and non-author/reader) friends! I couldn't do this without every single one of you.

ALSO BY WILLOW ASTER

The Single Dad Playbook Series

Mad Love

Secret Love

Reckless Love

Wicked Love

Crazy Love

Landmark Mountain Series

Unforgettable

Someday

Irresistible

Falling

Stay

Standalones with Interconnected Characters

Summertime

Autumn Nights

Kingdoms of Sin Series

Downfall

Exposed

Ruin

Pride

Standalones

True Love Story

Fade to Red

In the Fields

Maybe Maby (also available on all retailer sites)

Lilith (also available on all retailer sites)

Miles Apart (also available on all retailer sites)

Falling in Eden

The G.D. Taylors Series with Laura Pavlov

Wanted Wed or Alive

The Bold and the Bullheaded

Another Motherfaker

Don't Cry Over Spilled MILF

Friends with Benefactors

The End of Men Series with Tarryn Fisher

Folsom

Jackal

FOLLOW ME

JOIN MY MASTER LIST…
https://bit.ly/3CMKz5y

Website willowaster.com
Facebook @willowasterauthor
Instagram @willowaster
Amazon @willowaster
Bookbub @willow-aster
TikTok @willowaster1
Goodreads @willow_aster
Asters group @Astersgroup
Pinterest@willowaster

Printed in the USA
CPSIA information can be obtained
at www.ICGtesting.com
LVHW091924051024
792969LV00007B/788